W9-BVG-332

RAINBOW in the DARK

BY SEAN MCGINTY

CLARION BOOKS
HOUGHTON MIFFLIN HARCOURT
BOSTON   NEW YORK

Clarion Books
3 Park Avenue
New York, New York 10016

Clarion Books is an imprint of Houghton Mifflin Harcourt Publishing Company.

hmhbooks.com

The text was set in Bembo Book MT Std.
Cover design by Andrea Miller
Interior design by Andrea Miller

Library of Congress Cataloging-in-Publication Data is available.
ISBN 978-0-358-38037-5

Manufactured in the United States of America
1 2021
4500826930

for the ones who didn't make it back

CONTENTS

YOU CAN'T REMEMBER YOUR NAME

You find yourself in the dark one day, standing in the middle of the dusky ocean fog, and you can't remember your name. It's something random, like Luca or Jamie, but neither of those, and you're maybe like ages fourteen through seventeen, and you think you *might* be a girl? But you could also just as easily be a boy, or maybe neither? Also, you can't touch your pants. Every time you try, your hand is repelled like a magnet and there's a sound like *BRRZAP!*

More on that problem later.

~

Here are some other things you can't remember:

- The town you live in.
- The street you live on.
- The name of the school you go to.
- The names of any bands or celebrities.
- Or beverages.
- Or clothing brands.
- What the bottoms of shoes are called.
- Your brother's face.

- And probably a lot of other stuff that you aren't even aware of because you've already forgotten about it all entirely.

※

Honestly, the situation is starting to freak you out a little.

You're standing in the middle of the dark ocean fog, looking out at more fog, and it's like it just goes on *forever*. And that's all there is. Just the swirling fog, and you, and the absence of your memory. You think, *How did I get here?* But you can't remember.

What *do* you remember?

You need to remember *something*.

You stand in the fog, and you try to remember.

`mem00168w: [a bright new beginning]`

We're driving to our new home on the coast. Mom's got a job working as a night nurse, and she's telling us all about it, how excited she is, how hopeful for a bright, new beginning. She's doing that thing where she just talks and talks and talks. It's really beautiful, the way her mouth moves. The sunlight is shining through the window and reflecting off a phone charging on the dashboard. I'm in the front seat and my brother, CJ, is stretched out in the back, snoring. This is maybe a year after the divorce.

※

We're "relocating" to a little seaside tourist town with gray mansions stacked along the beach, two skate parks, five kite shops, and one super-market. The rents are impossibly high, and the only place we can find is a mobile home eight miles up the coast. I've never lived in a mobile home park before. The homes aren't mobile, and it isn't a park. There's the highway on one side and a gravel lot on the other, and there's nowhere to go but the beach, which is usually windy, rainy, or both. Like, *Thanks, I hate it.*

··

There's an old woman who lives in a yellow trailer by the gate. She's basically the unofficial greeter. I don't know her name, but in my head I have begun calling her "Muriel." She has a shiny, pink coat and a cat that I've named "Goldfish," and the two of them are usually out under the awning, Muriel in her metal chair and Goldfish on the ground underneath. She's a curious, I'd even say judgmental, kind of cat, watching me like she's deciding whether I'm worth the trouble of keeping around or not.

Pretty much every morning as I leave for school, I see Muriel and Goldfish, and Goldfish judges me, and Muriel smiles and waves. She has a really nice way of waving, just so utterly cheerful, stretching her arms up and twinkling her fingers, and sometimes Muriel's wave is like the best thing that happens to me all day.

One afternoon I come home from school and there's an ambulance by the gate with its lights on, and all the neighbors are outside, and a creepy old man I've never seen before puts his hand on my shoulder and tells me Muriel has fallen and broken her hip, and they are taking her away, and she smiles and gives me one last wave from the gurney, eyes sparkling, and that's the last time I ever see her.

··

Goldfish shows up a few nights later, meowing outside our trailer. I open the door, and she just hops up the steps and marches in like a queen, heading straight for the kitchen like she owns the place. Mom is all for keeping her. She loves animals, and I do too, and so does CJ.

The only reason we don't have a cat or a dog now is our sweet, ancient Booper died of cancer a year ago, just before the divorce, and Mom still hasn't really gotten over it.

But so here is Goldfish, and suddenly we have a cat. Or, at least, we are feeding a cat. Or *I* am feeding a cat. She's pretty aloof, and in some weird way this makes her instantly part of the family. She eats our food, lets me pet her sometimes, but mostly she just wanders around outside. She's always showing up in the randomest places: curled up on top of a mailbox, slinking out of a bush, crouched behind a paper bag. It's like she's still looking for her old spot under Muriel's chair.

`mem01171m (the van)`

My brother is a total hoarder, or maybe he's just messy, but either way he likes to live in filth and squalor. I don't know where he gets them, but he's always coming home with weird broken things. One day he'll have a little kid's bike with a missing chain, and the next day it will be a cracked djembe drum, and a week later the drum will be gone and he'll have, like, an empty fish tank and a skateboard.

Not long after we move to the coast, CJ gets this little electronic keyboard, halfway between a toy and musical instrument, and it immediately becomes the most annoying thing in the entire universe. It has all these sound effects, lasers, bells, falling planes, air raid sirens and humans shouting, and when I'm around, CJ likes to mash them all together, and it sounds like the end of the world.

A month later, CJ ends up with a van. It's a blue minivan, a total beater with a crushed bumper and missing rear window. Mom is aghast. But it's too late. The title is in his name. She lectures him on responsibility, safety, and maintenance, and in the end she lets him keep it. It's his first car, and it immediately fills with papers and trash. And the smell—like a wet dog rolled in a dead skunk and then shook all over the upholstery. I'm always trying to get CJ to clean it out or at least get an air freshener, because now this crappy hoarder van is how we get back and forth to high school.

`mem01172i (happysaddarktriumphant)`

It's Thanksgiving, and Mom is working, and CJ and I are supposed to order a pizza with the money she left on the table, but we don't really talk anymore and neither of us is hungry, so I'm just sitting in the living room looking at my phone, glancing out the window from time to time to see if Goldfish is going to show up . . . when I hear this distant song drifting down the hall.

I follow the song to CJ's room and stand at his door listening. At first I think it's music from a game or something, and I sort of like it—it's *interesting*—this disco beat with a keyboard sound over it. It's kind of happy, but then it gets sad, and right when I've had enough of the sadness, it gets dark, and then it turns triumphant, a crescendo of victory and joy, and in the final glorious moment, he messes up a chord, and everything instantly falls into a cacophony of frustration. It's totally my brother.

Later, when I see him in the hall, I ask him how he learned to play it.

"Play what?" he asks.

"The song you were playing. Where's it from?"

"I wrote it," he says.

"*You* wrote it?"

"Yeah," he says. "It sucks, I know."

"What?"

"You don't have to tell me."

"What?"

He's heading into his room. The door clicks shut.

⋯

I stand in the hall considering what I should do. It occurs to me we just had the longest conversation we've had all week. I almost knock on his door, but then I shrug and head back to the living room and take out my phone. In the back of my mind I keep thinking about how I really should tell him how actually his song is pretty great. Because it really is, and he's so sensitive and hard on himself all the time.

But then, I don't know what happens. I guess I don't tell him soon enough, and time passes, and the song starts to get annoying. CJ plays it *all the time,* like obsessively, so now I can't compliment him because it would only encourage him more.

For the entire winter, it's all he ever does, just messes around with that one song, over and over, rotating the same four parts — happy, sad, dark, triumphant — and when he isn't working on it, he's blasting it on his speakers, and I finally corner him in the kitchen and tell him, "Are you *trying* to make the most annoying song ever? Because congratulations you've done it." CJ laughs and flips me off, but after that I don't hear the song anymore. (Like I said, he can be really sensitive.)

`mem01907i (the fog)`

It's getting late. I'm out on the beach looking for CJ. It's urgent. The sun is going down, and the wind is sweeping a wall of fog in from the ocean, and it's starting to rain. Drops zip randomly from out of the twilight to

6

sting my face. It's too cold to be in this weather in just a hoodie. I pull my hands into my sleeves and hug myself against the wind.

This is stupid, I think. *He isn't out here.*

I text him again.

I try calling.

He doesn't answer.

I tell myself I should turn back but I just keep going.

And the fog. Here it comes.

It can happen so fast, rolling in from the horizon. It just keeps getting thicker, blotting out the sky and the ocean and the dunes and the trees, blotting out everything, hugging the world in a fuzzy, cold blanket.

Where is CJ?

I'm running now.

꙳

I'm—

꙳

Wait. Something is different.

SOMETHING ISN'T RIGHT

The beach. The sand.

Where's the sand? You look at your feet, and you are standing in grass. There is *grass* at your feet. What happened to the sand?

It takes you a moment to figure it out . . .

The fields. You must have strayed into the fields. That's what happened. There are some athletic fields near the beach, and you veered off in the fog without realizing it and just walked right into them. OK. Wow. Sometimes you are just so totally out of it.

❧

So you turn around and start walking back the way you came.

The fog is *so* thick. And the grass—it really needs to be mowed or something. It's, like, knee deep in places.

You walk some more. The grass is shiny and wet, and before long your shoes and socks are soaked.

Where's the beach? You should've seen something by now: a soccer goal, bleachers, a backstop—*something*.

You stop again.

Something isn't right. Something's missing . . .

The ocean.

Where's the sound of the ocean? The endless roar of the waves? You peer into the rolling, gray fog. The ocean has to be here *some*where, right? It's the *ocean*. You don't just lose track of an entire ocean.

As you stand in the grass and the fog trying to figure out where the ocean went, the wind begins to pick up.

It's really starting to blow now. The fog is beginning to move, a rush of ghosts hurrying past in trailing gowns. The light is beginning to seep through. It's getting brighter. You can see a little farther now, into the field.

And a little farther . . .

And then there's this massive gust, and it tears the last of the fog apart and sweeps it away in ghostly wisps, and you look around, and everything has changed.

THE FIELD

The fog is gone now, and everything else along with it: the hills, the trees, the highway, the dunes, the beach, the ocean . . . all of that is gone, and it's just the field now, just this endless expanse of knee-high grass stretching forever in every direction under an endless, blue sky. You shield your eyes with your hand and gaze into the vast, empty wilderness. The wind traces patterns over the grass.

You think — you don't know *what* to think.

For a moment you just stand motionless and stunned, like, *What . . . ?*

You try to remember what you were just doing.

You strain your memory.

It was evening, wasn't it? And you were on the beach looking for CJ, weren't you? You can't remember why, only that you were looking . . .

And then what?

This. *Here.*

You stare into the endless field, and the field stares back. You start to walk, sort of dreamily at first, because it's all so weirdly beautiful, but then you're like, *Wait, what's going on? What* is *this?* You turn in a circle, searching the distance for trees, houses, *anything*. You look out at the impossibly empty landscape. The wind traces patterns across the grass. The sun blazes overhead. The horizon is a flat line in every direction.

A thought swims into view from out of the panic:

OK. Right. I must be dreaming.

❦

"I'm dreaming."

You say it out loud, and your voice startles you, how real it sounds, how it resonates in your head.

"I am dreaming," you say again. "This is my imagination."

Nothing happens.

"Hey!" you say. "Hey, sleepy! Wake up!"

Nothing.

You pinch yourself. You twist the skin around until it starts to sting; you scrunch up your face and keep going until the pain turns white and you can feel your eyes watering. You let go and look at your skin where you pinched yourself. You watch as the white fills in with red.

"Ow," you say. "Ow, f█ck."

. . . ?

You try to say the word again.

"F█ck."

You can get the first sound out, that first *f,* and you can get the very last *ck,* but it's like something smears the *u* as it leaves your throat. The sound just disappears in the middle.

What?

You try again, same thing.

You can't say the word *f█ck*.

You really must be dreaming. What else could it be?

⋅⋅⋅

Suddenly you have to pee. It just hits you. Sometimes when you're stressed, it just comes at you, and you have like ten seconds to make it to a bathroom. This is one of those times. You look around. There are no bathrooms. You take a breath and wait for the feeling to pass. You try to say the word *f█ck* again. You start walking.

You concentrate on the landscape to forget about the feeling of having to pee.

Everything is so vivid and real. The wind on the grass. The gentle, green waves. The perfect detail of each individual stalk. And above it all, the yellow sun burning in the flickering sky. Yes, the sky is *flickering*. You see that now. It's like one of those old stop-motion videos, everything speckled and twitchy, and it looks so *real*, and it's so weird to be standing stunned in the presence of it all, it almost feels like floating, like you're here but you're somewhere else — or nowhere at all.

Or maybe it's just that you really have to pee.

⋅⋅⋅

Calm down.

You take a breath, wait for the panic to pass again. It doesn't really.

You take out your phone. Drop it. Pick it up.

You notice your hands are shaking.

The screen is blank. Your phone has turned itself off again. It's a thousand years old and always freezing up or turning itself off. So you turn it back on, and you manage to dial 911, but nothing happens. You press the numbers again. Nothing happens.

Right. Because you're dialing on the calculator.

You close the calculator and try again on the phone.
The screen flashes.

CALL FAILED. NO SERVICE.

You try again.
Same thing.
The clock says 6:01 p.m. You open the map. Nothing loads. You aren't getting a signal. You look at the empty grid and the spinning ball for a moment, and then you close the map and start a group text to your mom and your brother.

You can't get your hands to stop shaking. You keep making mistakes. The phone keeps autocorrecting.

> This I s an emergence somethings
> weird just harpoonED CALL ME PK
> EMERGENty !! call me

Close enough.
You press send, and the little bar moves halfway and stops.

MESSAGE FAILED. NO SERVICE.

You try again. *Message failed.*
And again. *No service.*
You put your phone back in your pocket and look around.
Part of you wants to scream and part of you wants to cry, but mostly you just really have to pee. You're hunched over now, legs crossed. You reach for your button and zipper, and something happens. *BRRZAP!*

A powerful force repels your hand, like a reverse magnet, and there's a sound—this sharp electrical sound like, *BRRZAP!*

You try again. Same thing. Your fingers are pushed to the side with a *BRRZAP!*

And part of your brain is like, *What?!*

And another part of your brain is like, *OK, so this must be a* nightmare *then*.

You try to dig your thumb into your waistband. Same thing. You grab your pant legs and try to yank them down, but they won't budge. You try the zipper again.

BRRZAP!

You're doing a little dance now. You're dancing and crossing your legs and tugging your pants all at once, and nothing is working, and you have a moment of almost transcendental clarity, in which you realize that in about five seconds you really and truly will not be able to hold it any longer.

⁂

It's been a while since you peed your pants. You can't remember the last time, actually. And as you feel the warm trickle down your leg, you think to yourself, *OK, so I am peeing my pants*. And then: *So I have now peed my pants*. The relief is so powerful, and it's a long moment before you think about the issue of cleanup.

OK. So how are you going to clean up if you can't take off your pants—or find any soap or water, for that matter?

But as you are considering all the options you don't have, something happens.

The feeling of wetness disappears. It's just gone. You look down at your pants. They're dry. They were just soaked with warm pee—you *felt* it, and now that feeling is gone, and it's like nothing ever happened.

Your pants are completely dry! It's beautiful and magical and the first good thing to happen in a while, and you stand in the middle of the endless field and think, *Ah. Great. Plus now I don't have to pee anymore.*

And then, *Wait. So did I just wet the bed?*

.ᴎ.

"Wake up!" you shout. "Wake up!"

You think about how crazy you must look, standing in the middle of nowhere shouting to yourself—but on the other hand, there's no one here to see you. You're completely alone.

"Wake up!"

The sky flickers silently.

"WAKE UP! WAKE UP! WAKE UP!"

Each time you shout, the silence grows more oppressive until finally you stop. Your mouth is dry. The sun is hot on your shoulders. The grass bends in the breeze.

OK, so now what?

4.

YOU ARE NOT HUMMING A SONG

They say when you get lost, you should just stay where you are, but it's too late for that. You've already been moving, and if you don't do *something*, you're afraid you might just start screaming, or crying, or both. So you start walking again. The grass rolls out endlessly in every direction. The wind traces patterns. The sky flickers. The grass swishes against your legs with a quickening rhythm as you begin to walk faster. And now you're sort of jogging.

Nothing changes. You aren't going *anywhere*. You may as well be on a giant grass treadmill. The wind blows. The sky flickers.

A little voice in your head is growing louder and louder. This conversation you're having with yourself, like:

All this grass. It's kind of starting to freak me out.

Yeah, hmm.

No, I'm serious.

I know. But just try to think about something else, OK?

Something like what?

I don't know. Count your footsteps or—

Count my footsteps? Are you crazy? We're going to die out here!

Don't say that! Just think about—just hum a song or something, OK?

A song? I can't remember any songs!

So you just start humming nonsense instead.

After a while, the nonsense turns itself into a song. You are humming a song. It goes like, *hmmhmmhmhmmmhmhmhmhmm*.

.

You walk through the endless grass humming the song.

Hmhmmmhmhmhmhmm

No. You are *not* humming a song. You can't be. This song has keyboard sounds. It has a string section. It has a drumbeat, like:

Boom, pish.

Boom, pish.

Boom, pish.

You are walking through the endless field, and a song is playing, and you can't tell if it's inside your head or not. It just keeps going. There's something familiar about it too, there's a pattern. It's like, *Happy part. Sad part. Dark part. Triumphant part.* Over and over, and you can't tell where it ends or begins, but it's *so* familiar. You *know* this song. Where have you heard it before? The answer is right there at the edge of your mind, fluttering around like a moth. You can almost grab it . . . and then it's gone. You can't remember the song.

5.

YOU ARE HERE

Dark . . . triumphant . . . happy . . . sad . . . Is it getting louder? It sounds like it's getting louder. It's like the song is right out in front of you now, emanating from hidden speakers, and someone is starting to crank the volume.

Then you see something. Way out on the horizon. A shape, a blurry dot. Something that is neither grass nor sky.

You are walking faster now. The song is getting louder.

The dot becomes a rectangle, and the rectangle becomes a box, a blue box, like the size of one of those things . . . what are they called? *Refrigerators.* Like the size of a refrigerator or a little smaller. You are standing in front of it now. It's just you and this blue box in the middle of miles and miles of grass, with the strange song blasting out like a soundtrack. The box is kind of shiny, and you can see your reflection in it. You gaze at your reflection, at the kid gazing back at you, this strange face you barely recognize.

⏣

There aren't any words on the box, but there is a button, a single dirty white button, and a slot.

You press the button, and instantly the music stops.

There's a scratchy sound, followed by a blast of electric static. Something inside the box whirs, and with a *BLAP!* a white slip of paper shoots out of the slot and drifts to the ground. You pick it up. There are three words printed on it:

PLEASE SCAN ID

You check your pockets. You don't have any ID. You press the button again.

The machine whirs and goes *BLAP!* and another slip of paper shoots out of the slot, and you almost catch this one before it hits the ground. You pick it up and read it.

PLEASE SCAN ID

"I don't have an ID," you say.

The blue box just stands there.

You slam the button a couple times.

BLAP!

Another paper. This time you catch it:

PLEASE HOLD

Music starts playing again — different music, some kind of generic ukulele thing or something. Hold music. You stand at the blue box and listen to the jangly strumming. You look at your reflection in the smooth, glossy metal. The expression on your face is strange; your eyes are too wide. You look totally bewildered.

The music stops. Something whirs inside the box again.

BLAP!

INSERT HAND INTO SLOT

Another slot has opened above where the paper comes out, some hidden, blue door you hadn't seen before. You peer inside. It's like a mail slot or something.

Insert my hand?

You think about it awhile.

Then you insert your hand.

The machine *BLAP!s,* and you feel a soft pressure begin to squeeze your arm just above your wrist, and it keeps squeezing, and by the time you try to pull back your hand, it's too late. The box has got you.

᠅

Maybe your adrenaline is all used up, because you don't feel scared, exactly, more just frustrated at how impossibly ridiculous this all is, standing here in the middle of nowhere with your arm held captive by a blue box.

But then you begin to feel something. A tickle on your wrist. You tug, but your arm won't budge. *At least it doesn't hurt,* you think.

And that's when it starts to hurt.

The tickle turns into a sharp jab—you can feel it stabbing you, and you make a sound you've never heard yourself make before, the *I'm getting stabbed* sound. But you aren't really thinking about the sound. Mostly you're just trying to save your hand from being chopped off by the blue box.

You are pulling with all your might, ramming your foot against the box for leverage. But you can't get your hand out. You can feel something piercing you, and you are screaming now. It's stabbing you over and over, and just when you feel like you're going to pass out or something, the box goes *click!* and your hand is released, and you go stumbling back and land on your butt in the grass.

⁂

You leap up, clutching your wrist. Look at what the box has done to your arm. There's a stamp, a thick, black stripe with words and numbers. You run your thumb across it and wipe away a thin smear of blood.

You've been tattooed.

> LK
> RAINBOW
> NOBODY
> 99.01

Rainbow? It isn't your name . . . it takes you a moment . . . it's something your brother called you, right? You remember that now. But why did he do it? You can't remember. To tease you? Or was it, like, affectionate? You just can't recall. What *is* your name, anyway? You search your memory frantically for the answer, and all you find is darkness, and now the box is *BLAPPING* at you again.

Another two papers have fallen to the ground. The first says:

FOLLOW MAP TO REFUGEE CAMP

And the other is a map. Kind of. Actually it's just a drawing with two dots. One dot says YOU ARE HERE. The other dot says TO REFUGEE CAMP. And that's it. No explanation of distance, or landmarks, or anything.

You press the button again. This time the box is silent.

6.

THE REFUGEE CAMP

You leave the box in search of the refugee camp. Across the grass you go. As far as you can tell, it's all the same in every direction. *This is crazy,* but you don't know what else to do except keep going and try not to think too much about how you can't remember your name. You walk and walk, and just when you're getting really sick of walking again, you see something. There's a space where the grass has been mowed, and in the middle of the mowed spot, there's a concrete square with a yellow cover on it about the size of a trashcan lid. There are letters stenciled on the lid: TO REFUGEE CAMP.

You kneel and grab the little handle. It opens smoothly on a hinge, revealing a hole in the ground, a big, black hole with a yellow metal ladder that plummets into darkness. You can't see the bottom.

You look down there for a long time. *So now this. Well, how much worse could it be?* You raise your gaze to examine the world outside the hole again, the endless waving grass and flickering sky. You take a breath and step onto the ladder. You stand a moment, gripping the rungs, and then you start down.

23

For a moment your eyes are even with the grass, and you watch the thin stalks bending in the wind. Then you take another step down. And another step, and another. Now you are completely in the hole. The wind disappears. The only sound is your hands and feet on the cool metal rungs.

Down the hole you go, rung by rung. The circle of light above you shrinks to a dot as the darkness grows. Then the dot disappears, and the darkness becomes total. You can't see your hands, the ladder, the walls of the hole, any of it. Black.

You keep going. The sound of shoes on metal rungs echoes in the darkness. You try to concentrate on the sound rather than the other things, like how this hole might have nothing at the bottom and that at some point you might have to climb back up, which has to be a long way by now. How long have you been going down for? *What if someone comes along and closes the lid?*

And still you go, down, down, until your fear becomes numb. After a while you notice that something has changed. The darkness isn't as dark anymore. You can almost see your hands again. You can sort of sense them there. And when you look down at where your feet should be, you see it—a tiny circle of light, way down below at the bottom of the hole.

The circle of light below grows larger as you climb down the ladder, until it is the same size as the hole you climbed into, and your first thought is that it must be the ceiling of some kind of enormous underground room or something, but as you pass through, you see that it is something else.

You are standing on a ladder in the sky.

And the hole above you, the hole you just climbed out of — the hole is just torn into the sky, and in it is darkness, and you are in the sky . . . you are standing on a ladder in the sky. Beneath your feet, the land is spread out like a distant, green quilt, and the ladder goes down, down, down, until you can't even see it anymore, and you've got that weird vertigo feeling in your stomach like you're going to puke or something, and for a moment, you just cling to the ladder with everything you've got.

OK, you think, *I climbed down into a hole in the ground and ended up in the sky.*

And yet it all seems so real. The ladder, the ground, the distance, the fall. You cling to the rungs, taking it all in, your bird's-eye view of the world below. Miles and miles and *miles* of green. The immensity of it all. The infinite horizon.

Your legs are starting to feel weird and shaky. You shouldn't have stopped. You start down again, descending from the sky like some kind of lesser god or goddess. One step, then another.

Down, down, down.

You begin to hear faint drums, an electronic keyboard. *Sad part, dark park, triumphant part, happy part* . . . You look down and see there's something below you now.

It's all a distant blur at first, but as you descend the ladder, the blur acquires edges, and the edges separate, and it becomes a series of boxes, and the boxes become tents. Row after row of green canvas tents. Hundreds of tents. A tent city alone in the field. The song is so loud now.

Ten feet above the ground, you come to the end of it, the final rung, and you pause. Once you drop to the grass, you won't be able to reach the ladder again. You'll be stuck down there, no way back up. You dangle for a moment from the bottom rung, feeling your arms and shoulders stretch, and then you let go.

Your landing is pretty good. You fall, but you don't get hurt. You get up and check your phone again. Nothing. You look up one last time at the yellow ladder hanging overhead in the blue, the black tunnel torn out of the sky, then you start walking.

～

There's another blue box in front of the tents. You press the button, and the song stops.

BLAP! A piece of paper:

PLEASE SWIPE YOUR WRIST

Swipe it where? You wave your wrist around in front of the box, and there's another *BLAP!,* and another paper appears.

WELCOME TO THE REFUGEE CAMP, RAINBOW
HERE ARE SOME MEMORIES
PLEASE KEEP THEM IN A SAFE PLACE

The box spits out more papers. They fall to the ground at your feet. You pick one up, and it's covered in a dense, unreadable script of numbers and letters, like some kind of code. As you look, you see that there's a pattern; the characters are broken into snippets, each one beginning with *mem.*

And as you are looking over this strange jumble, something weird happens.

The letters begin to jitter and vibrate, faster and faster. Their darkness blurs out across the page and the world around it, and then in a *snap!* it *all* disappears—everything, all of it—and it's all a blank, empty space, and for a moment there is just emptiness . . .

And then a light . . .

And then the memories.

mem00018c [the most beautiful]

I'm playing with a silk scarf in a patch of sunlight in our old house on Middle Street. I'm like four years old, and it's my aunt's scarf. She's visiting us. Her big brown eyes and smile. And the scarf—it's blue and red and iridescent in the sun and the way it floats and flows through the light and the shadows . . . I'm just mesmerized by it. It has to be the most beautiful thing I've ever seen.

mem01893i [rainbow]

It's late summer and I'm starting sixth grade and I decide that I would like to change my name to *Rainbow* because *Rainbow* is a cool/mysterious name that really captures my inner essence in an interesting and mysterious way, and also one of my friends already took the name *Wander.*

I ask everyone I know very politely and solemnly if they could please call me *Rainbow* from now on, and every single person goes along with it—even my teacher—all except CJ, who refuses with the resistance of a thousand suns to ever call me anything but the name our parents have given me.

The seasons change, winter comes, and I am older and wiser. I have realized that my inner essence can no longer be represented by a name like *Rainbow,* so I go back to my birth name—and this is the exact moment CJ starts calling me Rainbow and never stops. He can be such an ■sshole sometimes.

mem010016i (everyone dies)

It's the middle of winter. I'm six years old, CJ is like seven or eight, and we're in the living room having a deep conversation about life and death because our aunt—our beautiful, beloved aunt who married a rich d■ckhead and adorned herself with silk scarves—our aunt has taken her own life. She locked herself in the bathroom and swallowed all her pills and the d■ckhead found her the next day. Mom hasn't stopped crying. Our grandparents are driving up for the funeral. The whole world is just ringing with sadness.

I'm in the living room with CJ, and we're talking about death.

"Everyone dies," he says. "Everyone. All of us. Everyone who has ever lived or will live is going to die . . . Unless maybe scientists find a way to live forever."

"How?"

"I don't know," he says. "Maybe by like freezing you or putting your brain in a computer. But even then, if you kill yourself, they probably won't be able to save your brain in time unless you're near a body-freezing place."

"None of that is going to happen," I say.

"Why not?" he asks.

"Body-freezing place? It just isn't. Everyone is going to die."

CJ scowls. "That's what I said already! *Unless* the scientists think of something."

"What about our souls?" I ask.

"What about them?"

"Do you believe we have them? What happens to our souls?"

"Souls?" he says. "I'm talking about freezing brains."

"*I* believe in souls," I say. "But there isn't hell or heaven, just, I don't know, *empty space,* and no one remembers anything, or even is themselves anymore."

"Except for ghosts," says CJ.

"Yeah, maybe ghosts . . ." My gaze drifts to the window, aware of some movement. I see a maroon car pulling into the driveway.

"They're here!" I shout.

Our grandparents have arrived.

CJ and I rush to the door.

Our love for our grandparents comes from deep within our bones. Mom can't stand them, but CJ and I love every single thing about them —their constant bickering, the enormous shoes they wear, their old, soft hands. We haven't seen them in over a year, and now here they are, walking slowly up the snowy drive together, ancient and broken and beautiful, and as we step out to greet them, we forget for a moment in our sudden joy the reason why they're even here.

HELLO? IS ANYONE THERE?

You find yourself standing in a daze.

The papers fall from your hand. The memories.

They're fading fast in your mind, becoming memories of memories, drifting into the darkness, and all that's left is the memory of their light and a sort of empty, nauseous feeling.

Where am I?

You look around at the endless grass, the tents, the blue box, the slips of paper at your feet, and your confusion turns to disappointment and settles into a nagging fear.

Oh, right. Here.

You don't really want to look at them again, but it feels wrong to just leave your memories scattered on the ground, so you gather the little papers, fold them neatly, and tuck them into your back pocket. Then you turn your attention to the camp.

᛫᛫

Rows and rows of canvas tents, hundreds and hundreds, and not a sound but your own footsteps on the empty dirt path. Is everyone sleeping?

Some kind of afternoon nap? What time of day is it anyway? You take out your phone; it still says 6:01. You turn to the nearest tent and think about knocking to see if anyone's in there, but you can't really knock on a tent flap. You put your face up to the crack in the fabric panels instead.

"Hello?" Your voice is scratchy and kind of quiet.

You try again. "*Hello? Is there anyone there?*"

You untie the cord, open the flap, peek your head inside. Darker here. Sunlight filtered through canvas. Your eyes adjust, and you see four empty cots, a table, a lantern, a bowl, and a plastic bag with soap, toothpaste, and little bottles of shampoo. There's no one here.

You check the next tent. Empty.

And the next.

You go down one row and another, peering inside each empty tent.

"Is anyone here?" you call.

Silence.

More tents. All empty.

You appear to be the only person in the entire place.

⁌

The wind begins to pick up. It's gentle at first, tickling your face, stirring the canvas—but soon it's howling. You run into a tent to wait it out. You turn on the lantern, sit down on a cot, and listen to the canvas flap in the wind. It's the loneliest sound you've ever heard, and you're afraid you might start crying or something, so you get up. The bowl on the table has water in it, and you drink some and splash some on your face. The cold shock snaps things into focus again.

OK, I got lost. That happens.

I just happened to get <u>really</u> lost.

And I just need to get home. I just need to find my brother and get home.

I was looking for him, right?
Why was I looking for him?
You can't remember.

You were at the beach. You remember that. And then the field. And now here. So now what? You decide you will go back to the blue box and see if you can get some more instructions.

But when you open the tent flap, everything has changed. It's dark outside. Nighttime. Stars flicker in a moonless sky. A moment ago, the sun was basically overhead. Now this. You stand at the doorway of the tent, looking into the darkness, and then you go back inside.

．．

You tear open the plastic bag of toiletry items and brush your teeth and wash your face. You crawl onto the cot and pull the blanket up to your ears. Your mind is racing with about a thousand different thoughts. Like for example how the tent doesn't lock. What if someone tries sneaking in? But on the other hand, there doesn't seem to be anyone else around *anywhere*. You can't decide which is worse. You lie on the cot, thinking about how weird this all is. The wind has died down again, and in the darkness, there's no sound, nothing, just this immense and eternal silence. At some point, you sleep.

`mem01907j (the cave)`

CJ is eighteen months older than me. When we were little, we were almost best friends, but nowadays, he stays in his room and plays video games, and I zone out on my phone or wander around on the beach.

There's this one spot, maybe two miles up, where the sand ends and the cliffs begin. At the top there's a wooden railing and a sign that says DANGER. STAY BACK. Farther out, past the railing, there's a little path cut into the sandstone that supposedly leads down to a cave that faces the ocean.

I haven't been to the cave. The path has eroded completely away in places, and if you fell, you could definitely die, and if you didn't die, your phone would. It kind of freaks me out, which is maybe why I go there so much. I like to go up to the railing and look out over the immensity of the ocean and feel the waves below. It makes me feel so small and powerless, and at the same time sort of invincible in my meaninglessness, like some kind of lesser god or goddess of the ocean and sky.

.ı．

One night I'm especially lonely and restless, and the wood-paneled walls really have that closing-in-on-you feeling, and so I decide to drag CJ out on a walk with me. I find him in his room, maneuvering a warrior through a burned-out junkyard, pursued by monsters to a dance beat. I can't remember the name of the game . . . it's like all the others except with really big monsters, and CJ is totally cracked out on it. As far as I can tell, it's just a lot of walking—just on and on across an endless, burned-out grayscape, repeating the same eight animations over and over, searching in desperation for someone to kill.

"Hey," I say.

He doesn't answer, eyes pasted to the screen.

"Hey, you should come see something with me."

Silence.

I throw a pillow at him. It bounces off his head.

"Hey, I want to show you something."

"No thanks." He winces at something in the game.

I slide between him and the screen, and he cranes his neck to see around me.

"There's something cool you need to see."

"Move!" he says. "I'm gonna die!"

"Wow that would be just so sad."

"Move, Rainbow!"

"Ask me what it is," I tell him, "and I'll move."

" . . ."

" . . ."

"Fine," he says. "What is it?"

"Well, it isn't here. It's outside. We have to go for a walk."

"F█ck no."

"Just a couple miles."

"In your dreams."

"Come on," I say. "Walk or I never move for all eternity."

CJ is stubborn, but I am *more* stubborn and I can outlast him if it comes down to it. We both know this. The minutes pile up until finally he grunts and tosses his controller aside. "Congratulations, I died."

"Yay."

We watch as his bloody corpse is devoured by monsters, and then I say, "Come on. It's really cool."

And he must be feeling lonely too because finally my brother agrees.

⋱

It's clear but windy, the sun low in the sky, and CJ complains the whole way about how cold he is until finally I'm like, "OK! Can you please just shut up and let me enjoy the evening?"

And CJ turns to me and shouts, with the frigid wind blowing his hair all around his face, "Oh yeah, *this* is enjoyable!"

⋱

We get to the cliffs, and I lead him up the winding path, and as we step onto the top, the sun is setting over pink, sparkling ocean waves, and it's seriously the most beautiful thing in the entire world.

"So what's the surprise?" he says.

"This!"

CJ looks out over the water. He might as well be looking at a parking lot.

"People would pay money to be standing here right now," I tell him.

"What people?"

"Look at the waves! And the sunset! This is majestic, breathtaking beauty."

"Does the trail just end there at the edge or what?"

So I tell him about the cave — I heard about it from a kid at school — and of course he wants to go check it out.

"No way," I say. "Have you looked down there?"

We go to the railing and observe the trail and the crashing waves below.

"Even if you fell, I bet you'd survive," he says. "It isn't *that* far down."

"It isn't the *fall*," I say. "It's the waves bashing you against the rocks when you land."

"But so, the cave," he says. "Maybe there's treasure in there or something."

"You've been playing too many games."

"Nah. It's a known fact that caves usually have things like treasure or loot boxes or dead bones in them."

"Dead bones," I say. "As opposed to live bones?"

"Let's go check it out."

"No way. There's nothing there."

"But how do you *know?*"

"OK," I say. "Maybe there is. Maybe there's like an old wooden box, and inside the box is a glass bottle with a cork in it, and inside the bottle is a rolled-up scroll that says, *Hello, there's no way you're reading this because you fell off the cliff on your way here and are currently being bashed against the rocks.*"

"You're just scared," says CJ.

"Uh, yeah."

mem01608t ("The Eternal God/dess of Teen Depression")

The Eternal Heartbroken God and Goddess of Teen Anxiety & Depression is all forms, possibilities, genders, sexes, and manifestations all at once, but usually prefers the pronoun *she* . . . which might annoy her parents if she had any parents, but the Eternal Heartbroken God and Goddess of Teen Anxiety & Depression was born from the infinite primordial void of darkness, light, and the ethereal other, so there.

Usually, for brevity's sake, the Eternal Heartbroken God and Goddess of Teen Anxiety & Depression shortens her name to *the Eternal God/dess of Teen Depression,* which she has been told is still pretty emo.

The Eternal God/dess of Teen Depression is everywhere and every time all at once, but primarily alone in her bedroom with the curtains drawn.

The Eternal God/dess of Teen Depression is invested with powers beyond human comprehension, but mostly she just mopes around.

The Eternal God/dess of Teen Depression is too sad to exercise.

The Eternal God/dess of Teen Depression is too anxious to socialize.

The Eternal God/dess of Teen Depression once created 68 entirely new dimensions of time and space just to avoid going out.

In the beginning, the Eternal God/dess of Teen Depression actually really enjoyed being a god. Because being a god is obviously a lot of fun. She made all kinds of cool things, like light and love and stars and planetary worlds. And she filled her worlds with oceans and forests and flowers and magpies and koala bears and pandas and other strange and wondrous animals. But over time the flowers died, the oceans acidified, the strange and wondrous animals were eaten by other strange and wondrous animals, and the Eternal God/dess of Teen Depression began to realize that she was literally the only thing in her universe that would never end.

And she got really depressed.

The Eternal God/dess of Teen Depression is standing on a concrete pad, like the size of a playground, in the noonday sun. Music plays, some kind of bouncy, electronic polka, while an enormous cube of solid iron the size of a house or maybe a barn is raised by a towering crane high into the air.

Up it goes, growing smaller and smaller in the sky, until it fits neatly over the sun, a dark square ringed in brilliant light. It casts a square shadow upon the earth . . . and in the center of the shadow stands the Eternal God/dess of Teen Depression.

In her hand she holds a super-ergonomic remote control with a single red button positioned under her thumb.

The crane stops, and the music stops, and a voice says, "Ready."

~

(The Eternal God/dess of Teen Depression is a god/dess so yes, she could have made this whole thing happen magically with a wave of her hand, but the crane and a button are way more satisfying because they just are.)

~

The Eternal God/dess of Teen Depression stands in the shadow of the cube and takes a breath. She looks around at her creation. A bird goes *tweet*.

She thinks, *I created that bird.*

She presses the button.

The cable goes *shpwing!*

And the Eternal God/dess of Teen Depression looks up to see the dark underside of the cube growing bigger and bigger, wider and wider, the edges racing out in every direction, blotting out the sky as it plummets down, down, and there's a sudden final rush of wind, and—

mem01590i (your heavy use of expletives is distracting)

I get put in the wrong English class, but I don't know that at first. We're supposed to read a book, *One Hundred Years of Solitude* by Gabriel García Márquez, and then write an essay. I start out with a good attitude, but the book isn't what I imagined from the title, and I can't get into it, or I won't. Instead of reading the book, I fake my notes—it isn't hard, just circle some vocab or make a comment here or there—and I keep telling myself I'll start reading it, but I never do, and all the while the stress balloons in the corner of my mind until it's the week of the paper, which is when they inform me, *whoops,* I'm in the wrong class and offer to let me switch. So of course I say yes.

~

In my new class, they're in the middle of a different assignment, *personal narrative,* and the teacher hands me the instructions, two pages of dense text describing, basically sentence by sentence, what I'm supposed to write about.

OK.

I sit down in my room to start my paper. I can hear CJ's song coming down the hall—or maybe I've heard it so much it's in my head. I try to concentrate, but my words have a mind of their own and their own desires, and at some point they break free from the teacher's instructions, and I follow them down their own winding path, which turns out to be a story about an immortal being who has discovered that being immortal is actually a horrible curse and so is always thinking up crazy ways to die, just to try to experience a little nonexistence, but because she is immortal, she never really dies; she just keeps reappearing. And every time she comes back to life, she has a new foul catchphrase, like *"Fiddlef█cks! Not again!"* And at the end it was all a dream. And there are not one but *two* epilogues.

~

When I get the story back, the basic message is that I didn't understand the assignment *at all,* and, more than that, I managed to be both offensive and tediously edgy. My teacher has taken the time to black out almost every single swear word—and at the bottom there's a note:

Does not meet requirements. Heavy use of expletives is distracting. "It was all just a dream" is a cliché. The "epilogues" are unnecessary. Supposed to be real. See attached worksheet on comma usage to address grammatical errors.

My teacher is wrong about one thing. I didn't actually end the story with "It was all just a dream." The words were: "She was all just a dream of herself." Which is *way* more poetic.

It doesn't matter. I'm failing the class now. I take a pen and cross out the part about the dream and write a new conclusion: "This time she died. The end." And then, because I'm feeling really dramatic, I get a match and start burning pages in the kitchen sink, one after the other, and I get through page seven before I set the smoke detector off.

LUNCH IS A TURKEY SANDWICH

You wake, your head swimming with memories, and it takes you a while to remember where you are — and then you remember. The field. The camp. Your tent. Also, you really have to pee again. You lie on your cot thinking about how much you have to pee and how you don't want to get up, and how can any of this be real?

You get up and open the tent flap. Sunlight pours in. There's a tray at your feet, wrapped in plastic like they serve in a hospital. Scrambled eggs, toast, a blueberry muffin, a plastic cup of orange juice — along with a note that says COMPLIMENTS OF THE RED CROSS.

You set it in your tent and then you go back outside. When you try to unbutton your fly, your hands are repelled again, *BRRZAP!* Ridiculous. You can't think of any other option but to pee your pants again. So you do, and just like before they're all wet and sticky and gross, and then in an instant they're dry again. So at least there's that.

*

You eat your breakfast and throw the trash in a gray bin and return to the blue box and swipe your wrist again. The box goes *BLAP!* and spits out a piece of paper.

HERE ARE SOME MORE MEMORIES
PLEASE KEEP THEM IN A SAFE PLACE

"What are these for?" you ask.

The box doesn't answer.

⁙

You don't want to look at the memories again, you don't want the sickening feeling of being tossed back and forth between the past and here, so you fold the pages and put them in your pocket and wander the empty camp. The day inches by. Rows of tents cast shadows like teeth. The sky flickers. Your stomach hurts. You realize that you kind of have to go to the bathroom. Number two this time. That's right—you have to poop. You look around at the empty tents. As far as you know, there aren't any toilets. Not that it matters. You can't get your pants off.

You decide you will hold it.

You try to think about other stuff to distract yourself. You think about CJ. You're worried about him, but you can't remember why. You were out on the beach looking for him. But why? You can't remember.

You think about hide-and-seek by the river. You think about the dollhouse mansion you built together. You remember that one Halloween. You can see him sitting on his bed with his candy stacked around him like money. You can see him scoop up a fistful like he's going to shove the whole thing into his mouth, wrappers and all. You can remember him bringing the handful of candy to his open mouth . . . you can bring yourself right to that moment . . . but there's something wrong. When you try to remember his face, there's nothing there.

You can't remember what your brother's face looks like. You can see him from the back—his green shorts, his baggy T-shirt, his floppy hair—but you can't remember his face. *Where is he?*

You return to your tent. Lunch is a turkey sandwich. You set it aside on the table and curl up on the cot. You breathe in the canvas smell and listen to the creaking as you shift your weight and try not to think about how utterly lost you are or how much you have to go to the bathroom. You wish more than anything else that you could just sleep right now, but your stomach is aching too much. So instead you shift around uncomfortably on the cot until you can't hold it anymore.

You find yourself standing in the path between two tents trying to get your pants off.

BRRZAP!

BRRZAP!

BRRZAP!

But you can't get them off, and so there's nothing left to do but crap your pants, which is what you do, and while you are doing it, you keep thinking, *I am crapping my pants. This is a thing that is happening.*

A moment later, as you're standing in the aftermath of shame and relief, you feel a strange sensation and suddenly, magically you're all clean again, and you pause and take a breath.

Wow. OK.

You start to walk back to your tent, feeling actually pretty good about things. When you turn the corner, there's a kid standing there. He's about your age, dressed in jeans and a blue hoodie, and he's got a backpack and this purple sling across his chest, like he's all ready to go camping. Short brown hair, freckled cheeks.

"Saw you popping a squat," he says. "Didn't want to interrupt. So . . . are you Rainbow or what?"

9.

CHAD01

You're flustered beyond embarrassment at the sight of another human being, and for a moment you can't even think of what to say. You just stand there. You've got your phone out, like you're going to check it or something. You put it back in your pocket.

"So are you Rainbow or what?" he says again.

"Um, I think so?" you say.

"Well, I got a paper from the last call box, said I'm supposed to meet up here with a kid named Rainbow."

"Rainbow . . . Like on my wrist?"

"Yeah like on your wrist! Are you for real, or what?"

"Am I for real?"

"Yeah, let's figure this out." The kid claps his hands together. "Show me your toes."

"What?"

"Your toes," he says. "I gotta have a peek at your toes."

"You want to see my *toes?*"

"Yeah," he says firmly. "Before we go any further, I gotta see your toes. OK? Let's see 'em."

"Uh . . ." you answer.

"It's for a good reason," he says, fixing you with his eyes.

⁎

Fine, OK, whatever. You untie your shoe and slip off your sock and show the kid your toes.

He kneels and examines them very seriously, eyebrows knitted.

"Hmm . . ." he says slowly. "Yeah, OK. You're legit."

"Legit? What's that mean?"

"It means you're real. Toes are how you tell if someone's imaginary or not."

"What are you talking about?"

"Imaginary friends," he says. "NPCs. *People who aren't real.* You can tell by their toes. See that third toe there? If it's longer than the second toe, then the person isn't real. You're close there, but I'd say you pass."

The kid gives you a thumbs-up, and then he's pointing the thumb at himself. "I'm Chad01, Warrior rank three, XP 180."

"Chad—*one?*" you say.

"Yeah, see?" He pushes up his sleeve to show you the tattoo on his wrist. "It's actually Chad *Zero* One, but the zero is silent, so you say 'Chad-One.'"

"That's . . . a really weird name."

"Is it?" Chad01's eyebrows go up a bit. "No weirder than *Rainbow,* right? Which, by the way, according to the last call box, you and I are traveling together now. So what kind of skills you got?"

"Skills?" you say.

"Yeah. Archery? Grappling? Precognition?"

"Um . . . I'm not sure what you're talking about. What is this place?"

Chad01 gives you a look. "Whaddya mean 'this place'?"

"I mean *here*. *This place*. What is this?"

"This is the Refugee Camp," he says.

"But *where* is it? Where are we? What country is this?"

"Isn't a country. It's the *Refugee Camp*."

"I got here by climbing down from a hole in the sky."

"Yeah, no sh█t. Me too." Chad01 gives you another look. "What class are you, anyway?"

"Class? I don't know. I was looking for my brother. I was out on the beach, and I don't remember what happened after that. I just showed up here. What's going on? What *is* this place?"

He's really looking at you funny now. "Hey, can I see your wrist?"

You hold out your wrist, and as he reads it, his eyes narrow and his face gets kind of red.

"Seriously?" he says.

"What?"

"You're a *Nobody?!* The stupid call box tried to set me up with a frickin' *Nobody?!*"

"I don't get it," you say.

"Of course you don't! You're a Nobody! That's the point! Look at that—your mem is ninety-eight!" He stares at you. "I mean—*ninety-eight?* What, did you just get here?"

"Yes! Where is here? What is this?"

"Oh, wow. Where do I even begin?"

You tell this Chad01 kid he can begin anywhere, you don't care, you just want to know what's going on.

Chad01 scrunches up his face.

"OK," he says at last. "You see this? See your wrist here? Look at your wrist."

```
LK
RAINBOW
NOBODY
98.02
```

"The numbers changed!" you say. "It used to say ninety-nine."

"Yeah, duh," says Chad01. "But first of all, 'LK' is 'Lost Kid.' Everyone's got that. We're all lost. *Rainbow* is your name. *Nobody*—that's your class. You're a *Nobody,* meaning you're brand-new here, haven't even earned a class yet. OK, and the numbers: the first two are your memory, and the last two are your experience. As you gain experience, you lose memory, but you also earn more gold, and gold is how you get stuff, and getting stuff is how you get out of here."

"But where is here?"

"*The Wilds.* And a Nobody like you and a Warrior like me shouldn't be traveling together. So we gotta get this sorted out. We need a call box. Is there a call box around somewhere?" Chad01 looks at you intently. "You know, one of those blue things with the button?"

So you lead him to the call box. He swipes his wrist, jabs the button, and talks into the slot. "There's been a mistake. I was supposed to meet up with 'Rainbow, a Mystic and Scholar' and you linked me up with Rainbow, a f█cking *Nobody!*" He glances back. "No offense."

The box *BLAP!*s and spits out some papers.

HERE ARE SOME MORE MEMORIES
PLEASE KEEP THEM IN A SAFE PLACE

Chad01 crumples them into a ball and tosses it over his shoulder.

"What was that?" you ask.

"Memories," he says.

"Why'd you throw them away?"

"What are you, like, the litter patrol?"

"No. I mean, why wouldn't you keep the papers . . . if they're memories?"

"No one keeps them," he says. "Memories just make you more sad for home. I got only one I saved—it's about being on a canoe in the lake with my grandpa, and we caught a fish. That's enough for me. They say when you get home, you get all your memories back anyway."

"Who says?"

"Them."

"Who is them?" you ask.

"I don't know. Wizards and sh■t. You ask too many questions, Nobody."

"But you're saying we're *losing* our memories?"

"Um," he says. "Kind of."

"What do you mean, *kind of?*"

"*Jeez* you ask a lot of questions. OK, listen. As your experience goes up, your memory goes down. But you don't really *lose* it. It gets printed on the sheets. So you can read it. Only, it isn't really your memory anymore. It's like a memory of a memory. But it doesn't just *disappear*. The truth is, you *can't* escape your memories. Just wait and see. They're always popping up. You'll have memory flashes between levels, when you're sleeping, or just randomly. Everyone does. My advice? Forget what you can. Memories only hold you back. No need to add to the pain. Just forget that sh█t."

"And that!" you say. "What just happened there? Right when you tried to say 'sh█t'! *That*. How come my voice cut out in the middle? How come we can't swear?"

Chad01 rolls his eyes. "Look. I don't have time to explain *every little thing*. I gotta get this sorted out, OK?" He turns to the call box and slams the button again. "There's been a mistake! I was supposed to meet up with a Mystic and Scholar, see?" He takes a crumpled paper from his pocket and holds it up to the box. "See? *Meet up with Rainbow, a Mystic and Scholar.* I need a new quest, OK?"

The box *BLAP!*s and spits out another paper.

TO UNLOCK NEAREST PORTAL
CRY FOR YOUR BROTHER IN THE RAIN

"Wrong," says Chad01. "Impossible quest! I don't even *have* a brother."

"I do!" you say. "That's who I was looking for when I got lost!"

Chad01 spins to face you. "Yeah? Cool. You can have that quest, and I'll just get another one for me." He turns to the box again, then turns back to you and his expression momentarily softens. "I mean, no offense, but right now you should be training. Building up skills. Me, I'm doing some real next-level sh█t. It's dangerous out there. I've been at this a long time. My memory is in the *single digits*. I've put in my time, and I'm almost home, and just as a rule, I don't roll with Nobodies. But, you know . . . like I said, no offense."

"So you're just going to ditch me?" you ask.

"No! Not *ditch* you. Get you where you need to go."

"I need to go *home*."

"Well, duh," says Chad01. "You and me and everyone else." He slams the button again. "New quest!"

You can't believe it. This kid — the only person for miles — is just going to leave you here.

The box whirs and spits out a paper.

TO UNLOCK NEAREST PORTAL
CRY FOR YOUR BROTHER IN THE RAIN

"No!" Chad01 slams the button. "There's no brother here! There's no rain! *Give me a new quest!*"

BLAP!

TO LOCATE RAIN
WALK 10,000 PACES
IN ANY DIRECTION

Chad01 pounds the metal with his fist. The box shakes.

"GIVE ME." *Wham!* "A NEW." *Wham!* "QUEST!"

Wham!

There's a crackle of static. The machine whirs and spits out another piece of paper.

OUT OF ORDER

Chad01 *whams* the box two more times.

He looks out at the endless field.

"Sh■t," he mutters.

"So what do we do now?" you ask.

"Well . . ." Chad01 looks around again. "Well, *normally* I'd say we get a different ticket from the call box . . ."

But you broke it, you want to say.

He looks for a long moment at the sheet of paper in his hand. "I guess we're gonna count out ten thousand g■dd■mned paces."

TEN THOUSAND PACES

You find yourself walking across the endless field with Chad01. He's a fast walker, and it's hard to keep up and count at the same time. Grass swishes by in a blur. You make it to around five hundred before you lose your place. A minute later, Chad01 stops and turns to you.

"What's your count?"

"Um, five hundred and twenty?"

"Nope," he says. "Five hundred even. You gotta concentrate, OK? This is serious business. Ready?" He takes three slow steps. "Five oh one . . . five oh two . . . *five oh three*. Start from here."

And away Chad01 marches into the grass.

⚘

A couple hundred steps later, it occurs to you that you and Chad01 are different heights and, therefore, taking different-sized steps, so of course you have different numbers. And why would an exact number matter anyway? And why does it have to be the same number?

"Can't we just walk until it rains?" you ask. "Why do we have to count out every step?"

Chad01 stops and turns to you. "Just do what the box said. I don't make the rules. What's your count anyway?"

"Seven oh three?"

"Wrong. *Six ninety*."

"We're taking different-sized steps!" you say.

"What?"

"Your legs are longer! You're taking fewer steps to go the same distance!"

Chad01 blinks. "Let's take a break. Maybe we're dehydrated." He unstraps his backpack and offers you a canteen.

Water. You twist off the top and hold the canteen to your lips and tilt it up. The water is cold and good. You just want to keep drinking it, but you don't want to be rude and drink it all either.

"No worries," says Chad01, as if reading your mind. "Drink as much as you want. We got lots of water." So you drink a bunch and then wipe your face with your sleeve.

⋅⋅⋅

The refreshment puts you in a better mood, but as you follow Chad01 through the endless field, the mood burns away. You've already lost count again. How can it matter? You take out your phone to see if you're getting a signal. It's turned itself off again. You turn it back on. No signal. 6:01 p.m.

"What's your count?" Chad01 asks.

"What's yours?" you say.

"I asked first."

"Yeah, but I went first last time."

"Fine," he says. "Eight thousand and one. You?"

"Yeah."

"Yeah?" His eyebrows go up. "So you got the *exact same* count? Eight thousand and one?"

"Yeah, pretty much," you say.

"Pretty much." Chad01 shakes his head. *"Nobodies,"* he mutters.

⋯

Ten thousand paces is a long way, and your calves are starting to ache and the grass is looking like a great place to just collapse and take a little nap — and then Chad01 begins to slow.

". . . Nine thousand nine hundred and ninety-*eight*," he says. "Nine thousand nine hundred and ninety-*nine* . . . *Ten thousand*."

Chad01 stops. You stop. You look around. It's the same as everywhere else. Gently waving grass. Blue sky. Sun.

⋯

"Where's the rain?" says Chad01.

You've got your phone out, an automatic response, trying to check the weather app. Still no signal.

"What's so special about this spot?" you say.

"I don't know," says Chad01. "This is where it rains. You think we miscounted the paces? Or maybe . . . ?"

But as Chad01's speaking, a strange thing happens. Just like that, the sun whips across the sky and sinks below the horizon, and the light seeps out of the world, and in an instant, it's night. Swirling darkness. Stars twinkling overhead.

"What just happened?" you say.

"The sun went down," says Chad01.

"Well, yeah, but —"

"So here's what we'll do. We'll set up camp here and get some rest and see if anything goes down, precipitation-wise. Maybe give it until tomorrow afternoon. I *really* hope we don't have to recount our steps. Meantime, I'll start a fire."

Your eyes have adjusted somewhat, and you watch as he shrugs off his bag and rummages around and lifts out a couple small logs and a stick. He digs a little hole in the ground, crumples some dead grass in the middle, and lays his logs on top.

Chad01 takes the stick and mumbles something, a series of strange words, like some kind of foreign language, and then he blows on it, and the stick ignites like a reverse birthday candle. Crazy. Chad01 takes the stick and holds it to the grass, and in a moment you have a campfire.

"How'd you do that?" you ask.

"Do what?"

"The fire."

"Fire spell." He says it like it's the most obvious thing.

"How does it work?"

"Magic," says Chad01.

"What do you mean, magic?"

"I mean *magic*. Let's get set up. Lucky for you, I travel with lots of gear."

He reaches into his backpack and pulls out a green tarp, a sleeping bag, and then another sleeping bag, and then a pillow.

You help him spread the tarp on the ground. He plops the sleeping bags on top. "You can have the pillow. I got chairs too."

He reaches into his bag, pulls out two camping chairs, unfolds them, sets them in the grass. Then an umbrella. Then a big down quilt.

"How does all that fit in there?" you ask.

"What?"

"Your backpack—how does it fit all that stuff inside?"

"It's bottomless," says Chad01.

"Bottomless?"

"Yeah, see?" He reaches in and pulls out a djembe drum and drops it back in. "Holds as much as you want, never gets heavier."

"Your backpack is *bottomless?*"

"Yup. Bottomless *and* zero gravity. Check it out for yourself."

You reach in, and your hand keeps going, and then your arm, and then you're all the way up to your shoulder. You look into the backpack and discover a vast darkness, but after a moment, you begin to see objects here and there floating about, rope and clothing and pots and pans.

"Grab us something to eat," says Chad01. "I got some Chonk bars. That's actually *all* I got. There are two flavors: forest berry or chocolate peanut butter. See if you can find one. They're near the guitar."

⁂

You find the bars and grab two, both the same. Wrapped in white plastic with black words: CHOCOLATE PEANUT BUTTER CHONK BAR. No ingredients or nutritional facts or anything. Just those words. You hand one to Chad01 and open the other.

The bar is thick and chewy and tasteless, like a big wad of clay or something. But you're hungry and you make yourself eat it, and when you're done, Chad01 says, "Dig in the bag and grab yourself another. Get a couple if you want."

"I'm OK. Thanks."

"Yeah, good to pace yourself," he says. "And honestly, doesn't matter the flavor; they all taste the same. Trust me, before this is over, you're gonna be *sick* of Chonk bars."

11.

You sit by the fire and watch the glowing embers, the smoke rising into the darkness. You close your eyes and feel the cold breeze against your cheek, the way it gently lifts your hair. The fire pops and crackles. It's all so real and unreal and just *here*. You are in it. You have so many questions, you don't even know where to begin. Chad01 is sitting across from you, warming his hands.

"OK, but a bottomless backpack?" you say. "How is that even possible?"

He gives you a look like you're dumb. "Well, it's obviously a very special and rare magical fabric."

"Magic fabric?"

"Yeah."

"Is magic fabric also why I can't take my pants off?"

"Nah, *that's* because an evil wizard cast a spell."

"You're joking."

"No joke," he says. "An evil wizard cast a spell. Now no one can touch each other *or* themselves. I mean, you can shake hands, touch

57

each other's arms if you're gentle about it, even pat a shoulder—but watch what happens if you try to hug . . ."

He goes to wrap his arms around you, and the moment before you touch—*BRRZAP!*—an invisible force repels you both, sending you stumbling back.

"Yeah," says Chad01. "I remember the day that spell was cast. The biggest bummer was now you had to sh■t your pants. But then a *good* wizard came along and cast a *counter*spell, which makes the sh■t disappear."

"And you believe this. Wizards."

"Of course! And like how we can't swear? That was an evil wizard too! An evil wizard came along and cast a magical spell over all the levels, and now no one can say f■ck, sh■t, b■tch, or even d■mn, or p■ss, or ■ss—which is some real bullsh■t if you ask me. You *can* say 'crap' though, and 'hell.' See? Crap, crappy, crappity, hell."

"So basically your explanation for all this is *magic*."

"Yeah."

"You're saying magic is real."

"*Yes!*"

"That's crazy."

"Huh?" Chad01 leans back. "Whatever. *You* got a magical device. I've seen it. That magic mirror you keep checking."

"My phone? It's not magic."

"Sure, Rainbow," says Chad01. "And so how does this *phone* of yours work?"

"How can you not know what a phone is?"

"My memory, remember? But if you're such an expert in *phones*, then tell me how they work."

"I don't know. I'd look it up for you, but I'm not getting a signal. It's just—" You give it some thought. "Science and technology. Towers or whatever. Electrons. Satellites."

"Satellites?" says Chad01. "What's that?"

"You know, these big machines that float in the sky, and they send signals back and forth between—"

"What's a signal?"

"Like a *ray*," you say. "Invisible rays coming down from the sky. Energy. Light. Only invisible."

Chad01 tilts his head. "Invisible rays of light coming down from the sky?"

"Yes."

"You're telling me *that's* how it works."

"*Yes!*" you say.

"Well, that's magic!" says Chad01.

"Not really."

You take out your phone and try to check it again, but you aren't getting a signal.

"Tell you what." Chad01 pats the purple sling on his chest. It's like a little papoose or something. "You wanna see some magic? OK, I'll show you some magic. You ever seen a baby fuzzy glower before?"

"A what?"

"Most people just call them *fuzzies*. Mine is named Echo Joy, and no one touches it but me—got it? I bought it off a wizard. Cost me fifty thousand gold—*fifty thousand,* I sh■t you not. But here's the deal. Here's what the wizard said. He said, 'Return Echo Joy to the Lake of the Goldfish Moon, and it will give you one bonus poem of ancient wisdom and *unlock the portal home.*"

From the way Chad01 is looking at you, you can tell you're supposed to be impressed.

"And by the way," he says, "that's *guaranteed* by sacred wizard oath."

"Sacred wizard oath."

"Yep. You lucked out, Nobody. You just so happened to run into the one kid with the ticket outta here."

Goldfish Moon? Magic fuzzy? Sacred wizard oath? It's so ridiculous. Then you remember something. The cat.

"Hey," you say. "I had a cat named Goldfish. I mean, she wasn't mine at first, but then she was."

You tell Chad01 about the lady and the cat, Goldfish—at least as much as you can remember; it's kind of hazy—and when you're done, he sort of nods like, *Wow, thank you for sharing that totally not boring story about an old woman and a cat,* and then he says, "So do you wanna see the fuzzy or what?"

 ⁊

Chad01 unzips the top of his sling, and as he pulls back the fabric, a ray of shimmering light pours out, illuminating his face from below. He reaches in and carefully lifts out a small glowing creature, this little, orangish fuzzball with long, feathery, golden hair that glows so bright it's hard to look at directly. Its eyes are closed, and it's sleeping. It's really cute. Like, it makes your chest hurt how cute it is. You sort of want to eat it.

Chad01 holds his creature a moment, and then he opens his hands and lets go. And it just floats there—the creature floats, hovering in the space between you, cute and cuddly, as bright as the afternoon sun.

"Yeah, they can hover and even fly," he says. "But it gets better. Check this out." Chad01 runs his hand through its dazzling hair, and then he gives it a little spin, and the fuzzy pinwheels in the air, giggling in its sleep, shooting out little sparks. "It'll talk to you, too. Try it. Say, 'Hi, Echo Joy,'"

"Hi, Echo Joy."

"Little louder."

"Hi, Echo Joy!"

A tiny mouth appears. The fuzzy yawns, then opens its eyes, big and blue and bright.

"Hi," you say again.

"WHAT IS HI?" it squeaks cheerfully as it floats in the air before you.

"Uh, I was just saying hello."

Echo Joy blinks. "WHAT IS SAYING HELLO?"

"What is saying hello?"

"WHAT IS SAYING HELLO?"

"Um . . ." You aren't sure how to answer. "So . . . I, uh, hear Chad01 is trying to get you to a lake."

"WHAT IS A LAKE?"

"Well, it's like a large body of water."

"WHAT IS WATER?"

"Water? Um, I guess it's sort of like, uh—"

"Yeah," says Chad01. "Echo will keep you up all night with its questions. That's kind of all it does right now. Until I get it to the Lake of the Goldfish Moon. Then it's gonna give me the answers."

The little creature giggles. "WHAT ARE THE ANSWERS?"

Chad01 runs his fingers through the feathery halo of light. "Don't know yet, Echo."

"WHAT IS ECHO?"

"*You* are."

"WHAT ARE?"

"Never mind. We just gotta get you there."

"WHERE IS THERE?"

"Home." Chad01 cups his hands around the fuzzy and nestles it back into his sling. From inside you hear a little yawn followed by a sleepy, squeaky voice — *"what is home?"* — then silence.

"Little trick I learned," says Chad01 as he zips up the sling. "When it's in the dark, the fuzzy shuts up and sleeps."

⚡

"This is not happening," you say.

"What do you mean?" says Chad01.

"This isn't real. Wizards, magic animals, weird names with numbers. This is like — it's like a cartoon — or no, more like a video game or something."

"A *what* game?"

"Video game."

"What's that?" asks Chad01.

"You know — a *video game*. Where you control things with a controller?"

His face is blank. "No idea."

"How can you not remember video games?!"

"Look," he says, "I stopped reading my memories a long time ago. There's a lot I don't remember. But I can tell you this: The Wilds is not a game. This sh█t is for real. Pinch yourself if you don't believe me."

"I already did that," you say.

"Then you *know*," says Chad01. "The pain is what tells you it's real." He stretches, yawns, looks up at the sky. "No clouds yet. We should get some rest while we can."

"Sure," you say.

⚡

You can feel the cold air on your nose and cheeks, but your sleeping bag is warm. The fire is warm. A million stars are spattered in the sky above you. You lie in the darkness and search for familiar constellations, and then you remember that you don't really know any constellations, so instead you think about a god/dess who cannot die, then at some point you fall asleep.

`mem01093i (at some point you just disappear)`

I am seated in a yellow office with some decorative jars, feathery potted plants, and a poster of a lake under a blood-red sky at sunrise or sunset —I can't tell which.

After reading "The Eternal God/dess of Teen Depression," my teacher has referred me to the school counselor, which now that I think about it makes sense just based on the title, let alone what happens in the story. I'm sitting here looking at the poster of the lake, and the counselor is holding the copy of the story that my teacher sent her and asking me if I ever have any thoughts about hurting myself.

This isn't my first time seeing a counselor. I know the questions.

I tell her I know all about suicide and I am very sensitive to it.

I tell her about when I was six, there was a teenage boy with blue eyes who lived up the street. I used to play with his little sister. He shot himself in the garage, and there was a big funeral in the church and then his family moved, and the house was empty for a long time. The day they were moving, I remember playing in the yard with his sister one last time and how quiet everything was.

I tell her about my aunt, who was one of the most amazing people I ever knew and who also took her own life. She asks me the question again. "And do you ever have thoughts of hurting yourself?"

I tell her the truth, which is that at night before I go to bed, sometimes I'll sort of imagine stuff. "But only to help me get to sleep."

The counselor asks me if I would like to elaborate on what sort of stuff I imagine.

"Well . . . like the stuff I wrote about in the story, like the giant cube, and there's the blender jump, which is a diving board on top of this giant blender, and there's the helmet thing . . ."

And it all sounds really gross and insane coming out of my mouth, but the truth is I really do just dream them up as a way to fall asleep. There's something weirdly soothing about imagining my life being extinguished instantaneously as I drift off to sleep, because that's kind of what falling asleep is like, isn't it? At some point you just disappear.

I explain that I think the reason I wrote about this in my story was that I'd just transferred into the class and I was in a hurry and it happened to be the first thing that came to my mind, which OK, maybe says something about my general state of being, but really I was just in a hurry, the assignment was due, so I strung my bedtime daydreams together to make a story about a god who wants to end it all but can't.

But of course, in terms of self-harm, I would never do anything like that.

"It's not like I'm going to just go build a giant cube," I say.

The counselor tells me I'm creative. She tells me I need to be me but also never be afraid to reach out to others. She has big, honest eyes.

"I liked the epilogues," she says.

"What?"

"In your story. I liked how there were not one, but two epilogues."

"Yeah?" I scoot forward in my chair a little. It's almost embarrassing how thirsty I am for praise sometimes.

"Very creative," she says. "But listen."

She makes me promise that anytime I'm having any dark thoughts, I'll talk to her or someone I trust, and she's so nice about it, and on the one hand, I sort of want to grab her by her infinity scarf and yell "SO DO THESE THOUGHTS OF DEATH MEAN I'M CRAZY?" and on the other hand, I just want out of the office, so I reassure her again that it's all just a weird sleep thing—which it is—and I promise tonight I'll try to envision something nicer, like sunset clouds or tiny baby foxes with dragonfly wings.

12.

CRY FOR YOUR BROTHER

You wake up to the sound of gentle tapping. Something cold and wet touches your cheek. Then your forehead. It's raining.

"Chad01!" you say. "Hey, Chad01!"

"*Snnr* — huh?"

"It's raining!"

He scrambles out of his bag. "Right! OK! Let's do this!"

✵

Everything is shiny dark in the rain. Chad01 drops the last of his gear in the bottomless backpack and turns to you. "So now you just gotta cry for your brother, OK?"

"Me?"

"Yeah, you're the one with the brother!"

He's got a point, but you've got questions.

"What does that mean? Like just cry, or cry out his name, or what?"

"Try both!" says Chad01. "And hurry up and do it before the rain ends, OK?"

So you cry out for your brother. "CJ!"

Nothing happens.

The rain falls in the darkness.

"Maybe with a little more emotion," says Chad01.

So you cry louder.

"CJ!!!"

Nothing.

"OK," says Chad01. "Try *actually* crying then."

"How?" you say.

"I don't know. Think of something sad."

"This is ridiculous."

Chad01 shrugs. "Maybe, but it doesn't make it *not* true. Come on, whip up some tears so we can get outta here."

But you can't just cry on command. You're not an actor. You try to think of something sad. You think about the rain instead. It's sad, but not sad enough.

"I can't do this," you say.

"Sure you can!" says Chad01. "Cry for your brother. You miss him, don't you? Think about how much you miss him. You miss him, right?"

Something in you bristles. Of *course* you miss him. You miss *every-thing*. But you don't want to go there right now, in the dark, in the rain, and you don't like being told what to think.

"I'm done with this."

"One more try," says Chad01. "Third time's a charm!"

"This would be like the fifth time."

"Maybe you gotta do it more from the heart or something."

"I'm done."

"Look, the instructions were cry *for* him. Maybe you gotta feel it more. Try it with more emotion, OK? And hurry up. We gotta get this done before the rain lets up. Things move fast in this level. Let's go. Cry *for* your brother. One more time with feeling! Come on and—!"

"Enough!" you shout, or more like scream, because you've had enough, you don't want to hear another word from Chad01 on the subject of crying or your brother or anything else, really, and as the word leaves your lips, Chad01's face is suddenly illuminated in a brilliant radiance, and he smiles and points past your shoulder to a shimmery column of light rising into the rain.

"Portal's open! Good job, Rainbow! Way to cry for your brother!"

"I wasn't crying!"

"Sure seemed like it! Are those tears or rain?"

You wipe your eyes. "Rage tears."

"Cool," he says. "Whatever works. Come on, let's go!"

And Chad01 grabs your hand and pulls you into the light.

mem01861i (the darkness glows)

I'm like three years old, which would make CJ four or five. We're in the back seat of our old car and Dad is pumping gas outside. It must be autumn. I remember the dry leaves and sunlight shining through the window.

Dad gets in. I see a hand. He's got something for us, and then I see what it is, and it totally blows me away—he's holding these two giant glowing crystals, one green and one purple, beveled edges gleaming in the sun. I take the purple one and slide it onto my finger and hold it up to the light. It's magical, the way the darkness glows. I can't believe how beautiful it is.

We drive down the road and I look at my beautiful new ring and imagine how it will open portals to strange lands where I and a color-coded team of adventurer friends will rescue magical creatures from a series of evil but ultimately just misguided wizards. CJ won't stop bugging me: "Eat it! What are you waiting for? It's candy! Hey! Are you there? Can you even hear me?"

No. Just barely. Not really. I'm not in the car anymore. I'm somewhere else, walking along a windy ridge with my friends on a purple crystal adventure.

mem01168w (this stupid challenge)

I'm like fourteen, which makes CJ fifteen or sixteen. This is just before the divorce. There's this stupid challenge going around. There's a new flavor of Sour Patch Kids candy, translucent white Ghost Punch, and you're supposed to scrape the crystal powder into a pipe and record your reaction to smoking it. The fumes are supposedly really terrible, and everyone hacks and coughs and some people even appear to puke —but the twist is this: There's *also* a big rumor that everyone's really faking the coughing fits, and that it's all just one big in-joke, but the only way to know if you're in it or not is to smoke it for yourself and see. CJ likes Sour Patch Kids and doing dumb stuff, so the challenge is a perfect fit.

It's the middle of the night, and I wake up to a sound. A cough. Someone's coughing. Mom's working graveyard, so I get up to check in on CJ, and I smell this terrible burning smell coming from his room, and now I think the house is on fire, and I pound on his door and he's like, "F█ck off, Rainbow."

But I can't f█ck off because first I have to confirm that I'm not going to die in a fire. CJ swears that everything is OK, that I should just go to bed. His voice is all hoarse.

☙

The next morning, I get to watch the video. There he is, my brother, coughing and hacking like an idiot for all his literally dozens of followers.

"So . . . ?" he says.

"So you look like an idiot."

CJ raises his eyebrows. "Or maybe I'm just a good actor?"

I actually burst out laughing.

"I'm serious!" he says.

"*Maybe I'm just a good actor.* Come on! I *smelled* the smoke! It was *so* foul."

"Actually," he says. "Actually, *scientifically* speaking, there's only one way to *really* know for sure. You have to smoke some Sour Patch Ghost Punch powder yourself."

"Actually, no, that's not how science works," I say.

"Well, but *philosophically,* you'll never *really* know unless you have firsthand experience," he says.

"Yeah, guess not."

"And you're OK with that?"

"Very," I say.

CJ, smirking, closes his laptop. "Well I guess then I shall be forever the more wise."

"Oh my god, you are so dumb!"

13.

You find yourself standing on a long, sunlit walkway . . . like an airport or bus station, except there aren't any people. It's empty—no bustling noise, just a low hum. Also, the walls are moving. No, *you* are moving. You are standing on a moving walkway. That's what the hum is. It's carrying you down a corridor lit by fluorescence and skylights. A drinking fountain slides by, a fire alarm, a row of empty electrical outlets. Then there are windows, big windows on both sides of the walkway, and outside, the entire world is gray concrete. Nothing else. Just gray, empty concrete as far as you can see, drifting slowly past, like an enormous, abandoned runway.

"Where are we?" you ask.

"No idea," says Chad01. "Next level."

"And so what do we do?"

"We see where this goes."

Chad01 starts down the moving walkway. You follow. You're moving with the belt, and at first it feels like you're going fast, but after a while you get used to your new speed, and the illusion of progress is countered by the fact that the walkway appears to go on forever.

At some point a vending machine comes into view along the wall. Chad01 hops off, and you do too, and the walls seem to smear like ink as your brain adjusts to the change in motion.

There's a soft and very cute whimpering sound.

"Echo's hungry," says Chad01. "Let's get some grub."

He takes some gold from his backpack and buys a dozen chocolate peanut butter Chonk bars, which is the only thing for sale. You watch as the little metal spirals drop the bars one by one into the bin below.

You hop back on the moving walkway, and Chad01 tosses you a Chonk, and then he unzips his sling and lifts out the little glowing creature, whose floating presence lights up the corridor like a beam of sunshine. Chad01 takes some chewed-up Chonk from his mouth and feeds Echo Joy. The little fuzzy makes humming noises while it eats. The cuteness is almost unbearable. Outside, the endless concrete drifts by.

"OK," says Chad01. "All done?"

"WHAT IS ALL DONE?" says Echo Joy brightly.

"You are, cutie."

"WHAT IS CUTIE?"

"You. You are." Chad01 nestles the fuzzy into his sling.

You hear a tiny yawn, a sweet and sleepy voice muffled in fabric: *"What is you are?"*

.ı.

You follow Chad01 down the walkway. You walk and walk. Outside, the sun sinks lower, the concrete darkens, the sky turns purple, then black, and more lights come on, all at once, a series of bright panels stretching endlessly ahead and behind you. Finally it's time to rest.

Chad01 grabs your sleeping bag out of his bottomless backpack, and you lay it out on the moving walkway and crawl inside. You watch the lights gliding past overhead. What happens if the walkway ends and you're asleep? What if it spills you off a cliff or something?

You have this sudden urge to be close to another human. You look over at Chad01. He's on his side, breathing soft and slow. He must be asleep. You scooch closer to him in your bag until you're lying on your back next to him, and the lights sweep by overhead, an endless illuminated river, and you yawn and turn to nuzzle up against him and —*BRRZAP!* the invisible force throws you back, and Chad01 shouts and scrambles out of his sleeping bag to his feet.

"Ah! What is it?! What's going on?" He looks around, scanning the empty corridor, the moving walls. "Oh. OK. I musta fallen asleep. I dreamed a horrible creature tried to bite me . . . everything OK, Rainbow?"

"Yeah," you say.

Chad01 crawls back into his bag. "Nighty-night."

`mem01869a (our common suffering)`

After the move, I don't have a lot of friends. Or really any friends. Not in real life, anyway. Before the divorce, I was friends with CJ, but not really anymore. We've changed. The thing that should have brought us together has only pushed us apart. Don't ask me why. I'm just a kid.

The only friends I have now are online, in a game I play sometimes at night. It's an ancient adventure game with ridiculous campaigns and no final goal, and almost no one plays it these days, and that's kind of why I like it. Mostly I just hang out with some other players and chat about school and life.

There's four of us, and we're all from different places, but we've got the same problems—loneliness, frustration, boredom. Even in the game, I'm not much of a talker—they call me "The Storyteller" as a joke. But I do chime in now and again, and I listen and I care and I find comfort in our common suffering.

It's kind of a repetitive game, but that's what makes it good: the reliability of it all. Just another late night, four lonely travelers wandering the randomly generated worlds, wishing *this* was our life, this low-res landscape of pastel colors and intermittent lag, where there is no homework, no depression, only endless polygon trees, save points, and the occasional NPC.

14.

THE WANDERING SONG

You wake up and open your eyes as the memory fades. Daylight. You're on your back. Ceiling tiles, fluorescent arrays, and skylights drift past. You've been in motion all this time, gliding along the moving walkway. How far have you gone? You glance back at the tunnel receding behind you.

♪

You start down the corridor again with Chad01. You walk and walk. You think, *What is the point of walking if we're moving anyway? Where are we even going?*

And then you hear something. Music.

♪

"Do you hear that?" you say.

"Hear what?" says Chad01.

"The song."

"What song?" he asks.

"The *song*. You know—it's like . . . happy part, sad part, dark part . . . ?"

"Oh, wait," says Chad01. "Does it go like, dah, dah-dah-dah, duh-dah dah *dah*?"

"Yes."

"The Wandering Song!" he says. "That means we're near a call box . . . look, there it is."

A blue box comes drifting into view. You and Chad01 hop off and scan your IDs, and the machine goes *BLAP!* and spits out a paper.

TO UNLOCK NEAREST PORTAL, PULL ANY FIRE ALARM

Chad01 shakes his head. "F■ckin' typical, right? Walk two days to find we had the answer all along . . . and look, there's one right there." He's pointing to a fire alarm on the wall beside you. "You can have the honors."

"How can you remember fire alarms and not phones or video games?"

"Beats me. Do you wanna pull it or not?"

Of course you do. You've always had the urge to pull a fire alarm, and now here you are. You grip the metal handle and pull down. An alarm begins to sound, *BOOOOP! BOOOOP! BOOOOP!,* and the sprinklers go off, raining down from the ceiling, drenching you instantly. The sound is furious. You stand in the falling water, covering your ears.

"There!" Chad01 shouts.

You see it down the hallway. A column of light shimmering in the spray, brilliant white reflecting off thousands of tiny drops.

BOOOOP! BOOOOP!

The alarm is so loud you can't hear the sound of your feet as you splash off after Chad01 through the mirrored water, like running through liquid silver. You follow him into the light, and in a flash, you are gone.

Her latest creation stands in splendor on the boundless, whispering prairie: an enormous hippo-like creature with mighty jaws that can crush a watermelon like a balloon. The Eternal God/dess of Teen Depression knows this for a fact because she's tested it just to be sure. She has fed her magnificent beast the following items so far:

two watermelons

four coconuts

five pumpkins

five squash

various other hard-shelled gourds

one bowling ball

It might as well have been eating grapes. This creature has *really* strong jaws. All you have to do is tickle its chin. Because here's the thing: this beautiful, resplendent animal, which she has just now decided to call Quincy (scientific name: *Hippogantua masticae*), has a peculiar automatic reflex: when its chin is tickled, its jaws slam together like a trap.

The Eternal God/dess of Teen Depression takes this stunning creature out for a jog on a sunny autumn afternoon and then feeds it some yummy sugared grapefruits and tucks it into its giant, comfy bed and sings it lullabies until it finally yawns, and when it does, the Eternal God/dess of Teen Depression slips her head in the beast's mouth, reaches down, and tickles its chin.

Crunch.

Back again. As soon as the Eternal God/dess of Teen Depression is dead, she is alive again. Broken, she is whole again, popping instantly back into existence like a reverse bubble.

"This bites," she says, not swearing for once because suddenly she's got other concerns.

In her brief absence, the Eternal God/dess of Teen Depression's problems have multiplied. Now our sweet enormous Quincy is traumatized because it is a peaceful herbivore and was just tricked into literally bursting a head, and the Eternal God/dess of Teen Depression reincarnates to find the poor creature just sort of standing there shivering with one eye twitching, so she turns gentle Quincy into a happy fluttering bug and gives unto it a friend, another fluttering bug, and the two bugs flutter off and are eaten by a bird who dies in a snowstorm that night and is devoured by a wandering fox who is hit by a school bus the next morning in whose next-to-last row is seated a kid whose father will not make it to a single one of her soccer games the entire season.

15.

MACHINE FOREST

You find yourself standing on a wooden dock on misty water. The hall is gone, and the moving walkway. The sprinklers are gone. The alarm is gone. You lower your hands from your ears. You're completely drenched. Water pours from your fingertips to the dock. It's dark out, but not completely. Twilight maybe, or early morning. The light almost seems to be coming from the mist.

Above you, the sky is shrouded. Shadows of trees loom hazy along the shore, vines hanging like necklaces. Wooden boards creak underfoot as you shift your weight. The water under the dock is scummy, and there's a chemical odor, like fertilizer or gasoline.

Chad01 is muttering something to himself as he wrings the water from his hoodie.

"Where are we?" you ask.

"F█ckin' machine forest."

"What's that?"

"*This,*" he says. "What you see. Nasty, overgrown, nowhere to go. Lots of levels are like this. It pops up and takes over. The other

problem with machine forests is it means there's probably night screamers around."

"Night screamers?"

Chad01 peers into the darkness. "We can't go in the forest anyway.
It's too overgrown. Let's see where the water goes, yeah?"

He opens his backpack and pulls out a suitcase . . . a lamp . . . a
whisk . . . and then two wooden paddles, a bicycle pump, and a big wad
of rubbery plastic that turns out to be a giant inflatable swan. He pumps
up the swan, grabs it by the neck, and eases it off the dock into the water.
Then he dumps everything else back in the bag except the paddles.

He's holding one out for you.

"All aboard."

⋅⋏⋅

You pull your oar through the dark water. It's quiet, no birds or insects
or frogs or anything, just the gentle sound of paddling as the swan
drifts through the mist. The gasoline smell rising into your sinuses.

"What are night screamers?" you ask.

"Don't even worry about it," says Chad01.

"But —"

"Look, there's the other shore, I think. More machine forest."

Dark shapes loom in the distance again. There's a small beach
among the tangle of trees. You wade ashore. Chad01 drags the swan
up onto the sand, opens the little plug, and leaps on top, slowly sink-
ing down as the swan deflates. He crumples it up and stuffs it into his
backpack along with the paddles.

⋅⋏⋅

You start up the path, Chad01 in the lead. It's darker here, branches
gathered in a dripping canopy overhead. Everything is wet, the pebbly
ground slippery, each footstep ringing out with an odd metallic sound.

It isn't pebbles. You can see that now. The path is covered in bits of metal—screws and washers, stuff like that—grinding and clinking underfoot with each step.

A vine brushes against your face and you push it aside. It has a strange texture, slippery like wet rubber. You grab another one. It isn't a vine. None of them are. The vines—they're electrical cords, cables, and hoses.

And the trees, they aren't trees. They're metal. They're all around you, rising into the shrouded sky, towering stacks of dark machinery, balanced on top of one another as if by a crane, all of it overgrown with slippery, black moss. It's warm and humid. The machinery is literally dripping. You feel a drop hit your cheek, then your arm. It isn't water. It's something else, something dark and slippery.

"What is this?" you say.

"What's what?" says Chad01.

"The forest is, like, dripping stuff."

"Don't be afraid. Just keep your eyes on the trail, OK? Don't look around."

So of course you start to look around. At first it's just dark, unidentifiable shapes, but then some of it becomes familiar: hoses . . . fan blades . . . pipes . . . And then you see what appears to be a tuft of hair sticking out from oily gears. It's everywhere you look now, tangled in the machinery—dark, bloody hair, and bits and pieces of what look like *meat*.

"Chad01?" you say.

"Don't be afraid," he says.

"Chad01, the forest—"

"Shh!" he says. "No talking. Just walking."

The path turns, and you are in a denser place now. The forest closes in and oily, black liquid drips like rain from the canopy overhead. It's even darker, the mist grows thicker until you can't see the ground—but you can hear it now, the squish of mud and then the slap of shoes on puddles, and the cold, oily bog water runs into your sneakers, soaking your socks, and everything smells like gasoline and rotting meat.

The bloody stuff drips, *ploink . . . ploink . . .* into the water.

"That way," says Chad01. "Come on."

He splashes ahead, running now, and you follow after through the foul chemical air. The fumes are making you sort of giddy. The machine forest is deep and misty, and you see things in it, and you can't tell if they are real or not. A hut with a chimney. A telephone pole. You could swear at one point you catch a glimpse of a sunny glade filled with flowery, white stalks of tall grass.

Suddenly the ground is dry again, the bog is gone. The machinery opens up to reveal a gray sky. You start up a hill. The ground gets looser as the path gets steeper. Bits of metal slide under your feet and go clinking down the slope as you climb. The path levels off and the machines close in again overhead. You follow Chad01 down the winding trail, walking and walking, until suddenly he stops. Two figures in matching black hoodies are blocking the path. A boy and a girl.

"Outta the way," says Chad01. "Coming through."

"*Shh,*" says the girl.

"What?"

"*Shh!*"

"Are you *shushing* me?" says Chad01. "Don't shush me. No one shushes me."

"There are night screamers about," the boy whispers. He has dark eyes and bushy eyebrows and round cheeks. The girl has similar features, but on her they are wilder somehow. Her eyebrows are even more severe. Her hair is long and dark and messy, with glass beads and faded cloth and dry flowers entwined in it, a stray lock falling across one eye.

"Night screamers?" says Chad01. "Who cares? I ain't scared."

"Someone is," says the girl.

"What makes you say that?"

"I can feel it."

"Hey," you say. "Hey. Will someone tell me what night screamers even are?"

"You don't know about night screamers?" says the boy.

"Rainbow here is a Nobody," says Chad01.

The boy's eyes widen. "Oh . . ."

"What are night screamers?" you ask.

"Don't worry about it," says Chad01. "Literally. Just. Don't. Worry."

"Night screamers sense fear," says the boy.

"So all you gotta do is not be afraid," says Chad01.

"But why would I be afraid?" you ask.

"Don't even worry about it," says Chad01. "No reason."

"Well, *actually* . . ." The boy fixes you with his dark eyes. "*One* reason would maybe be the fact that if you *see* night screamers, you will become riveted in terror and die screaming with blood running out of your eyeballs and a—"

"OK, OK, that's enough," says Chad01. "We don't need a lecture. As long as you aren't scared, nothing happens. Let's go, Rainbow."

"I really wouldn't," says the girl.

"Thanks for the tip," says Chad01. "Let's go."

"What about the night screamers?" you ask.

"Ugh! You're *still* on that?" Chad01 wheels around and fixes you with his gaze. "Look—*Rainbow*. There's nothing to be afraid of. OK? Even if you do see one, *all you gotta do is cover your eyes.* Like this, see? Peekaboo. That's all. Plus, not to mention, you'd have to stare a *long* time before you even start to—"

"Three seconds," says the boy.

"What? Longer than *that*," says Chad01.

"Not according to my wiki."

"You got a wiki?" says Chad01.

"Yes."

"Is it complete?"

"No," says the boy. "None of them are complete."

"I'll give you four hundred gold for it," says Chad01.

"It isn't for sale."

"Five hundred."

"Sorry. Not for sale."

"Five-fifty," says Chad01. "Final offer."

"Listen," the girl whispers. "We haven't exactly got time to stand about chatting. *They're going to locate us.*"

"That's your problem, not mine. Let's go, Rainbow."

"Um," you say. "Maybe we should listen to them."

"These clowns?" says Chad01. "Are you serious? They probably aren't even real! Let's go." He shoves past the boy and then the girl.

"Watch it," says the girl.

"Forget it, Lark," says the boy. "No more fights, OK?"

"Ha!" Chad01 laughs. "Yeah, hold her back. I'm *so* afraid."

The girl smiles. "Oh, you're tough, then," she says.

"Nah. I'm actually sh■tting my pants over here."

The girl steps up to him. "We've got a tough guy on our hands, have we?"

"Lark . . ." says her companion. He turns to you and Chad01. "It's just . . . we'd really rather you tried avoiding the Screamers—for all our sake."

"And I'd really *rather* you kiss my ■ss," says Chad01. "How about that?"

"How about you try shoving me again?" says the girl.

"Yeah, OK."

Chad01 steps forward—and the girl grabs his arm and pulls him *toward* her, and whispers something in his ear . . . and he drops like a stone to the ground. You watch the whole thing sort of dumbfounded, and you're too slow to realize that now it's your turn, the girl is grabbing your arm, she's whispering strange words into your ear, and the last thing you feel is gravity take hold as everything goes black.

16.

SOUR

You wake to find yourself tied to a tree with an orange extension cord. Chad01 is bound up next to you, head slumped forward. It isn't a tree, it's some kind of metal beam. Right—the machine forest. You hear a sound and look over to see the boy and girl standing a ways off, partially shrouded in darkness, talking quietly to each other.

With a snort, Chad01 wakes up.

"Hey!" he says. "Hey! What's going on?"

"*Shh!*" says the girl.

"Untie me!"

She comes over and presses her hand to his mouth to quiet him. In her other hand, she's holding his sling by the straps, the one with Echo Joy sleeping inside.

"That's my sling!" Chad01 says, wriggling his face free. "You better not—"

There's a sound in the distance. A long, chilling screech, somewhere between a laugh and a scream.

After a moment, it stops.

The boy has joined you now. "Listen," he hisses. "We don't have much time before they find us, OK? So here's the rundown. I'm Owlsy —I'm a scholar—and this is my twin sister, Lark, a mystic. We're on a quest to return the purple crystal power ring to the City of a Thousand Days and Nights. Do you have any relevant information, or would you like to join us?"

"Hell no," says Chad01. "Here's your *information*: that's a garbage quest. I can tell you one thing, you aren't getting home with a power crystal."

"According to my wiki, we have ninety-three percent odds."

"Your wiki can bite my d■ck."

You remember something. "Hey," you say. "Hey, Chad01. That paper you showed me when we first met. Weren't you looking for a mystic and a scholar?"

"Yeah, but instead I got a Nobody."

"Maybe it was three separate people," you say.

"What?"

··

The boy digs into Chad01's pocket, removes several sheets of paper, flips through them until he finds the one you were talking about, and reads it. "'Meet up with Rainbow, a Mystic and Scholar . . .' Hm . . . a sentence in need of an Oxford comma for sure . . . We haven't been to a call box in a bit, but it would seem that this paper is talking about us, wouldn't you think, Lark?"

"I thought it was just Rainbow," says Chad01.

"No, I think it's three separate people," says Owlsy.

The girl, Lark, sort of shrugs. "Why not?" She's barely whispering now. "Why wouldn't the call box try to link us up with a Nobody and a Flaming ■sshole?" She turns to Chad01. "That is your class, isn't it? Level Four Flaming ■sshole?"

"F█ck off."

"Oh, and he's witty, too. Let's see what's in the bag, shall we?"

"DON'T YOU DARE! NO ONE TOUCHES—MMPH!" The hand again.

"*Shh.*"

Lark opens the top of his sling, and the light pours out as she lifts the fuzzy's glowing body into her hands. The orange feathery hair, tipped with luminescent gold. Shiny, blue eyes gaze back. Its tiny mouth opens, and it giggles.

"Wow, you are *cute!*" Lark turns to Chad01. "This thing is *really* cute!"

"WHAT IS REALLY CUTE?" it says.

"You, but you should probably be quiet so we aren't—"

"WHAT IS BE QUIET SO WE AREN'T?"

From out of the forest comes another laughing scream.

"WHAT IS AHHAHAHAHAHA?" echoes the fuzzy.

Owlsy turns to you. "How do you shut it up?"

The fuzzy giggles. "WHAT IS SHUT IT UP?"

"Shh!"

"WHAT IS SHH?"

"Untie me!" says Chad01. "Untie me and I'll shut it up!"

"Not until you promise to be civil," says Lark.

"I ain't promising sh█t!"

"WHAT IS PROMISING SH█T?"

Another scream rips through the air.

"Fine," says Owlsy. "We'll set you free, but that means we're a *team* then, OK? From here on out, we help each other." He looks at you, then Chad01. "Is that a deal?"

"Whatever," says Chad01.

"Yes or no."

"*Fine*. Just untie me."

"And you, Rainbow?"

"Sure," you say.

᠅

So the twins untie you, and Chad01 takes the glowing fuzzy in his arms and strokes its wispy fur and shoves it back into the sling, where it yawns and promptly falls asleep again.

"Listen," he says. "If any of you *ever* touch Echo again—"

"I have a suggestion," Owlsy whispers. "Rather than stand about chatting, why don't we—"

"Don't need your suggestions," says Chad01. "Didn't ask for them, didn't n—"

Before he can get the rest of the sentence out, another shrieking howl rings through the darkness. It's crazy close. Your ears are ringing with it, skin crawling. You turn to the others, like, *What now?*

Chad01 catches your eye, blinks.

"Fine," he says. "Let's go."

᠅

You are running down the trail. Metal clinks underfoot. Cables and cords whip past. The forest is so overgrown in places it's like you're in a tunnel. You catch a glimpse of something that looks like a bloody eyeball. You tell yourself it was just your imagination. You run until your legs are burning. Finally, in a clearing under the dripping machines, you stop with the others, hands on knees, and catch your breath.

The forest is silent, no more laughing screams.

"OK," Chad01 whispers. "No one be afraid anymore—*OK?*"

"Here's the deal," says Owlsy. "Lark and I know how to get out of this level. We just need some sour."

"Sour?" says Chad01. "How much you need?"

"How much do you have?" says Lark.

"None. I usually just pay in gold."

"Gold won't work here," says Owlsy. "Only sour."

"What's *sour*?" you ask.

"A magic powder," says Chad01.

"Grass dust," says Lark.

"Technically it's a pollen," says Owlsy. "Found on tall clusters of white grass blossoms. And very rare. You see, sour grass has adapted so it will only grow out of the foulest of oily bogs, and then of course you have to catch it when it's in bloom."

"Tall white flowers?" you ask. "I think maybe I saw some."

"What? Where?"

"Earlier. When we were running down the path, me and Chad01. I'm not sure, but I thought I saw a little, like, glade, and there was this grass with, like, white flowers and—"

A laughing scream cuts you off. This one is shorter than the others, just a quick cackle, but *loud*.

Lark touches your arm. "Will you show us the flowers?" she says.

⚬⚬

You're leading everyone back down the trail now, suddenly less sure of yourself. You saw the flowers, right? Earlier with Chad01. A little glade with grass in bloom? But what exactly is a *glade* anyway? This whole thing is just—

Another scream. Evil laughter. Even closer.

Now you are sprinting through the mechanical trees, cords and hoses whipping past your face, and the metal clinking under foot making such a racket anyone could easily follow you. Where is the glade?

Where are the white blossoms? Did you just imagine it? You smell oil and gasoline, and before long, you are walking through the bog again. And then you spot them.

"There!"

"Brilliant!" says Owlsy.

You find yourself standing at the edge of a clearing with tall grass growing up out of the bog, and the grass is covered in white blossoms, like cattails in bloom, and as you splash over to them, a sweet, fruity odor mixes with the gasoline, and you can see that the blossoms aren't blossoms at all, they are—you can hardly believe it—they are Sour Patch Kids. Yes, it's true. You hold one in your hand, a little gummy caked in sour sugar. All around you, the grass has these big, white stalks covered with sugary, translucent candy.

"These are Sour Patch Kids," you say.

"What?" says Chad01.

"Sour Patch Kids. It's a candy. Ghost Punch flavor, I think."

"Well, actually, no," says Owlsy. "*Actually,* sour is a very powerful and dangerous plant. The way it works is, if a person smokes the crystal pollen, they can temporarily see and unlock the nearest portal. However, they may only do this *once*. If they smoke sour again, they achieve even more powers, but at the same time they become hopelessly addicted and—"

"I'm pretty sure it's candy," you say.

"*Um . . .*" says Owlsy. "No offense, but you're still a Nobody, so—"

"I've *seen* them before. I remember them from home!"

Owlsy nods. "Well, yes, but you've got to understand. Items from memory often appear in the Wilds. It's not an uncommon phenomenon. In fact—"

"Hey," says Lark. "How about we finish this conversation later?"

"Well, but Rainbow needs to know about Keepers," says Owlsy. "This is important. You see, Keepers are—"

"They're junkies," says Chad01.

"Lost Kids like us," says Owlsy. "But they made the mistake of smoking sour more than once. Now they're extremely powerful and also extremely addicted, and this can make them extremely dangerous. People call them *Keepers* because they will often guard a locked portal and demand sour in order to—"

The conversation is interrupted by a laughing scream in the distance.

"Enough chitchat," Lark hisses. "Let's go."

You hurry with the others into the stinking bog, gathering Ghost Punch Sour Patch Kids and stuffing them into plastic baggies supplied by Chad01.

"Awesome," he says. "Got enough here for the next hundred Keepers! Where to now? Where's the Keeper?"

"Back that way," says Owlsy.

"Where we just came from?" Chad01 asks.

"Yep," says Lark.

"But that's where the screamers are," you say.

"Very true."

"Well, not *necessarily* true," says Owlsy. "Screamers are superfast. So they could *actually* be anywhere by now."

THE HAND

Out of the bog and back to the main trail. Back up the other way again. You run and you run, following the others through the looming machinery, and then there's another laughing scream. This time it's in front of you. You skid to a halt. Owlsy holds up his hand, unnecessarily, for silence. The back of your neck feels like it's got electricity going through it. You stand, holding your breath, as the scream fades into the darkness.

⠼

"This way," Lark whispers.

You follow her down a side path you hadn't noticed before. It comes to a dead end in a dense thicket of machinery, but then you see it: a white panel midway up the pile of junk, like an oven door. Lark stretches on her tiptoes to open it, then lifts herself up and disappears inside. Owlsy goes next. Then Chad01. Then you.

⠼

It's like a tunnel inside, and it smells really, really bad, this warm, foul breath of rotten meat and sweat and pee all mixed together. You have to fight not to gag as you follow the others. Deeper you go, tracing your hands along the low ceiling. Everything is wet and slimy. You can't see a thing.

The tunnel seems to widen into a cave, and the others suddenly stop.

"Hi," says Owlsy. "We've brought you the sour."

⁂

In the darkness, no one answers. But you can feel it—there's someone else here.

"So yeah." Owlsy clears his throat. "We've returned with—"

"I heard you the first time," says a voice, the voice of a girl maybe, low and raspy. It could be any age. It's barely a whisper. "You said a couple hours."

"Well, yes, but—"

"It's been all day."

"Right. We got a bit sidetracked, but we're here now, and we've got it."

"You brought others here to take my loot. I should just let the screamers have you."

"If the screamers get us," says Owlsy, "they'll get you too."

"No they won't. I'm the one who brings people here."

"Do you want the sour or not?" says Lark.

⁂

From out of the darkness a hand slowly appears. It's so close. Way closer than you expected. From the acoustics, it sounded like the voice was in the back of the cave. But it's right here in front of you, dirty, waiting. Owlsy places his baggie on the open palm, and the disembodied hand withdraws into the darkness. It reappears, empty.

"More."

He hands over another baggie.

The hand returns.

"More."

"Unlock the portal."

"..."

"Unlock the portal!" Owlsy says again.

"I already did."

"Where is it then?"

"More."

"Give him yours, Lark," says Owlsy. "You too, Rainbow."

You hand the Keeper your baggie of sour.

"You've got more. I can smell it."

"You've had enough," says Owlsy. "That's more than double what we promised. Tell us where the portal is."

"On the island," says the voice.

"What island?"

"The one in the middle of the bog, duh."

"And how are we supposed to get there?"

"How should I know? Swim."

The figure moves, and there's a *snick* and a sudden flash of light. And you see it, a face floating in the dark. Pale skin. Black eyes.

"Run!"

Chad01 is pulling you back down the tunnel and out of the cave, and when you're safely outside, everyone stops.

"What's going on?" you ask.

"The Keeper is smoking the sour," says Chad01.

"Those fumes are deadly," says Owlsy. "Lark and I have used up our one turn, and I assume Chad01 has by now as well . . ."

"Yeah," says Chad01. "I escaped a dragon maze that way."

"Right," says Owlsy. "And so if any of us catch just one more whiff of it, we'll become like that kid in there, totally addicted and—"

A scream sounds from the forest.

"Awesome," says Lark.

"We need a boat," says Owlsy.

"I've got a boat!" says Chad01.

"You've got a boat?"

"It's a swan!"

"Great! Let's go!"

18.

THE FEAR

At the edge of the dark water, Chad01 pulls a pumpkin from out of his backpack, then a unicycle, then the bicycle pump, two paddles, and then the inflatable swan. Screams echo in the forest behind you as he pumps furiously and the swan balloons slowly into existence.

With the four of you aboard, it dips low in the water as you push off from the shore, with Chad01 and Lark rowing.

Even though you're in the bog now, the screams seem to be growing closer.

"Can night screamers swim?" you ask.

"Yes," says Owlsy. "And fly," he adds.

"They can *fly?*"

"Doesn't matter," says Chad01. "Just don't think about it! You just gotta not let yourself be afraid!"

⸕

Chad01 and Lark paddle the swan across the misty water, and the laughing screams grow closer and closer—and then suddenly they stop. There's a moment of silence, but only a moment, and then the sound

97

of whispering begins. This evil whispering in the mist all around you, from every direction.

"They may have located us," says Owlsy.

And that's when you see it: a dark shape creeping toward you, skimming over the water like some kind of evil cloud.

"There!" you say. "Look!"

The others turn their heads to where you're pointing.

"What?"

"Where?"

"There!" you say again. "Right there!" You can't see what it is exactly, just this dark shape moving toward you. Something unspeakably horrible and evil.

"Well don't *look* at it!" Chad01 yells. "Someone cover Rainbow's eyes!"

Cold fingers blanket your face. "Don't look! Don't be afraid!"

But even in the darkness behind the hands, you can see it — or more like feel it — moving closer and closer across the water, gaining on you.

Images flash through your mind — horrible shapes, glowing eyes. Or are they right there in front of you? You can't tell.

"Rainbow!" Chad01 says. "Rainbow, can you hear me? They can't find you if you're not afraid! Don't be afraid!"

You can't speak. If you open your mouth, the darkness will hear you and devour you and everyone. You can sense it, hovering near you, listening for you, calling out your name. *Rainbow, Rainbow, where are you? Come out, come out, wherever you are . . .*

"Breathe!" says Lark. "Take some deep breaths. We're almost there!"

You feel the swan bump up against something.

Come out, come out and play with me!

"*Rainbow,*" says Chad01. "Stay with us. Don't give in to the fear!"

He sounds afraid.

"Where's the portal?" says Owlsy. "I don't see a portal!"

"Are you certain this is the right island?" Lark asks.

They all sound afraid.

"Well, it's got to be here *somewhere.*" You feel the hands fall from your face.

"What are you *doing?* Cover Rainbow's eyes!"

It's too late. You don't want to open your eyes, but it's like something is prying your lids apart. This irresistible force. And just as Owlsy places his hands over your eyes again, you see it. Just a glimpse. A dark form. And the face — the way it's twisted. Open mouth. Teeth. Tongue. Howling laughter.

No.

It's —

You can hear another sound, this terrible moaning.

"Guys? We're losing Rainbow!"

You wriggle and squirm and kick and flail as the moaning sound grows louder. You realize, finally, that it's coming from your own mouth.

The face. The twisted, screaming face.

"There!" calls a voice. "The portal! Down the path! Let's go!"

"Wait! My swan!"

"Forget the swan! Grab Rainbow!"

You feel them pulling you. But the face. It's coming for you.

It already has you. It's here.

So this is what it's like to die.

A sort of good thing happens: the counselor convinces my English teacher to let me redo "The Eternal God/dess of Teen Depression" so I won't fail the class. I just have to get a printed copy in by 3:00 p.m. on the Friday before finals week. It's an in-service day for the teachers, which means kids don't have school. Of course, I've waited to do everything at the last minute. Like the very last minute.

It's 2:36 p.m. and I've just printed the final page, and I'm pacing around the trailer waiting for CJ to show up with his van and give me a ride into town. He took off earlier to "run some errands," and I've texted him and called him twice, and he hasn't answered. I've tried calling Mom, but her phone is off for work. It's eight miles into town. I scan through a mental list of any other person in the world who could give me a ride — and come up with an answer of zero.

I call the school. It goes to voicemail. I start to leave a message, but then I decide I should just email my teacher, so I hang up, but then I can't find her email.

Just as I'm about to lose it, I hear the crunch of tires outside. So typical. A door slams shut, and I can see him out the window, walking up the drive with a bag of chips in his hand like it's just the most chill day ever in the history of humankind.

I whip open the front door and rush outside. "Hey! You said you'd be back an hour ago!"

My brother pauses on the walk. "Well, I got into some—"

"You got *snacks!*"

"I was at the gas station! I got a flat!"

"So why didn't you answer your phone?"

"I was fixing the flat!"

"You could have texted me—it isn't that hard!" I stare into his skull wishing I could explode it with my eyes.

There's much I want to say right now, but I need a ride from him, so I take a breath and find a calmer voice. "Did you even read my messages? I need to be at school like *right now*."

"Sure, you bet," CJ says as he slides past me.

"Wait, where are you going? Come back! I need to go now!"

"Chill out! I just gotta get something." The words drift over his shoulder as my brother disappears into the trailer, and I stand absolutely still for a furious moment, and then I decide that OK, I will just take his f■cking keys and drive myself. I've got my permit.

I'm about to run in after him when the door opens and my brother appears, holding what appears to be a clear plastic binder, which he hands to me.

"You're welcome," he says.

"What?"

"For your paper. You know—so it looks good when you hand it in."

I stand there a moment completely dumbfounded. My brother can be surprisingly thoughtful when I least expect it. I mean, I don't need a clear plastic binder. My teacher has actually expressly forbidden us from handing in our work encased in any kind of ornamental exoskeleton including folders, envelopes, and clear plastic binders. Really one of the last things on Earth I am in need of right now is a clear plastic binder. But yeah, OK.

CJ is looking at me. "So do I get a thanks or what?" he says.

"Or what," I say. "Can we *please* just go now?"

.•.

We climb into the van and start down the road. I check my phone again. I can hardly believe it. We've actually still got enough time, maybe even a couple minutes to spare. I slide back into the seat and take a breath, and CJ makes the second turn onto the main road, and that's when I see them. In the distance on the wet black pavement. Two cats, standing in the left lane doing their cat thing, some kind of cat showdown. One of the cats is black, and the other one is orange, and I recognize her right away, and my foot goes down to slam on the break, but of course I'm not the one driving, and in the same moment I yell, "Cats!"

And CJ says, "Ha, right," and swerves the van *toward* them.

⁂

We're still at some distance when he swerves the van, and he's only joking—at least that's what he'll say later—and OK, it's true, he only swerves it a *little* and then jerks the wheel back the other way. But this only confuses the cats. They dash off in one direction and then careen back the other way, orange chasing black, and I hear myself yell, "Agh!" as CJ jerks the wheel and slams on the brakes, but it's too late, we hit one, *THUMP*, I can feel it—and there's this terrible drawn-out screeching *crrrunch* as the van slides into a metal utility pole and we jerk to a stop.

⁂

There's a lot to think about, but for the moment I'm not thinking; I'm just experiencing. I'm living in the *oh wow*-ness of having just witnessed a series of events go impossibly wrong, one after another. I'm just looking. It's all coming at me in flashes.

⁂

I'm running back up the street. There's something there. A dark stain smeared across the wet pavement. A lump near the curb. A little mound, like clothing, an old orange sweatshirt left in the rain. It isn't a sweat-shirt. It's Goldfish.

Her head is twisted around, her hair is sticking out, and her mouth is open like she's screaming, but there's no sound, she isn't moving. She's dead. It's crazy. CJ couldn't have hit her more perfectly for maximum death. My brother just killed our cat dead on the street. *My cat.*

19.

ICE

You find yourself standing with the others on a large sheet of frosty ice, like an iceberg or something, in the middle of a stormy ocean. The lake is gone. The forest is gone. And the darkness. And the screamers. And you aren't dead.

A cold wind claws at you, tearing into your memories of the van, the crash, Goldfish. You feel sort of nauseous.

What is this place?

You look around. Steely waves break across the edges of the ice, sending spray into the air. Beyond this, as far as you can see, in every direction, nothing but the choppy water and the still, gray sky. You stand shivering as your memories fade.

"You OK?" says Chad01. "That was close. Screamers almost gotcha, didn't they? I *told* you not to be afraid."

⁂

Owlsy has his wiki out. He flips through the pages of the little book.

"OK . . . there's an entry here. Let's see, uh . . . *When the ice melts, the portal will unlock.*"

"When the *ice melts?*" says Chad01. "Seriously?"

"Seriously."

"What else does it say?"

"Nothing." Owlsy scans the gray sky. "We just need a little sunshine, that's all."

"We're going to need more than sunshine to melt this," says Lark.

"What we *need* is a *boat*," says Chad01. "I can't believe I left my g█dd█mn swan back there."

⨋

"You should try manifesting again," Owlsy says to his sister.

"You can manifest?" says Chad01.

"Of course she can," says Owlsy. "All mystics can."

"Why didn't you guys tell me before? So manifest us a portal outta here!"

"It doesn't work like that," says Lark.

"She's a rank-two Mystic," says Owlsy. "She can't simply *manifest* a portal. It isn't that easy."

"I thought you said that's what mystics did!" says Chad01.

"Well, no, it's more complex than that." Owlsy's got his wiki out again. "OK, here it is: Mystics. *Mystics are a rare class with above-average empathic abilities and below-average faith. A rank-one Mystic may possess limited and hazy precognition. A rank-two Mystic, in addition to precognition, may on occasion, with random fidelity and low accuracy, manifest Sour, Portals, and Keepers. Rank-three Mystics may, in addition to the ability to*—"

"Yeah, yeah, we got it." Chad01 turns to Lark. "So are you gonna *manifest* or what?"

"Don't get your hopes up," she says. "This hardly ever works. I don't even have a stick or somewhere to sit."

"Got you covered." Chad01 shrugs off his backpack and pulls out a coffee mug, a basketball, a table lamp, and then a small stick, which he hands to Lark. Next, he grabs some sleeping bags, two wooden chairs, two folding chairs, and a doormat that says WELCOME. "Might as well get comfortable for the show."

 ⚓

You climb into a chair and pull a sleeping bag up to your chin. You're between Chad01 and Owlsy, while Lark sits cross-legged on the welcome mat in front of you. It's good to be off your feet.

Lark takes the stick and holds it to her lips. She whispers something, and it bursts into flame. She lets it burn a moment, and then she blows it out and leans forward, bending her neck so that her wild hair falls over her eyes. She begins to draw a large circle, about the size of a bicycle tire, in the ice with the ash-tipped stick. She draws another circle over this one. And then another, moving faster and faster, drawing that one endless circle, and her body begins to shake, and she's breathing loud, and then suddenly with a sort of gasp she just falls over, mouth open, eyes rolled back in her head. You're up on your feet, ready to help her, but Owlsy takes your arm.

"She'll come out of it in a moment," he says, as Lark convulses on the ice.

"Dang," says Chad01.

"Mm," says Owlsy. "Yes, this is why she never wants to do it."

 ⚓

And then just like that, she snaps out of it. She blinks and sits up and wipes the drool off her face.

"I couldn't—" she says. "I couldn't really—I think maybe I saw us, and I think I saw the city, but I don't know. That's it."

"City?" says Chad01. "What city?"

"The City of a Thousand Days and Nights!" says Owlsy. "The level we're looking for! If we can get there, we can get home! This is good news. *Very* good news!"

"Right," says Chad01. "The stupid crystal quest."

"Exactly! If we return the purple crystal power ring to the City of a Thousand Days and Nights, we will be rewarded one million gold, which happens—"

"A million?" says Chad01. "No way."

"Yes way!" says Owlsy. "One million gold. Which is the *exact* same price to use the home portal that is in the very same city."

"According to your wiki."

"Yes."

"And you have the crystal?"

"Of course! Would you like to see it?" Owlsy digs into his pocket and pulls out a little cloth bag. He unties the ribbon and loosens the top and very carefully dumps the contents into the palm of his hand.

You recognize it immediately. The big, sugary crystal. The green plastic hoop. "That's a Ring Pop," you say.

"Ring Pop?" says Chad01.

"It's candy."

"You think *everything* is candy," he says.

"It is!" you say. "You wear it on your finger and suck on it."

"Suck on it?" Owlsy laughs. "Ha. No. Believe me—no. It would be *beyond* foolish to touch your lips to a power crystal. Within this stone lies enough power to light up a single city for *years.*"

"It's a piece of candy on a plastic ring," you say.

"Awesome," says Lark. "This is too good."

"No," says Owlsy. "No way. I can assure you this is *not* candy."

"I told you," says Chad01. "Crystal quests are *the worst!* You can all

107

forget about that anyway. I got the ticket home right here." He pats his purple sling. "Real live fuzzy. Guaranteed by wizard oath. Which reminds me. Before we go any farther, I gotta see your toes."

"Toes?" says Lark.

"Yeah. Let's get it over with. How's about the two of you show me your toes?"

"How's about no?"

Chad01 crosses his arms. "Well, I gotta see 'em or I can't go any farther with you."

"Oh really?" Lark gestures at the rippling immensity around you. "And where are you going to go? Or did you not notice that we're stuck on an iceberg in the middle of an ocean?"

"Ice floe," says Owlsy.

"What?" says Lark.

"This is an ice *floe*. An ice*berg* would rise higher from the water."

Lark turns to her brother. "Oh, well, thank you. That's very useful information."

"I gotta see your toes," says Chad01.

"Take a dive in the cold, cold water," says Lark.

"Here," says Owlsy. "You can see mine if you want." He unties his shoe, slips off his sock, and wiggles his toes in the air. "Ta-dah."

20.

IT'S ALL STORIES

Chad01 grabs Owlsy's ankle. He peers intently. His nose wrinkles in disgust. "Just what I thought! Hey, Rainbow—see that? Look at his third toe."

"What about my third toe?" says Owlsy.

"Well, it's like a quarter inch *longer* than your second toe."

"And the significance of that would be . . . ?"

"The *significance* is you're imaginary. And I bet your sister is too."

"Because—*why?*"

"Because that's how it works!"

Owlsy sits up in his chair. "You mean to tell me—you mean to tell me that you believe you can ascertain whether a person is real or not by the length of their *toes?*"

"D■mn right I can *ascertain*."

"Wow," says Lark. "And how did you come to such rare wisdom?"

Chad01 gives her a look. "A wizard told me."

"Would this be the same wizard that gave you the magic fizzy?"

"Nah. Different wizard. And not a fizzy, a *fuzzy*. Its name is Echo Joy, and it's our ticket out of here."

"My friend, you put a lot of faith in wizards," says Owlsy.

"Yeah, and what do you put your faith in?"

"I don't need faith. I have a wiki."

Lark laughs. "A book and a fuzzball. You're both crazy."

"Yeah?" Chad01 turns to her. "And what do *you* believe in?"

Lark's smile fades. "I believe we're never getting home. I believe no one *ever* gets home. I believe it's all just wishful thinking . . . and the truth is it only goes on and on and on."

"Well, that's ridiculous. Nothing goes on and on forever."

Lark shrugs. "Nothing but this. It's like the exception that proves the rule."

"No way," says Chad01.

"Way," says Lark.

The ice slowly rises and falls in the gray, choppy water.

"OK, but I've *known* Lost Kids who escaped the Wilds," says Chad01.

"And you saw this with your own eyes?"

"Pretty much."

"Right," says Lark. "So if you saw it, then why didn't you just exit too?"

"Well, maybe not *directly* with my own eyes. But I *know* a kid who saw it."

"It's all stories."

"Wrong." Chad01 pats his sling. "This fuzzy? *This* is how we get out of here. This is some *real* magic. Guaranteed. Just gotta get my dude to the Lake of the Goldfish Moon. Boom. Splat. We're home."

"Sure," says Lark. "Everything's going to be just—"

"Hey." Owlsy is standing now. "Look—do you see it? Is that land?"

"Where?"

You're all standing now, straining to see in the distance. There's something dark rising out of the water.

"Trees?" you say.

"Those aren't trees," says Lark.

"Another machine forest," says Owlsy.

Right. You can see it now, the towers of junk.

"Know what that means," says Lark. "Probably—"

"Shh," says Chad01. "No one be afraid, OK? Just don't think about it."

But when someone tells you not to think about something, it's almost impossible not to. You think about the screamers. You think about the face you saw. The mangled face and the eyes and the open mouth. And as you do, an evil scream comes laughing across the water. Then another.

"Hey," says Chad01. "What did I just say? No one be scared!"

There's something in the distance. You can almost see it. Something dark on the water. More screaming.

"They're swimming, aren't they?" says Lark.

"Very possibly," says Owlsy.

"You two aren't helping," says Chad01. "Talk about something else!"

"Like what?"

"I don't know! Picnics or something."

"Picnics?!"

Another scream. Crazy close. You're searching around frantically. You don't see anything but ice and choppy, gray water. Chad01 looks worried. The wind is blowing freezing, wet spray across the ice. And then you see it. A darkness on the water. Eyes. You see the eyes. You

hear a scream. It isn't the screamer. It's you. You are screaming. You
are—

`mem01901i (what kind of a person)`

I'm standing with CJ on the side of the road looking down at Goldfish.
I don't know how long it's been. It feels like we've been here forever. I
have memorized the pink pads on the underside of her back paw, the
curve of her tail. Everything is so vivid. The dark smear on the pavement. Orange fur trembling in the wind. A car alarm is going off in the
distance.

And then, I don't know what it is, but something snaps me out of it.
I tune back in. He's talking. My brother is talking.

"It was an *accident!*" he's saying. "I was—I didn't mean to—I was
only f█cking joking!"

It takes me a moment to even find the words.

"What kind of a person f█cking *jokes* about killing a cat?"

⁌

I'm heading back up the road. I just want to get away. I just want to
bury myself in my bed. I'm being a child, and I know it, but I just want
to leave.

I can see the gate to the trailer park ahead. And then I remember
something. There was a *reason* I was in the van with CJ. We were going
somewhere, right?

School. My English assignment. The deadline.

⁌

So now I'm running back up the road. It's all starting to feel like some
kind of nightmare. I can see CJ in the distance, standing in the same

spot in the street, and I'm about to shout to him when I see the van. I hadn't really looked at it until now. It's crunched up against the pole, the hood is all crumpled, and the front wheel is angled underneath like a broken foot. It's leaking something black. The alarm is still going off. I check the time on my phone. It's too late. There's no way.

21.

CRACK

You wake in a puddle of water to a blazing sun.

"Rise and shine!" says Lark brightly. "I had to put a sleep spell on you. Otherwise you were going to get us all killed. Because of the Screamers. Who are gone now, by the way. So you don't have to be afraid anymore . . . How's it going? You look terrible."

You lie there, remembering your assignment, the van, Goldfish . . . and as the memories fade in the brightness of day, you begin to realize how hot it is. It's got to be like ninety degrees. You sit up and rub your eyes. The ice is mushy. Puddles have formed, a deep crystal blue. Flocks of white birds circle the blue sky. You look around, kind of stunned.

"On a positive note," says Owlsy, "as we drifted away from the machine forest while you were napping, the sun came out."

"The iceberg's melting," says Chad01.

"Well, *floe,*" says Owlsy.

"Yes, thank you, professor," says Lark.

"We should actually be thankful it *isn't* an iceberg," says Owlsy. "If it *was* an iceberg, there would be *far* more ice to melt, the vast majority of it underwater, meaning the melt time could be orders of magnitude longer than what we are currently facing, a scenario which in my opinion—"

There's a loud *CRACK!* and the ice shudders. You watch as a fissure snakes through the white—and then a section splits off.

"Watch out!" says Chad01.

Another *CRACK!* and it splits again. "This is much faster than I'd anticipated," says Owlsy.

CRACK! and then *CRACK!* again, the ice breaking off until the four of you are stranded on basically a dinner table, bobbing up and down on the shimmering water of the endless ocean.

"Now what?" you manage to say.

Lark shrugs. "Who knows? Sea serpents, maybe? Or like some kind of v—"

CRACK! You are plunged feet first into the freezing water.

Your body screams, every nerve zinging with pain. You kick and thrash furiously, gasping in the frigid waves, struggling to keep your head above water. Your clothing is a dead weight pulling you down. You can hear someone shouting your name. You turn to see Chad01, the twins, and a shimmering column of light. The light is growing quickly, a blizzard of obscuring radiance that torches the water and the chunks of ice and Chad01 and Lark and Owlsy—and then you.

There's flash, and you are somewhere else.

mem01902i (go away)

I'm in my room sitting on my bed with the green quilt pulled up to my chin, staring at the wall, and all I can see is what happened, just playing over and over in my mind. Her body. The blood on the road.

⁂

There's a knock on my bedroom door. The handle turns, the door swings open. CJ steps inside.

"Hey," he says quietly. "So, um . . ."

"Go away."

He doesn't, of course. "Look," he begins. "I'm really sorry, OK? And I just — I just wanted to ask what you thought we should do with, uh, Goldfish."

"Where is she?"

"I put her in a bag," he says.

"A bag?"

CJ nods. "Yeah, and I was wondering what you thought we should do with —"

"What *we* should do?"

"Well, yeah . . ."

"We?" I'm standing now. I'm marching over to him. I'm squaring up to my brother and I'm staring him in the face.

"This is all *you! You* did this!"

"I'm sorry!" he says. "You gotta tell mom it was an accident!"

"No." I lock eyes with my brother. I really want him to feel what I'm about to say. "I'm done with this. OK? You're on your own. I don't care what you do. Throw her off the cliff — throw yourself off while you're at it! I don't care! You killed my cat, you made me fail my class, and I'm done with you! OK? SO JUST GO AWAY!"

CJ stands there in the doorway. His lips part. "Rain —"

"GO!"

116

I shove him back into the hall and slam the door.

I stand alone in my room, hating the world, and my brother, and school, and most of all myself for being so stupid and lazy. Because if it wasn't for me, we wouldn't have even been out on the road in the first place. I look at the stupid tiles on the ceiling. I scream.

DON'T EAT THE FLOWERS

You find yourself standing in an endless field of purple flowers. The sun is low in the sky, the light is golden. As far as you can see, in every direction, it's just thousands—millions—of flowers gently swaying in the golden-purple light, radiating a sweet, chemical aroma like two-in-one shampoo and conditioner. You take a deep breath. The sun feels good on your cold skin. You close your eyes and turn your face to the light and just bathe in it all for a moment.

Then you hear a sound. It's like *Ding!*

"What was that?" says Chad01.

"Good news," says Owlsy. "That beautiful, euphonic tone means my wiki has just updated." He takes it out of his pocket, flips through the pages. "Let's see . . . uh, here we are. OK, first off, the flowers are poison and to be avoided. *Deadly in very high doses. Avoid ingestion if possible . . . symptoms may include gagging, nausea, and violent loss of equilibrium.*"

"Yes," says Lark. "Because we were about to eat the flowers."

"I'm only reading what it says."

"Read something useful."

Owlsy skims the page, murmuring to himself, then snaps the wiki shut.

"And?" she says.

"There's a shop that way. In the direction of the setting sun, which is perpetually setting in this level. The kid who runs the shop is a Keeper."

"Ugh," says Chad01. "I hate Keepers."

"We've got the sour," says Owlsy. "It should be easy."

Lark rolls her eyes.

"How far?" you ask.

Owlsy sort of grimaces. "It didn't say."

"No worries," says Chad01. "Just don't eat the flowers."

⚡

You start off through the endless evening of purple flowers. You walk and walk, and nothing changes; it's just flowers and flowers and flowers, purple sunlit flowers in every direction. Your hoodie is hot. Your back is sore. Your legs ache. You consider plopping down among the fragrant blooms and staying there forever. It would be so nice to just give in to oblivion.

"There!" says Chad01. "I see it!"

A lamppost and a little cart are standing side by side on the horizon of flowers. An old-fashioned circus cart, painted in stars and moons, with yellow wagon wheels. As you get closer, you can see a large sign with black letters.

SH■T FOR SALE

A kid in a black hoodie stands behind the counter, intent on something in his left hand. You draw closer. He's got a piece of string, a shoelace, and he's busy tying and untying it in knots, using just his left hand, fingers dancing.

"Hiya," says Owlsy brightly. "You must be the Keeper here."

The kid doesn't look up from his one-handed knot.

"You got anything for sale?" says Chad01.

For a moment there's no response, and then the kid grabs a piece of laminated paper and slides it your way before returning to his shoelace.

ITEM	PRICE
HEALING SPELL PACK (2)	3000 GOLD
CHONK BAR REPLENISH (1)	~~800~~ SOLD OUT
ONION (1)	~~10~~ SOLD OUT
SAW (1)	400 GOLD
WOODEN LADDER (1)	400 GOLD
PORTAL	5000 GOLD OR 10 SOURS

"Three *thousand* gold for *two* healing spells?" says Chad01. "Seriously? That's robbery!"

Lark sets some coins on the counter. "One healing spell pack, please."

"Save your loot," says Chad01. "You could get a way better deal literally anywhere else."

"Yes, but you see" — she motions to the endless flowers waving in the breeze — "there isn't anywhere else, Chad01."

.ıٔ.

So Lark buys the healing spell pack and Owlsy purchases the saw. The kid slides each item across the counter, never looking up from his knot. Then Chad01 buys the ladder. You watch as he just drops the whole thing into his backpack.

"You gonna carry that saw?" he says to Owlsy. "Just put it in my bag. In fact, I should be carrying *all* your stuff. This backpack doesn't get any heavier, you know."

So everyone puts their stuff in Chad01's bag—everything except ten Ghost Punch Sour Patch Kids, which Owlsy drops in the kid's open hand.

"One portal open, please."

The kid flips over the price list to reveal what's written on the back.

TO UNLOCK PORTAL
EAT 1 PURPLE FLOWER

"And there it is," says Lark.

"The flowers are poisonous," Chad01 says to the kid, but the kid doesn't answer.

"We could divvy up the task," says Owlsy. "A quarter for each of us. That way we can spread out the poisonous effects. Come on, let's find the smallest one."

You pick the smallest purple flower you can find, and even so, it's pretty big, and the blossoms are surprisingly tough—finally Owlsy has to saw it in quarters with his bow saw—and you wonder how you're going to eat something so hard, but the instant it hits your tongue it dissolves into a bitter goo, and you choke it down.

The effect is almost instantaneous. First comes the gagging. Followed by a throbbing nausea. Then a sickly green feeling in your gut. As you're clutching your stomach, about to heave, you see something —a brilliant column of light shooting down from the lamppost.

"Look!" you say.

Lark turns to look and falls down into the flowers with a *crunch*. Chad01 lets out a yelp as he falls too, and then the ground comes rising up for you. You're enveloped in flowers, soft at first, but in the next moment hard and scratchy as you slam into the earth.

"It's the violent—" says Owlsy as he crunches into the purple blooms. "Violent loss of equilibrium! Everybody crawl for the portal!"

You manage to get up on your knees, but after a couple steps, the earth comes slamming up again. You try again. You fall again. You give up on crawling.

Rolling and scooching through the grass, fighting back the gagging desire to puke, you make your way with the others to the light.

And all along there's been a sound, and you haven't registered it yet, but now you finally do. The sound of quiet laughter coming from the booth. "Heh heh heh."

". . . f■cking hate Keepers," says Chad01.

With a final scooch, he pushes himself into the light and disappears. Then Owlsy and Lark.

One last look at the flowers, the endless waves of purple.

Then you.

`mem01309w (ski trip)`

We're going on a plane. Our family is flying to the mountains in the middle of the country where Mom's rich sister lives, and we're going to stay in her condo and spend three days skiing. I'm seven years old, and I've never flown or skied or any of it, and I have never been this excited in my entire life. Ski trip!

We get to the airport to find the plane is delayed. Seriously, majorly delayed. They might not be able to get us on a flight until tomorrow. But they don't know yet.

Dad is furious and stomps off to a bar, and our mom sits there biting her nails, but I don't care and neither does CJ. We've never been in an *airport* before. Which it turns out is just basically an enormous playground. The two of us chase each other up and down the moving walkways, not full-out running but pretty close, dodging between people and bags until Mom grabs us each by the arm and marches us back to the chairs.

.⋅.

And then finally the plane. It's louder than I expected, and my brother and I fight over the window seat. According to the ticket it should be mine — I have verified this — but CJ gets there first, and Mom lets him keep it because it turns out she is clinically terrified of flying and is sitting there with her face in her hands rocking back and forth, praying. So I end up in the middle seat, CJ gets the window, and then it's time for takeoff.

.⋅.

Later, the beverage cart comes. CJ and I both order ginger ales, and it just isn't my day because I instantly spill the entire thing in my lap, and by this point Dad has had it with us, and leans across the aisle and swears at us under his breath that basically we are going to be in so much trouble when the plane lands it isn't even funny.

.⋅.

So we're sitting there in stony silence, me in the middle seat, and the only drink I have is on my pants, and I'm honestly about to cry, and then out of the blue CJ does something completely uncharacteristic, which is to slide *his* ginger ale onto my tray, and as he does he gives me this weird look of sympathy, and I almost throw the drink in his face, but I don't.

⁊

And later, skiing. The bunny slope.

The first thing I do is immediately and monumentally crash in the most ridiculous and painful way possible, skis and poles flying in every direction like a cartoon, and after that my whole perspective on the day changes. I have the fear now. This snow is not soft and fluffy. This snow is trying to murder me. I tighten up on my skis in anticipation of the next inevitable fall, and each trip down the slope becomes worse than the last, a frantic game of trying to avoid killing myself.

⁊

CJ figures it out right away, of course, and as he sweeps gracefully back and forth, I find myself growing cranky and jealous. It's like, *You get the window seat <u>and</u> you're good at skiing?* He glides up beside me, offering advice, but I won't listen because I'm being a brat.

I pass the afternoon angry and frustrated, tumbling again and again.

One thing, though, I don't give up. That's kind of who I am. I can be very stubborn.

And finally, after like the hundredth time, I sort of get it.

I don't know how it happens, but for a moment everything just clicks.

It's so wonderful. The weightless freedom, giving in to the speed. I glide down the slope, and as the fear dissipates, I am suddenly aware of the expression on my face, my wide-open smile, and I feel myself blush with self-consciousness, but then it's like, *Hey, let's enjoy this.*

There's only one small, tiny problem: I don't really know how to stop or slow down. I mean I *do,* but I *don't.* And I'm going fast enough now that it feels like if I bail, I might break something. And then I see the barriers. A line of bright orange barriers at the end of the run. I am heading toward the barriers.

There's a gap in the barriers, and I manage to turn toward it and go sailing through, and one problem is replaced with another, as I'm still moving, only out-of-bounds now, and there is a man in my path, an older man in a puffy blue jacket, who at the last second dives to the side like an action hero.

And I'm *still* going. The snow whooshes by. I'm heading to the lodge now, the restaurant patio. Diners turn their heads from their burgers with mild concern as this gawky figure comes sailing toward them.

At the last moment I bail, tumbling along the snow, skis and poles all over, gliding to a rest near the patio railing. I lie there, spread-eagle on the snow. A plane sails across the blue.

~

I hear him calling my name, and then he slides expertly to a stop, spattering snow onto my face. His eyes are wide.

"Hey," he says. "Hey, are you OK?"

And then he sees my expression, how bewildered I must look, and he starts laughing, and in a moment we are both laughing. CJ laughs so hard he almost falls over, and that makes me laugh even harder, and it's probably one of the best moments of my life, crashed out in the snow after I almost killed a bystander and myself, looking up at the sky and my laughing brother.

PREPARE FOR SKI QUEST

You find yourself standing with the others on a moving walkway under harsh fluorescent lighting. White tile, gray carpet. A drinking fountain glides past.

Owlsy snaps his wiki shut. "There isn't an entry for this level."

"Don't worry," says Chad01. "I think Rainbow and I have been here before. Follow me."

He hops off the moving walkway and goes to the wall and a red box marked FIRE ALARM.

"Check it out." Chad01 pulls the lever.

The sprinklers turn on, instantly drenching you as the alarm cries *BOOOP! BOOOP!* up and down the corridor.

"And why did you do that?!" Lark shouts.

"To open the portal!" shouts Chad01 back. "It worked last time. Remember, Rainbow?"

"Well, actually," Owlsy chimes in. "Just because something works in one level doesn't mean it —"

"I know that!" Chad01 yells. "You think I don't know that?"

BOOOOP! BOOOOP! BOOOOP!

The sound is deafening. There's no way to turn it off.

✻

You dash along the moving walkway with the others, trying to outrun the screaming alarm, but the alarm won't stop, and the water keeps falling.

BOOOOP! BOOOOP! BOOOOP!

You slosh along the corridor. The water is beginning to puddle at your feet.

Now it's at your ankles.

"If this keeps up, we're going to drown!" Owlsy shouts.

"Look!" Lark is pointing down the corridor. There's a call box. No song this time. Just the relentless *BOOOOP! BOOOOP!* of the alarms and the SHHHHH of spraying water.

Everyone swipes their wrist, and Chad01 slams the button, and suddenly it all stops. The alarm stops. The sprinklers stop. Everything is so quiet, just gentle dripping from your sodden hoodies.

A machine whirs, and the box goes *BLAP!* and spits out a paper. It flutters down to the water, and Owlsy scoops it up.

TO UNLOCK PORTAL EVERYONE MUST
COMPLETE SKI QUEST

"What's a *ski?*" says Chad01, pronouncing it like "sky."

"*Skis,*" you say. "You don't remember skis? They're, like, these special boards you strap to your feet, and you then slide down a mountain on the snow."

"That sounds extremely dangerous," says Owlsy.

"Great, so all we have to do now is find some skis," says Lark.

"And boots," you add. "You have these special boots."

"Right, and boots," says Lark. "And a snowy mountain too, right? Easy peasy. Has anyone seen a snowy mountain about?"

⁂

You continue down the corridor, and then you come to a sign hanging by chains from the ceiling.

PREPARE FOR SKI QUEST

Below the sign is a rack of boots and skis and poles.

"Must be for us," says Owlsy.

"Oh, you think?" says Lark.

The four of you take off your shoes and drop them into Chad01's backpack.

While you're putting on your boots, Chad01 reaches over and yanks the sock from Lark's foot.

"Hey!" she says.

"Look at that! Ya see that? Right there. Look at her toes!"

"Give me back my sock!"

"Imaginary! Just like Owlsy! I knew it! Here's your sock, NPC."

Chad01 tosses Lark her sock and she snatches it out of the air.

"One would expect our feet to be similar," says Owlsy. "We are twins, after all."

"Imaginary twins," says Chad01.

Lark aims the bottom of her foot at Chad01's face. "Look at that blister. You see that? Tell me that's not real!"

"The wizard told me—"

"Chad01," she says, "if a wizard told you to kiss my ▪ss, would

128

you? Take a big sniff of my blistery foot and tell me that isn't real. Go on."

"Hell no."

"Aw, come on, Chad01. Give it a sniff."

Lark grabs him by the back of the head and pushes his nose into her foot. He shoves the foot away, twists around, and tries to wrap her in a headlock, but she slips easily out and goes to tackle him and —*BRRZAP!*—the two of them are thrown stumbling to the ground.

"The hell do I care?" says Chad01. "You do you. Be real if you want."

"Wow," says Lark. "Thank you. It's such an honor to have my existence approved by such a wise and knowledgeable expert as yourself. So glad to know I'm allowed to be real."

"Real enough to be a pain in the ■ss," says Chad01, picking himself up.

⁂

Everyone puts on their boots. This was a mistake because now you have to walk in them. It's like wearing a brick. The four of you clomp down the tunnel in your big boots like newborn giraffes, and then the light begins to change, and there's another sign:

SKI QUEST 200 PACES

Ahead, the concrete wall is lit up in a brilliant blaze of white light —sunlight. The tunnel has come to an end.

Just before the opening, there's a final sign.

TO OPEN PORTAL
ALL LOST KIDS MUST
SUCCESSFULLY LAND

THREE (3) JUMPS
IN A ROW
WITHOUT FALLING

Somehow, the tunnel has led you to the top of a precipice. You find yourself looking out from a hole at the peak of a giant mountain. You're so high up, the bottom is invisible, lost in a swirl of cloudy fog below.

Another thing: the mountain is green with grass.

"I thought you said skiing involved snowy mountains," Lark says.

"It usually does," you say.

Owlsy squats and feels the grass. "A bit squishy."

You touch it too. It isn't real. It's this rubbery, green material, with soft, nubby blades like a sea anemone. And it's covering the mountain: this vast green slope going down down down into the clouds. There are trees too, and rocks, big veins of gray and black.

"Ugh," says Chad01. "I hate heights."

"Good thing about the clouds, then," says Lark.

"Why?"

"You don't have to see the bottom."

⚉

You click on your skis and take your poles and stand with the others on the edge of the tunnel at the top of the rubbery, green heights. Bright sun illuminates the clouds below. Your mind is busy with questions and doubts, but the mountain is quiet. You stand, skis jutting out over the concrete lip, casting your shadow on the green.

"Ready?" says Lark.

"No," says Chad01.

"Count of three," says Owlsy. "One . . . two . . ."

"I SAID I WASN'T READY!"

"Three!" Lark shouts, pushing off from the concrete and zooming down the green.

Owlsy follows after her, then Chad01, then you.

Down you go.

24.

SKI QUEST

The nubby grass whizzes past in a blur under your skis, making a sound like *ssszzzzzzzzz*. Below, the mountain is shrouded in cloud. You're kind of surprised at how well you can balance, but on the other hand, you can't remember how to slow yourself or turn. It's just down down down the mountain, faster and faster, the wind pushing against your body and face. So wild you forget to be scared. Ahead, you can see the others gliding in more leisurely arcs. You're about to catch up to them when they disappear into the cloud bank.

And then you do too.

Wet cold stinging your cheeks. You can't see anything but white. Everywhere, all around you, the rushing white. And then the white opens up and you are looking down another long, green slope, only this one has rocks, or more like boulders, and you watch in horror as one of them races up to meet you, and you squeeze your eyes shut and bail.

You are in the air now, every fiber bracing for the collision, but instead you feel yourself bounce, and you open your eyes to see the grass and sky spinning around you as you bounce and tumble down the mountain and then a tree rushes up and you cascade into a heap against its pillowy trunk.

The others gather around you.

"Are you all right?" says Owlsy.

"That was some tumble you took," says Chad01.

You pick yourself up, dust yourself off. You feel all right. Two bright, dark eyes are looking at you. "Good job," says Lark. "A beautiful wreck."

··

You start down again.

The grass is soft and springy, and when you fall (which you do, over and over), you are trampolined back into the air, and you go bouncing harmlessly down the mountain, and the only pain is walking back up to retrieve your skis each time. Lark and Chad01 are natural athletes, and before long, they're making wide cuts along the slope, sweeping back and forth all around you. Even Owlsy is getting the hang of it.

··

You follow them into another cloud bank. The cold white envelops you. It's just you and the sound of your skis on the grass, *ssszzzzzzzzzz* . . . and suddenly the clouds whip away, and you are staring down another vast green bottomless slope. It's like the mountain never ends. You must be *miles* in the air.

You're almost getting the hang of it. At least you aren't crashing.

And then you see something in the distance. White rectangles with the number "1" on them. No—not rectangles. *Ramps.*

"These must be the jumps," says Owlsy.

··

Chad01 is the first to successfully complete a jump. You watch as he shoots off a ramp and lands wobbly and askew on the slope, and in the same moment, the next ramp in front of him changes from a *1* to a *2,* but he isn't so lucky with that one and lands on his back and bounces down the mountain, and the number *2* on the ramp changes back to a *1.*

✵

Lark is the first to complete three in a row. You don't see the first two jumps, but you catch the third. She hits the ramp perfectly, is airborne like a bird surfing above her shadow, then joins the slope again. She whips into a sharp turn, skidding to a halt. Bells are ringing out from the sky above, and a voice thunders over the mountain.

QUEST COMPLETED, LARK!

Not long after that, you hear the voice again.

QUEST COMPLETED, CHAD01!

Now it's up to you and Owlsy.

More cloud banks. More mountain. More jumps. You haven't had the courage to go off one yet. As you struggle with fear and mechanics, Lark and Chad01 are having a blast, playing chicken with each other, carving back and forth across the green, absolutely fearless. Lark dips her shoulder and plows into Chad01's side, and the two of them go tumbling together down the mountain, pinballing off the trees and flipping into the air.

Bells ring again.

QUEST COMPLETED, OWLSY!

It's just you now.

You aim for a ramp. At the last second, you bail. You try again. You fail.

Every time you go for a ramp, the fear seizes you — the weightlessness of it, the slope spread out below — and you become totally useless and scrunch up your eyes or gawk in horror. But either way you keep screwing up the landing.

The others are skiing next to you now, harassing you with words of encouragement.

"Don't worry about falling!"

"Keep your eyes open!"

"It might help if you bend your knees a bit more!"

"Lean into those turns."

Down you go.

Another jump.

It's steeper than most and you're moving too fast.

You shoot off the edge too high in the air. The slope falls away from under your skis, and you catch a glimpse of your shadow drifting like water along the contours below. Too fast. Too high. You feel the sickly loss of gravity and close your eyes.

You open them again just in time to see the green slope meet your skis. Your knees bend, your hand touches the slope. And still you're skiing. Ahead, all the jumps now say *2*.

If I don't do it this time, I'll never get it.

You aim for the next jump, feel the ground leave you again. You brace yourself, every muscle tightened in fear, but at the last moment, you remember to relax and just go with it . . . and you're on the slope again. The others are cheering.

Now all the jumps say *3*.

You aim for the next one, decide it's too steep, sweep to the left and barely miss it, only to see another, steeper ramp in front of you. You hit it straight on.

Air. Flight.

And then with a *whump,* you are back on the green, wobbling but still going, and bells are ringing from the heavens.

QUEST COMPLETED, RAINBOW!

It's glorious. You haven't felt this good in . . . you can't remember when. All the fear is gone now. You've got the hang of this skiing thing. You could do this all day long—just sailing down the mountain, weightless, fearless, and, for the first time in a long time, totally happy.

So of course you instantly cross your skis and crash and go bouncing down the mountain (you still haven't figured out how to stop) and when you're gathering your skis, you look up the slope to see a shimmering column of light rising out of the green.

"Nice!" says Owlsy.

You gaze at the mountain spread out below you one last time. Endless miles. All that green. You fight the urge to just push off and sail down forever, then you head back up the slope and follow the others into the light.

`mem01292m (snow)`

My family moves to the country for a year, over the hills to a little house on the edge of town, out where the farms are, and there is a little river running through our backyard and cottonwood trees as big as buildings. I'll be starting fifth grade in the fall, but right now it's early summer and everything is good. Dad has a new job. Mom is taking online classes, and CJ and I are left to ourselves.

It's one of those in-between times, when the two of us aren't really friends or enemies, we're just sort of living in the same house. He's gotten into gaming, but I'd still rather be outside. I spend a lot of time reading under the cottonwoods. It's lonely but serene. Sometimes I just sit and stare at the river. There's something magical about moving water. Little puffs of cotton go floating past, tracing the hidden current.

⁂

Mom and Dad talk about going camping and make it as far as purchasing a tent, which we then set up in the backyard under the cottonwoods. I really want to spend the night out there, but I'm a little too afraid to do it by myself, and CJ wants to do it by himself, but Mom and Dad don't trust him, so we both end up in the tent together and I get to smell his farts and listen to his game music because he forgot to bring headphones and he's too lazy to go back in the house and get some.

It doesn't matter. It's really cool to be in a tent: the way it filters the light, the soft shuffling sound my sleeping bag makes, the glow of the screen on the nylon bubble—all of it. I snuggle up in my bag and fall asleep dreaming I'm being pulled on a sled through a starlit arctic wasteland.

⁂

Deep in the middle of the night, I wake up. Even with the streetlight still on, it's somehow darker now, emptier. The wind is up, the tent door flapping. CJ is passed out and snoring, tablet on his chest. I go to fix the flap, and when I look outside, it's snowing. I can't believe it. There's snow everywhere.

I crawl out onto the lawn. The wind is so warm. And the snow —it isn't snow—it's the cottonwoods. The wind is blowing the cotton from the cottonwood trees, and it's drifting down through the street-lights, all lit up like sparks. And there's just so *much* of it. A blizzard of cotton drifting down through the light and into the darkness again, falling silently onto the tent, the lawn, the river.

✦

I stand there, struck by the beauty.

I have to share it with someone, so I wake up CJ, and it's like waking someone into a dream. He's cranky at first, complaining that I woke him, but then he looks outside and sees the cotton in the light. It really is that beautiful—beautiful enough to shut my brother up. Flurries of incandescent snow drifting down from the sky. Neither of us says a word. There's a spell over everything.

The night is strange, magical—bright and mild and dark and deep all at once—and it feels like the summer snow could go on forever, that if we just stand here and don't move for long enough, the world will silently bury itself in fuzzy, warm love.

25.

THE DESERT

You find yourself standing in a broad landscape under an intensely deep-blue sky, so deep blue it's almost purple, and then it *is* purple. You watch as the sky flickers back and forth. Blue. Purple. The sun is a crackling ball of white-hot fire. It's actually shooting off sparks. You're in a desert of some kind—powdery, gray ground dotted with clumps of dry grass and gray-green brush as far as you can see, ending in a distant line of mountains, bluish-purplish peaks, almost the same color as the sky.

You watch the scene as your memories fade.

". . . f█cking hot here," says Chad01.

"Yes, and bright," says Lark.

A chime rings out from Owlsy's back pocket—*Ding!*

"Great," he says. "Wiki update." He takes out his book and flips through the pages, then he stops and reads, *"Sometimes life is a nightmare."*

Chad01 gives him a look. "What?"

"Sometimes life is a nightmare. That's the entire entry."

"Wow," says Lark. "Thanks for the tip."

Owlsy turns to his sister. "So why don't *you* do something useful then?"

"Like what?" she says.

"You could try to manifest."

"Ugh."

"Why not?"

"Does it ever work?"

"Sometimes," says Owlsy.

"Well, I need a stick."

"Got you covered," says Chad01, grabbing a basketball, a toaster, a shoebox, and finally a stick from his bag. "Here."

Lark takes the stick and begins to trace circles in the powdery, gray earth. Her body starts to shake and shiver. She tips over sideways and lies there convulsing. A moment later her eyes regain their focus.

She looks up at you, then Chad01, then Owlsy. She's oddly serious.

"I saw it," she says.

"Saw what?" her brother asks.

"The city."

"Of a Thousand Days and Nights?" says Owlsy. *"Here?"*

"Not here . . . Close. Maybe the next level, I don't know. There's a portal, I think."

"Which direction?" says Owlsy.

"Toward the mountains," says Lark.

"What about a moon?" says Chad01. "Did you see a moon? Or a lake?"

"No," she says. "Sorry, Chad01."

⁘

The sun burns down from the flickering, moonless sky. There isn't a breeze, and you're roasting in your hoodie. You unzip it and sling it over your shoulder. Powdery dust rises at each step. You are walking

140

with your friends through the brush toward the jagged, purple mountains. Is it OK to call them your friends? You've completed quests together, you've helped each other, so yes, you decide, *friends*. They're all you've got now. It's a lot better than having nobody at all.

"Hey," says Chad01. "Check it out. A path."

You've come to the edge of an empty, two-lane road, dotted down the middle with a yellow line, running through the desert before fading into the distant mountains.

"A highway!" you say.

"A what?" says Chad01.

"You know — a highway. A place with cars."

"What's a car?" says Owlsy.

"Seriously? You don't remember *cars?*"

Their faces are blank. Lark shrugs.

So you tell them about cars.

"And they go *how* fast?" Chad01 asks. "Sounds a little far-fetched to me."

"What?" you say. "After all the weird sh█t out here, *cars* sound far-fetched?"

"Well, but I get what Chad01 is saying," says Owlsy. "It's just the amount of magic required to propel such a —"

"Cars aren't magic!"

"Uh, wrong," says Chad01. "*Everything's* magic."

You start down the highway, continuing in the direction of the mountains. It's even hotter now, heat radiating in waves off the black pavement. The sweat pours down your temples and drips from your nose.

The others are walking right in the middle of the road, side by side, following the dotted yellow lines, but your instinct is to walk on the shoulder, just in case there's any traffic.

"Why you walking way over there?" says Chad01.

"In case of cars."

"You're really hung up on these car things, aintcha?"

"They're big and they go fast. If you get hit by one, it could kill you."

"Not me. I got reflexes like a cat."

"Cats get hit by cars all the time."

"Not this cat," says Chad01.

"Hey," says Lark. "What's that up there?"

"What?"

"*That*. Don't you see it? That thing. That blue thing there. Way up the road, do you see it?"

"A call box?" says Chad01.

"No," says Lark. "It's bigger than a call box."

ROAD TRIP

As you come closer, the details fill in. The crushed bumper. The peeling chrome. The black plastic bag duct-taped to the window. It's your brother's van. Just chilling on the side of the road on an empty highway in the middle of a desert. You go up to it. The door is unlocked. The van is empty, but you recognize the smell. You're not sure if you're relieved at this or not. You sift through some of the junk on the floor — taco wrappers and empty soda bottles — like you're looking for some kind of clue.

You step back out onto the road again.

"This is CJ's."

"What?" says Owlsy.

"My brother. This is his van."

"What's a van?" Chad01 asks.

"This. *You* know — like a car."

"So *this* is a car?" says Owlsy.

"Yes!"

"Ah, I see." Owlsy nods. "When you were telling us about cars, I was imagining something a *lot* bigger. I get it now. It wouldn't take *too* much magic to make this go."

"It isn't magic!" you say. "But what's it doing here?"

"Magic," says Chad01.

"It's like I told you," says Owlsy. "Items from home sometimes appear in the Wilds. Things from deep in our psyche. Once, for example, Lark and I found ourselves wandering through a tunnel made of our mother's underwear."

"That wasn't her underwear!" says Lark.

"I'm pretty sure it was."

"How's it work?" Chad01 asks.

"What, the memories?" says Owlsy.

"No, the van!"

"Get in," you say. "I'll show you."

᠃

Chad01 and Owlsy sit in the back. Lark takes shotgun, and you sit in the driver's seat, trying to remember how to drive a car. You know how to drive a car, right? Of course you do. You've had lessons, right? It's just — how does it start?

"A key," you say.

"What?"

"I need a key."

"What, like this?" Your brother's keychain dangles from Owlsy's outstretched fingers.

"Where'd you get that?"

"It was sitting here in this cylindrical depression."

"You mean the cup holder?"

"Yes. *Cup holder.*"

᠃

You slide the key in the ignition and grip the steering wheel. You're starting to remember how this works now. There's a gas pedal and a brake and—oh, right. Seat belts. You remember seat belts.

"Everyone, buckle up."

"Buckle up what?" says Lark.

So you show them how the seat belts work. Then you scoot your seat forward a little, adjust the mirrors, put your hands on the wheel, and take a deep breath. You turn the key, and with a squeal, the engine rattles to life.

"Cool," says Chad01.

"Ready?" You press the gas and the engine revs up, but the van doesn't budge. You press the pedal harder. The roar grows louder. You are still not moving.

"It's very loud!" says Chad01 approvingly.

Why isn't it moving? You're forgetting something. Some essential step. You fumble around with the controls, and a light starts blinking. A mist of fluid sprays onto the windshield, and the wipers sweep back and forth.

"That's pretty," says Lark, tracing the path of the wipers with her fingertip.

You stare at the controls, trying to remember how to get it to go.

The shifter. Right. You have to put it in DRIVE.

～

As the van lurches forward, everyone cheers. You press the gas harder and steer into the right lane and go shooting down the road maybe a little too fast, brush whizzing by in a blur, and so you tap the brakes —or try to—but they're more sensitive than you expected, and you come skidding to a stop on the pavement, tires screeching, and it's a good thing you made everyone wear seat belts.

You sit for a moment in the wafting odor of burned rubber.

⁙

Chad01 catches your eye in the rearview mirror and nods. "Very cool. Let's do it again, no stopping this time."

"Yes," Owlsy chimes in. "Truly a wonder of magical engineering, Rainbow."

⁙

You start down the road again, and after a couple miles, you begin to feel comfortable. For once in your life you're in the driver's seat. Literally. You ease the gas pedal down and begin to go faster. After all this time walking, it feels like you are absolutely flying.

You soar along the empty highway, the black bag rippling and snapping in the wind. The road doesn't bend or curve; it just flows out in a straight line through the unchanging landscape. The sun sparks white in the blue sky.

"Maybe a bit too fast?" says Owlsy.

"Hell no!" says Chad01. "Faster!"

"It's hot in here," says Lark.

"Yeah that too," says Chad01. "We're roasting back here."

"But are you sure we should be going *this* fast?" Owlsy asks.

Then you remember about air conditioning.

You turn it on and take Lark's hand and move it toward the vent. "Feel that."

"Oh," she says. "Yes. Nice."

"What is it?" says Chad01 from the back.

"Mm, that's nice."

"What is it?"

"The coolest breeze," says Lark. "Can't you feel it?"

"I can't feel sh■t."

"I wonder if we shouldn't slow down a bit," says Owlsy.

"What do all these buttons do?" says Lark.

.ıl.

You remember about the radio. You turn it on, and amazingly a song is playing. It's something heavy, with a scratchy guitar and a man screaming unintelligible words from the top of a windy mountain.

"Cool song," says Chad01. "Turn it up."

"Is this the only song it plays?" says Lark.

You hit SCAN and the digits on the display cycle through, stopping at last on 106.8, where a woman is singing over a bouncy beat and synthesizers.

"Better," says Lark.

Chad01 sticks his head up between the seats. "This is crap. Go back to the first song."

"Wait," you say. "If we've got radio, that means maybe there's news and stuff."

"News?" says Owlsy.

"You know—*the news*. Maybe we can find out where we are. Or, I don't know . . ." You hit SCAN again, and the numbers cycle back to the first station, that same heavy song.

"*No sign of the morning coming!*" the voice shrieks.

"Yeah!" says Chad01. "Keep it here!"

"No, the other one!" says Lark.

"What about the news?" says Owlsy.

"Turn it up louder!"

"Make it end!"

"I wonder if—"

"Stop!" You mash the power button, and the radio goes silent. "If everyone's going to shout, we can't hear *anything!*"

Silence. No one speaks. It isn't really like you to raise your voice, so when you do, it sometimes comes out a little more forceful than you intended. You drive in silence for a while, watching the blur of the road.

"Sheesh," says Chad01 at last. "Turn it back on then."

But when you turn up the volume, his song is over, and another has started, barely audible over the static. You hit SCAN and the numbers cycle through, and now it doesn't stop. It just keeps scanning. You try the stations manually. Nothing.

"Well, that sucks," says Chad01.

⁂

"Yes, I like this," says Owlsy. "This is a good and reasonable velocity."

While you were messing with the radio you let your foot off the pedal, and as you speed up again, you remember about gas. You look at the dash — the needle is hovering just above the E, and there's a little illuminated gas can.

And yet the van just keeps going, and you begin to wonder if maybe it *is* magic — and right as you're having this thought the engine cuts out and you drift to a stop on the shoulder.

You turn the key. Something clicks and tries to catch but doesn't.

"We're out of gas," you say.

"Gas?" says Lark.

"It makes the engine run. *Gasoline,* it's called."

"Never heard of it," says Chad01.

"Is it some kind of crystal?" says Owlsy.

"No," you say, "more like a flammable liquid."

"So some kind of *magic juice*," says Chad01.

"Maybe we can find some," says Owlsy.

"No, we need a gas station," you say.

"Maybe we can find one of those," says Chad01.

You look around at the empty desert and flickering sky. "Maybe."

27.

FIRE SPELL

You leave the van on the side of the road and head in a silent line toward the distant mountains. The purple ridges don't look any closer than when you first started out. The desert is endless. Not a gas station in sight. Your mind is filled with questions. Your brother's van — what was it doing here? And your brother — where is he? And what is this place? And how will you get home? And on and on as you march through the desert.

You walk and walk, and at a certain point the highway just ends, the black pavement becomes a dirt road, and you follow the road until it becomes a trail, and then the trail disappears and you're walking through the brush again, the same as before.

⚡

Echo Joy begins to whimper, and Chad01 takes the glowing creature out and sets it floating in the air as he feeds it some chewed-up Chonk. Then he returns it to his purple sling.

The sun is low in the sky now, and Owlsy suggests you set up camp for the night. Chad01 passes around the canteen, and while Lark makes a fire ring out of small rocks and Chad01 sets up the bags, you gather wood with Owlsy. There really isn't much actual wood, just dead bits of brush here and there, but you manage to gather enough of it. It's good to have a task. It keeps your mind off the other stuff.

Lark takes a small branch in her hand, mumbles a string of soft words, and blows. The stick bursts into flames. Chad01 adds more brush until you've got a roaring fire.

"How does that work?" you say. "When you blew on the branch like that."

Lark turns to you. "Everyone knows the fire spell, don't they?"

"Not Nobodies," says Chad01.

"Well, but they can learn it," says Owlsy. "Would you like to learn the fire spell, Rainbow?"

"I can learn it?"

"Absolutely," he says. "Most spells must be purchased, but not this one."

"It's very basic," says Lark.

"First you need to memorize the words," says Owlsy.

"Only, they aren't words," says Chad01. "They're more like sounds, and they're always grouped in fours, no matter what the spell is.

"Very straightforward."

"Right," says Chad01. "So repeat after me: Wan . . . shay . . . wen . . . ah . . ."

"Wan shay wen ah?" you say.

"Right. Sah . . . shay . . . tah . . . dah."

"Sah shay tah dah."

"And now: dah . . . nah . . . sah . . . hay . . ."

"Now dah nah—"

"Not 'now'!" Chad01 laughs. "You don't say the *now* part."

"Groups of *four*," says Lark.

"Like this," says Owlsy. "Dah . . . nah . . . sah . . . hay."

"This is silly."

"No it's not," says Owlsy. "Dah nah sah hay."

"Dah nah sah hay."

"Good. And finally: Ahn . . . so . . . tay . . . *dah*."

"Ahn so tay *dah*," you say.

"Correct. And what you do is you say them all together."

"It's easy," says Chad01. "See?" He raises a stick to his lips, closes his eyes and whispers the words. He blows on the tip and a flame leaps up. "Ta-dah. Magic." He tosses the stick in the fire.

᙮

You give it a couple tries, but it's hard to remember all the gibberish.

"You know," says Owlsy. "When I learned the fire spell, it was taught to me as a story."

"Right," says Chad01. "The story."

"It goes like this," says Owlsy. "*Wan shay wen ah*—When she went out.

"*Sah shay tah dah*—Saw she the dark.

"*Dah nah sah hay*—Darkness saw her.

"*Ahn so tay dah*—And so they danced."

"*Danced?*" says Chad01. "I always heard it as, 'And so they *died*.'"

"Well, *danced* is better," says Lark.

"But why would someone just suddenly dance in the dark?" says Chad01.

"Why would someone just suddenly die?" says Lark.

"Maybe she fell in a hole she didn't see."

"Or maybe," says Lark, "she felt liberated by the, like, anonymity provided by the cover of darkness and therefore decided spontaneously to express herself through rhythm and movement."

"Nah — fell in a hole."

"It doesn't matter," says Owlsy. "You just need to memorize it. Repetition. That's the key. You need to be able to say the words smoothly without thinking about it while still remaining precise."

⁂

You take a stick and try again, but you're tired, and after the conversation it's all a confusion in your mind. You keep accidentally saying the story instead of the spell. You're not sure whether to think *danced* or *died,* and the stick just sits there in your hand, totally not on fire.

Even so, saying the words comforts you in a way. So while the fire flickers and pops, you whisper strange words to the stick.

There's nothing crazy about this at all, you think, and when you look up and see your friends' shadowy faces in the orange light, you're surprised by how hopeful their eyes are. You whisper the words.

`mem01632a (eight months of dave)`

After the divorce but before we move, Mom dates a fake and fraud named Dave. How do I know he's a fake and fraud? I can just tell. Sometimes that stuff is just apparent. I'm not being biased. He's like a ghoul or a psychic vampire or something, all wrapped up in this, like, happy-go-lucky, weepy bro stoner dude.

I don't know. I can't quite tell *what* he is, if it's creepy or dishonest or both, but anyway CJ and I get to endure eight months of Dave, and then one afternoon I find mom crying in her bedroom. It isn't the sad, discouraged crying; it's like the angry, determined, I'm-going-to-make-a-change-now crying, which is even worse.

Dave is gone. But before he left he stole her wallet and credit cards and our dad's antique stereo that he supposedly left behind for me and CJ, plus all of our family's leftover Easter candy. The police come over that afternoon, and Mom keeps saying sorry to them. It's just like her to feel the need to apologize for being robbed. I'm embarrassed for her, and angry that stuff like this happens, and totally elated that Dave is gone —basically all the feelings at once—and after the police leave I'm sitting in my room, sort of catatonic from it all, and my mom comes in, and she's smiling, and it's sort of a crazy smile, but there's something noble about the effort.

"Here." She hands me a chocolate egg. "He missed one."

28

WHERE IS IT

Morning. You wake to the sound of Chad01. The memories swirling in your mind are replaced by shouting.

"WHERE IS IT?" he's yelling.

"Hm? What?" Owlsy mumbles groggily from his bag.

"WHERE IS IT? WHERE THE HELL IS IT?!"

"Where's *what?*" says Lark.

"MY BACKPACK! MY BOTTOMLESS F■CKING BACK-PACK! IT'S GONE!"

Chad01 is scrambling around, but there isn't anywhere to look—just dirt and brush. You climb out of your bag and help in the search, but there aren't any tracks or signs of it or anything. It's just gone.

"What the hell?" he says.

"Perhaps some kind of large bird . . ." suggests Owlsy as he flips through the pages of his wiki.

"Some kinda *bird?!*" Chad01 bellows. "Are you sh■tting me?!" He lifts his foot and stomps a nearby bush, snapping the dry branches. He wrenches it from the earth with his hands, winds his arm back, and chucks it out into the desert, where it lands silently in a puff of dust.

"WHERE IS MY BACKPACK?"

You rest your hand on Chad01's shoulder, but he shrugs you away.

"Maybe it just fell into itself," says Lark.

"What?"

"It's bottomless, yes? Maybe it collapsed into itself and disappeared."

Chad01 glares at her. "You think that's *funny?* All our gear was in there! All our food and water and sour and gold and—"

"Yes, I'm fully aware of that, but does throwing a tantrum—"

"WHERE IS IT?!"

"NO ONE KNOWS!" she shouts back.

"Enough!" says Owlsy. "The backpack is gone. We'll need to find water as soon as possible. We can't waste energy bickering."

⁂

You trudge through the brush with your sleeping bag slung over your shoulders. Owlsy is in the lead, then Lark, Chad01, and you. The mountains are as far away as ever, distant, purple ridges below a flickering sky. How long can a person go without water? You don't want to think about it. So you think about your brother instead, how you yelled at him after the death of Goldfish, but that's just as bad if not worse, so finally you just think about nothing but walking.

⁂

You walk and walk, and the sun sinks into the horizon, the purple mountains turn yellow in the last light, and a cold evening wind sweeps across the dry brush. You stop for the night, and Lark lights a small fire and you sit there with the others, warming your hands as the darkness deepens. Your mouth is pasty and your side is aching, and you keep having to shift positions. When's the last time you had a drink?

The fire pops, sending a burst of sparks into the air.

"Sorry about the backpack," says Chad01 out of nowhere. "I should have kept it closer to me."

"No worries," says Owlsy.

"At least we've got our sleeping bags," says Lark.

No one says much after that. You're too tired. You can't stop thinking about water. The wind is cold. Stars come out to form strange constellations. Nothing moves. No satellites, no airplanes or shooting stars.

You close your eyes. You try to sleep.

mem01612h ("The Eternal God/dess of Teen Depression")

Here she is again, back again from dying but never being dead . . . the Eternal God/dess of Teen Depression!

Today we find her sitting upon a throne of her own creation. On her head rests an enormous and strange helmet. From a distance it would look like a cactus or maybe a sea anemone. But the spines aren't spines — they are guns, hundreds and hundreds of guns, and instead of pointing out, the guns point *in,* all of them aimed at a place in her mind where the darkness is. Every trigger of every gun is connected to a string, and every string is connected to a rope connected to a little chain that dangles before her with a plastic knob on the end, like the pull cord on a lamp.

The Eternal God/dess of Teen Depression takes the cord in her hand.

The Eternal God/dess of Teen Depression takes a breath and pulls the cord.

There's a very loud sound.

OUT TO LUNCH

You wake up in the predawn cold. Someone is shaking you.

"Rainbow! Hey!"

It's Chad01.

"Hey, you were screaming in your sleep," he says.

You sit up in the waning darkness. Chad01 whispers the spell and lights the fire again, and you watch the last of the stars fade away as the sky turns from black to blue. The twins snore softly in the dancing light. The air is still and cold. Then, in the same instant, Owlsy and Lark wake. They sit up and stretch, mirroring each other, and then Lark yawns and says, "Another beautiful day, yeah?"

✴

You start off again, sleeping bag draped over your shoulder as before. The pain in your side is back, or maybe it never left. You dig your fingers under your ribs, and the throbbing moves to a different spot. You try not to think too much about water or food. You walk. The sky flickers; the desert is woozy under your feet.

✴

You come to a beat-up call box. No music this time — it just appears suddenly in the distance on the path. There's a sign taped over the slot:

OUT OF ORDER

The sign seems unnecessary. One side of the box has been crushed in like it was hit by a car or something, the rest is spray-painted in random silver and white swirls, and some of it looks like it was maybe on fire. There's a big wad of chewing gum on the button. Chad01 slams it a couple times, and nothing happens.

"Lovely," says Lark.

You move on.

⁂

You walk until your legs are burning, but the mountains don't get any closer. Your thoughts drift here and there, always returning to the same thing. Water.

⁂

Gradually a form takes shape in the distance. Something gray hanging in the sky. Some kind of weird cloud. No, not a cloud. An enormous cube. You've seen this cube before. You've imagined it.

"What *is* that?" says Chad01.

"The cube," you say quietly.

"The *what?*"

"From my dreams." You explain your trick of falling asleep by imagining a variety of complex but instant deaths, including being crushed by a cube.

"You dream about dying?" says Lark.

"Not really dream," you say. *"Imagine."*

"And this helps you fall asleep?" says Owlsy.

"I'm not saying it's healthy."

᠅

As you walk closer, the cube grows, and a concrete pad takes shape underneath, maybe the size of a volleyball court, sitting alone in the desert below the suspended cube. Trash and broken bottles glitter in the light. There's a huge pile of clothing, all different shapes and colors, like the biggest pile of laundry ever, and also a metal barrel, some other random trash, and in the very middle of the pad, a red door standing upright by itself.

You go to the door with the others. There's a note taped to the splintered wood.

Out to lunch
Don't touch my sh■t
— the kid

"Keeper nest," says Chad01.

"Right," says Owlsy. "They're always mucking around in filth like this."

"So what do we do?" you ask.

"We wait," says Owlsy.

"And then we deal with the Keeper," says Chad01.

"It's going to be lovely," says Lark.

THE KID

A single fly buzzes lazily in the air. Heat radiates off the concrete. The mountains shimmer in the distance like a mirage. No one's really talking. You're all thinking about water.

Your lips are cracked. When you lick them, you taste blood.

The wind picks up a little, and the fly drifts away.

"There," says Lark.

You follow her gaze to the distant figure walking slowly toward you through the brush. If he notices you, he doesn't acknowledge it. He's got olive shorts and a dirty brown hoodie with the hood up. And he's got some kind of a bag, a white, plastic grocery sack dangling from his left hand.

⁂

The kid walks onto the concrete pad, and when he's about halfway, he stops and just stands there. His clothes are torn and filthy. And his hoodie—he's pulled the strings as tight as they will go, and in the scrunched little circle, all you can see is his nose and the top part of his mouth. The rest of his face is concealed, eyes hidden. The bag he's carrying has a smiley face drawn on it in black marker, with x's for eyes.

He stops there, halfway on the concrete, so you and the others get up and approach him, and as you draw closer, you hear a whimpering sound, and at first you think it's the kid, but no. It's coming from inside the bag. There's something in there, maybe the size of like a half-deflated volleyball, and it's whimpering.

"Hi," says Owlsy. "We just arrived a bit ago, and we were wondering if we might ask for your help unlocking a portal . . ."

No answer. The kid just stands there, face hidden. The thing in the bag whimpers. The sun blazes down. He must be so hot with his hood tied like that. For a moment, you aren't sure if he's going to speak, if he can. But then he does.

"Gold or sour."

"Um . . ." Owlsy responds. "So that's sort of the issue. We had some, but our backpack was stolen. Perhaps we could work out some other sort of deal? Is there some other way we could help you out in exchange for you unlocking the portal?"

"Gold or sour," says the kid again.

The thing in the bag whimpers louder.

"Listen," says Chad01. "We already told you—we don't have any gold or sour. The hell you got in that bag, anyway?"

The kid sort of shrugs.

"Hey, I asked you a question. What's in the bag?"

"My heart," says the kid.

"Your *what?*"

"Let's go," says Lark. "We're wasting our time here."

"Know what I think?" Chad01 steps up to the kid. "I think you should let whatever is in that bag free."

"I think I'll pass on that." The kid stands there, face hidden in his hoodie. The thing in the bag whimpers louder still.

"No, you don't get it," says Chad01. "I'm not asking you. I'm *telling* you."

"Ha, yeah," says the kid. "So, hey, by the way, I just remembered something funny—wanna hear it? Weren't you all telling me about a backpack you lost? I just remembered something. I *found* a backpack. Yes, I did. Just the other night. It was blue and bottomless and full of sour and gold."

"That's MY backpack!" Chad01 lunges at the kid, but in the same instant the kid disappears, and Chad01 goes stumbling across the concrete, and the kid reappears five feet over from where he was originally standing.

"Finders keepers," says the kid. "Losers creepers."

"I didn't *lose* it," says Chad01. "You *stole* it!"

"And it's *weepers!*" says Owlsy.

"What?" says the kid.

"I believe the expression is, 'Finders keepers, losers *weepers.*'"

"Wait." The kid leans back a little to look at Owlsy from the darkness of his hoodie. "Are you calling me a f█cking *liar?*"

The words ring out in the desert air, and for a moment no one says anything. It's like an evil wind passing by.

"Wow," says the kid at last. "I'm getting cranky. I need my medicine."

He's holding a lighter and a pipe now. In the end of the pipe, you see the white crystal sour. The kid sticks the pipe in the opening in his hood and brings the lighter up. *Snick.*

⁂

"Run!" says Owlsy.

You are sprinting with the others across the concrete pad, away from the magical, addicting smoke. You stand at a distance and watch the kid. The opening in his hoodie is barely bigger than the pipe. Smoke comes pouring out of the hole like he's some kind of alien machine.

"OK." The kid takes the pipe and taps the ashes into his hand and blows them into the air. "All better. I'm a jolly old elf again."

When you're certain all the smoke has cleared, the four of you return.

"OK," says the kid. "So I was thinking. About the backpack— I think you might be right."

"Of course I'm right!" says Chad01.

"Not you—*him*." He points to Owlsy. "About the expression. I think you're right. I think it *is* 'Finders keepers, losers weepers.' I must've just forgotten. I'm always forgetting things. There's a lot to forget, you know? Like, what were we even talking about?"

"MY BACKPACK! WHERE IS IT?"

"Oh," says the kid. "Right. It's behind the red door."

Chad01 runs to the door and looks around. "There's nothing behind it at all!"

"Well, you gotta open it."

So Chad01 tries the door. "It's locked."

"No kidding?"

"So unlock it!"

"Gold or sour."

"QUIT YOUR SH█T AND GIVE ME MY BACKPACK!"

"Easy, Chad01," says Owlsy.

The bag whimpers.

Chad01 springs forward and socks the kid in the gut, and his hand is repelled—*BRRZAP!*—but it must have had some impact because the kid lets out a sound like *nnuhhhhhh* as Chad01 snatches the bag out of the kid's hand. But when he rips it open, there's nothing there. He turns it inside out—nothing—empty. The whimpering continues for a moment and then drifts away on the breeze.

The kid shakes his head. "Great. Just great. There goes my heart. I was going to eat that!"

"What are you even—"

And that's as far as Chad01 gets, because the next thing the kid does is reach his hands up and stretch out the opening of his hoodie so all of you can see his eyes.

His eyes. You've never witnessed anything like it. Two dark holes, like open, screaming mouths, dark beyond dark, full of pain and sadness and fury and this sickening hate so strong it instantly makes you nauseous. You can feel the bile rising in your throat.

You can feel it coming on.

It's like you're going to puke.

.ᴧ.

And now you actually are puking—everyone is. You're puking so hard it hurts, your stomach cramping with each heave, and for a moment the desert is filled with the sounds of heaving and gagging and vomited Chonk slapping onto the concrete.

When it's over you're left with the taste of it in your mouth. Your throat burns. You wipe away the tears.

"Hey," says the kid. "Can I ask you a question? I think there's something wrong with my eyes. Did you see what just happened to you all? I mean—is that normal? And not just you—me too. It's like every time I look at myself in the mirror, I end up puking my guts out." He readjusts his hoodie so all you can see is his nose again. "Better? I don't want to see you all puking up all your insides—I mean, I do and I don't." He tilts his head and you catch the faintest glimmer of a dark eye. "Maybe if I get bored later I'll take it off and watch you puke some more."

He lifts his hoodie just a little. You shield yourself from the howling gaze.

"I need another smoke," he says.

31

THE PLAN

The four of you gather together in the desert, away from the dangerous sour fumes and out of earshot of the kid.

Owlsy closes his wiki. "Nothing more here."

Lark sighs. "Guess I'll try manifesting. Anything to avoid this creep."

···

Chad01 breaks a stick from a bush, and Lark sits and lights it on fire and draws the concentric circles. Her body begins to shake, and she leans over and begins to fall—backwards this time—and Owlsy leaps in and catches his sister.

···

Lark blinks in the light. "The portal to the city," she says. "I saw it."

"Saw it *where?*" says Owlsy.

"*Here*. Like right around here. Hidden but close."

"Can you unlock it?" says Chad01.

Lark shakes her head.

"Only the Keeper can," says Owlsy.

"OK," says Chad01. "I got an idea. So here's what we do. I'll take an old shirt from his pile of laundry and use it like a blindfold, yeah? So I'll be immune to his gaze. And then you just tell me where to swing, and I'll beat the crap out of him until he unlocks it."

"Brilliant," says Lark. "And what about the part where he disappears and reappears?"

"What about it? You got any better ideas?"

"What, other than fighting him blind?"

Suddenly an idea comes to you. "What about the sour?" you say.

"What?" says Chad01.

"That's how you open a portal, right? And you told me a person can inhale the fumes once before they're addicted, right? And you all have smoked it before—but I haven't . . . So what if the next time he smokes, I run up to him and—"

"*No,*" says Owlsy. "You should save that ability. It's only good once. For dire situations only."

"And this doesn't count?" says Chad01. "We're out of *water.* The Keeper is *insane.*"

"It's Rainbow's decision anyway," says Lark.

"I *know* that!" says Owlsy.

They're all looking at you now, the three of them pasted lonely against the desert. Tired eyes, dusty faces, cracked lips.

"Yeah," you say. "I'll do it."

⁂

So you make a plan.

"We'll talk with him, humor him," says Owlsy. "And as he becomes agitated, he'll want to smoke, and that's when you run in. OK, Rainbow?"

"Breathe in the smoke," says Chad01.

"You don't need much," says Owlsy. "All it takes is the littlest bit."

"But you gotta get *some,* OK?" says Chad01.

"What happens after I inhale?" you ask.

"Don't worry," says Lark. "You'll know what to do."

"Get ready," says Chad01. "You're going to see things you never saw before."

⁓

You return to the kid, who is done smoking for the moment.

"Newsflash to your mom," he says.

"What?"

"Mr. Sunshine is back." He does a little jig, spins around. "I was thinking, maybe we could make a deal: if you all stay a little while and play a game with me, I'll give you back your bag and unlock the portal. How's that sound?"

"No games," says Chad01.

"What is the game?" says Owlsy.

"Uh . . ." The kid digs into his pocket and pulls out a wad of paper. "I'm always forgetting, so I have to write them down . . . OK, how about Cook Off? That could be fun. Every contestant prepares one dish, which we then judge based on three factors: presentation, creativity, and flavor profile. Um, I don't have a kitchen, so we'll have to barbecue I guess."

He walks to the oil barrel, takes out his lighter, and touches it to the inside. Flames shoot up, followed by thick, black smoke and a terrible odor of burned plastic and hair.

"As for ingredients, uh . . ." He reads from his paper. "There's just one we need. A single fuzzy glower. Gimme that fuzzy in your sling and we'll get started."

"*What?!*" Chad01 sputters. "IF YOU THINK THAT'S HAPPENING, YOU'RE OUT OF YOUR MIND!"

"No." The kid points a finger at you. "Rainbow is."

You have a sudden urge to slap his finger away, but you don't want to see his eyes again. How does he know your name?

"Hey!" he says. "It just came to me! I know a *really* fun game we could play — and you don't even have to cook anything! It's called One Precious Memory. You wanna play that?"

"I was wondering," says Owlsy. "What if perhaps we struck a different deal? What if, instead of playing a game, we let you keep our sour and gold, but you returned the backpack and opened the portal — and in return we agreed to come back at a later point with even *more* sour? If you just trust us, we could be your friends in this situation. And really, it would be worth it to have more, wouldn't it?"

The kid stands there, eyes hidden in his hoodie.

"Could you?" he says at last.

"Could we what?" says Owlsy.

"Really be my friends?" says the kid.

"Hell no," says Chad01.

"Yes, of course!" says Owlsy. "Of course we can." He gives you all a look. *Come on, guys.*

The kid raises his hoodie a little so you can almost see his eyes. "ARE YOU MY F■CKING FRIENDS OR AREN'T YOU?"

"Uh . . ."

"Why you gotta make me so angry, anyway?"

He's holding his pipe again. The wind nudges a crumpled wrapper along the concrete. Lark glances at you, like, *Ready?*

The kid flicks the lighter.

"Now!"

The others head one direction, and you dash toward the kid, but you've made your move too fast. He sees you coming, and he hasn't lit the sour yet, and his eyes scream out from the hole in his hoodie, his sickening gaze, and your stomach clenches and you stoop over in pain. The emptiness. The cruelty.

Still you can feel him looking at you. Your skin is crawling, your eyes water. Convulsions ripple through your gut as your body tries to vomit, but there's nothing left to throw up.

mem01613t ["The Eternal God/dess of Teen Depression"]

The Eternal God/dess of Teen Depression scribbles over the story she's been writing and rips out all the pages of her spiral notebook. Then she takes the spring, uncoils it, and jabs it into the naked skin of her wrist. She presses the wire into her god flesh and twists it around.

Hi, I am pain.

The blood appears, a bead of bright red. But the pain is white.

The Eternal God/dess of Teen Depression sits there while the blood drips from her wrist and onto the white tile. It just keeps coming. She closes her eyes, but she doesn't pass out, and when she looks again, she is standing in a puddle of blood. It's pouring out of her. She puts her hand on her arm, but it just keeps coming, pooling on the floor now, covering her shoes. She can feel it soaking into her socks, seeping between her toes.

*It's up to her knees now.

This is very gross, she thinks.

The blood keeps rising.

Her waist. Her chest.

Now comes the moment of buoyancy. She is floating in it.

The Eternal God/dess of Teen Depression is floating in the blood, she is kicking her legs to keep her head up.

The blood keeps rising. It's nearly to the ceiling.

The Eternal God/dess of Teen Depression presses her lips up to the last bit of air. Gasping. Drowning in it. She is drowning in her own blood. Screaming in the blood. She is—

32.

ONE PRECIOUS MEMORY

Finally the kid withdraws his horrible gaze, and you collapse to the ground. The wind scutters a plastic wrapper across the concrete. You pick yourself up and gather with the others again in the desert.

"We need to fight him," says Chad01. "We need a coordinated attack."

"He's too powerful," says Owlsy. "Maybe if we had water, we could stay longer and wear him out, but in this state? No. I don't think we have a lot of choice in this situation."

"What are you suggesting?" Lark asks.

"The City of a Thousand Days and Nights is *literally* the next level, yeah? You said you saw it. We just need to get through this *one* thing. What did he say the game was? One Precious Memory? How bad can it be?"

"You're kidding, right?" says Lark.

"We might as well just *see,*" says Owlsy.

~

You return to the kid, who is still standing where you left him, arms at his sides, hoodie cinched up over his face.

"OK," says Owlsy. "So to recap, the deal is this: if we play your game, you'll unlock the portal *and* give Chad01 back his bag. Is that correct?"

"You bet."

"Do you swear by it?"

"For sure," says the kid.

 Owlsy considers him. "And you do realize, of course, that if a Keeper *swears* by a deal and then reneges on that deal, the Keeper loses *all* accumulated power?"

"That is how it works," says the kid.

"So let's see it, then," says Chad01.

"The game?" says the kid.

"My backpack."

"OK." The kid snaps his fingers, and the red door swings open. You see Chad01's blue pack, hanging from a hook. The kid snaps his fingers again and the door slams shut. A lock clicks.

⠒

"OK, here's how it works." The kid is holding a deck of playing cards now. He fans them out, grimy and worn at the edges. "Very simple. Everyone goes once. When it's your turn, you pick a card. You do what it says on the card. While you're doing that, you will remember a special and beloved memory from home, and then you will forget that memory forever. That's why they call it *One Precious Memory*. Once everyone has gone, the game is over."

"Do we get to choose the memory?" says Owlsy.

"No."

"And what, exactly, is on the cards?" says Lark.

"Dunno," says the kid. "You gotta pick one to see."

"This is a terrible idea," says Chad01.

"Agreed," says Lark.

"Only one way to know for sure," says Owlsy brightly. "I'll go first." And with that he slides a card out of the deck and flips it over for everyone to see.

SNORT A LINE OF RED ANTS

Owlsy considers the card a moment, then turns to the kid. "So what exactly does this entail?"

"Well, I'll show you," says the kid. "We gotta go to the ant hill. It's just over there."

"Lead the way," says Owlsy.

"Seriously?" says Lark.

"I wouldn't do it," says Chad01.

"Hold up," says the kid. "I just remembered something. I'll meet you at the ants. See the little hill? It's right over there. I'll be right back. I gotta get the syrup."

.ʌ.

The ant hill turns out to be a little pile of tiny pebbles laid over a crack in the concrete. You see a couple red ants walking along the fissure, exploring the canyon's edge.

"You don't have to do this," says Lark.

"If we get home, it's worth it," says Owlsy.

"I don't trust him," says Chad01.

"Trust doesn't matter," says Owlsy. "He swore on the deal. He's bound by wizard law now . . . But listen. If this game works like he says it does, I'm going to remember my memory before I forget it. So when I start to remember the memory, I'm going to recite it aloud, yeah? That way you can tell it back to me later and I won't lose it. Understand? And,

Lark, if it's the memory about Mom and us and the bunk beds, you already know that one, right?"

"Yeah, yeah," she says.

⁛

The kid returns with a brown bottle with white letters that say SYRUP. He drizzles a thick stripe along the concrete, ending at the ant hill. "Now we wait."

In a moment the ants are pouring out of the hole, gathering along the line of syrup. They keep emerging, more and more of them, growing thicker by the second.

"OK, and here's your straw." The kid hands Owlsy a straw. "No fakesies. If you don't snort, it doesn't count."

You gaze with the others at the twitchy mass of bodies, legs, and pinchers.

"Ew," says Lark.

"Don't do it," you say.

Owlsy says nothing as he slowly drops to one knee, eyes glued to the ants.

"Ready, steady, spaghetti," says the kid. "Anytime now."

Lark kneels beside her brother. "Listen to what Rainbow said. You don't have to do this."

"You really don't," says Chad01.

Owlsy sort of shrugs. "If we go home, it's worth it."

He plugs one nostril, inserts the straw into his other nostril, and hunches over. He stays like that for a moment, holding the straw just above the ants, watching the seething line.

Then in one quick and steady motion, sweeps the straw along the skittery strip of ants, and snorts the line.

⁛

"Gaah! Ughh! Ksnnrk!"

Owlsy is on his feet again, hands clawing at his face, huffing and snuffing and trying to blow the ants back out his nose. Then the blood starts. It's like a fountain of it, pouring out of his nose and mouth, mixing with spit and ants all down his chin and onto his hoodie and shirt.

"The store!" he shouts through the blood. "We're at the store with the balloons and she's got — she's got —"

"Who?" says Lark. "Who are you talking about? Mom?"

"Yes! She's got — she's — snnrrkkk." He's pinching his nostrils, snorting and coughing. There's blood everywhere, running down his pants and his shirt.

The kid nods once like he's seen it all before.

"He's got an ant in the sinus," he says. "That would be my guess."

NOW EVERYONE LOATHES YOU

Eventually the bleeding slows and Owlsy gets the last ant out. He wipes his face with his shirt, leaving a dark smear. "The memory—what was it? What did I say?"

"I don't know," says Lark. "You only got as far as 'mom and the store with balloons.'"

"What store? What balloons? I don't remember that."

"I don't either," says Lark.

"Yep," says the kid. "That's how the game works. Gone forever. Dust in the wind. Who's next?"

You all look at one another.

"I'll go," says Lark at last.

"No, I will." Chad01 steps past her and grabs a card from the kid's deck. "Stupid game anyway, might as well get it over with."

He flips the card and reads it.

"No way," he says.

"Play a stupid game, win a stupid prize," says the kid.

"What's it say?" asks Lark.

"Nuh-uh. No."

"What *is* it?"

Chad01 holds up the card:

DRAW THREE (3) MORE CARDS

"No way," he says again. "Not fair. I'm not doing it."

"You gotta," says the kid. "That's how you play the game."

Chad01 stands there looking at the kid and the cards in his hand. "This is totally unfair," he says at last.

And it *is* totally unfair, but Owlsy has already completed his turn —it feels like you're all kind of in it now.

The kid stands there. Screaming eyes.

"Fine," says Chad01. "I'll *look* at the cards. Doesn't mean I'll do them."

✌

With that, he snatches three more cards from the kid's deck, gathers them in his palm, and flips the top one over.

BRUSH YOUR TEETH

"What, is that a joke?"

"No," says the kid. "You're a joke."

"What am I supposed to do?"

"Brush your teeth."

"Brush my teeth?" says Chad01. "And that's it?"

"That's it."

"This is stupid."

"No," says the kid. "You're stupid."

"F█ck off." Chad01 flips over the second card.

FACE PUNCH SURPRISE X3

"The hell does *that* mean?"

"It means," says the kid, "you get three surprise punches in the face."

"Who's gonna do that?"

"Me."

"You?" Chad01 laughs. "*You?* You ain't gonna do sh—"

The kid wheels around and socks Chad01 in the face. He just *splbaps* him, *BRRZAP!* on the chin, and his hand is repelled, and Chad01's face goes whipping the other direction, and it's horrible, you can feel it in your own face, the pain of it, and it's so real, and you watch helplessly as Chad01 stumbles back, dropping his cards, just managing not to fall.

Lark turns to the kid. "Hey!" she says. "This is not what—"

"This is *not* the game we agreed to," Owlsy finishes.

Chad01's eyes are watery, but after a moment he sort of smiles. "No worries. You think that hurt? That didn't *even*—"

This time it's even faster.

BRRZAP! The kid swings and knocks Chad01 to the concrete. He lands hard but springs back up and lunges at the kid, and the kid unleashes his terrible gaze. Chad01's hands go up as he tries to shield himself, but he isn't quick enough, and in a moment he's bent over heaving, but nothing's coming out.

"Looks like you're all empty," says the kid after a moment.

"Go to hell," says Chad01.

⁂

"Let's get out of here," you say. "Let's just go."

"Nah," says Chad01. "That's all right." He turns to the kid. "Punch me again, you sick f█ck. Come on."

"Well, I can't," says the kid.

"Why not?"

"It wouldn't be a surprise."

Chad01 wipes his mouth on the sleeve of his hoodie and looks at the kid for a long time. "You're not a good person," he says at last, and picks the final card up from the concrete where it landed face-down. He flips it over.

NOW EVERYONE LOATHES YOU

"What is this nonsense?"

"The truth," says the kid.

"What do you mean?"

"Now everyone loathes you."

"Who does?" says Chad01.

"Everyone," says the kid. "Them. Me. All of us. *Everyone*."

"I don't get it. What am I supposed to do?"

"Nothing," says the kid.

"This is so stupid," says Chad01.

"No," says the kid. "*You're* stupid."

You hear a sound. Someone snickering. You can't tell who.

"Whatever," says Chad01. "I drew the stupid cards. My turn's over."

"No it's not," says the kid.

"Yes it is!"

"You still have to brush your teeth."

"I don't have a toothbrush. You stole my backpack—*remember?*"

"You can use mine." The kid digs in his pocket and pulls out a toothbrush, grimy, chewed-up, and yellow. The bristles are fanned out, nearly flat. He's got a little tube of toothpaste, too, and he squeezes some onto the brush and offers it to Chad01.

"Nice!" Owlsy guffaws.

"No way!" says Chad01. "I'm not touching that. You want me to brush, you get my toothbrush from my bag."

The kid doesn't answer. He just keeps holding out the toothbrush.

"Look," says Chad01. "I'm not—"

"F■cking just *do* it!" a voice cries. "Shut up and brush your stupid f■cking teeth and get it over with so we can get out of here! *OK??*"

It takes you a moment to realize who said it. *You* said it. You're kind of stunned—but on the other hand, you're starting to get really annoyed with Chad01, the way he won't stop whining, and you know you're all just going to end up bent over heaving again, and you don't want to go through that anymore, you just want this nightmare to be over with, and right now it's all Chad01's fault.

"Look at that thing!" he cries. "It could have diseases!"

"*You're* a disease," says Lark.

"Shut up," says Chad01.

"You shut up!" says Owlsy. He turns to you and Lark and rolls his eyes. "Ugh. God. What a complete sh■thead Chad01 is. And stupid too, isn't he? From the moment I met him, I can't believe I didn't instantly realize what a complete and utter waste he was."

"An absolute f■ckstain," Lark agrees.

"It cannot be denied."

"And ugly too."

"Oh my god, yes!"

It feels good to hear them talk like this, to know you're not alone in your sudden loathsome feelings. Chad01's had it coming for a long time. You look at him standing there, red-faced and useless. He's so, *so* pathetic.

Finally Chad01 takes the brush. He puts it to his mouth. He isn't looking at any of you, but he won't turn away either. He's too proud. It's disgusting.

"Little circular motions," says the kid. "Don't forget to get behind your molars."

ᴧᴠ

At first it's normal, just a person brushing his teeth. But then something happens. His mouth begins to foam. He gags and spits on the ground, and you can see in his spit there are these little white pills, two of them, only they aren't pills. He picks one up. This little white square.

"My tooth!" he cries.

"*Teeth,*" says the kid. "There's another there."

"Good one!" Owlsy laughs.

Lark laughs too. And you join in the fun. You are all laughing except Chad01. Chad01 looks like he might cry. It's beautiful.

"MY TEETH!"

"They're free to roam now," says the kid. "Can I have my toothbrush back?"

"YOU TRICKED ME! THE TOOTHBRUSH MADE MY TEETH FALL OUT!"

"No. Your teeth fell out because I punched you in the mouth."

"What?" says Chad01. "No. You never punched me in the mouth."

"Yeah I did."

"When?"

"Just now."

BRRZAP! The kid socks Chad01 in the mouth. Chad01 falls backwards, gets up, and spits out another tooth. His hand is at his lips, his face red, blood and spit dribbling down his chin. His eyes are wide, like he can't believe what he's seeing.

It's just so glorious.

Everyone is laughing at the cruel joke, and you keep laughing until you realize that the kid is laughing with you, and then you stop and it's just the kid who is laughing.

"Wait!" says Chad01. "The memory! It's coming to me! It's me and Grandma. It's like a cold but sunny autumn day, and I just got home after school, and—"

"La, la, la." Lark puts her hands to her ears. "La, la, la, can't hear you!"

"I just got home, OK? And she was there in the room, OK? And—"

"Yeah yeah," says Owlsy. "We get it. You and your grandmother. The end."

"Stop! I need you to hear this! My grandma, she—"

Chad01 blinks.

His face is blank.

He blinks some more.

"Wait, what just happened?"

"Forget it," you say.

"Looks like he already has!" says Owlsy.

Everyone laughs some more except stupid Chad01, and then you all stop laughing and just look at Chad01 and his stupid fat face and stupid nose and stupid, gross toothless mouth. Oh, how you utterly loathe him. For how weak he is. For how dumb. For how ugly and gross, with his bloody mouth and missing teeth. You think, *Maybe if I just stare at him long enough I can get him to cry.*

Instead, Chad01 begins to plead.

In a way, it's even better.

"Lark," he whines. "Those heal spells you bought—remember? In the field of flowers? Can I—"

"Yeah right!" Owlsy laughs. "As if she'd waste a heal spell on an ▆sswipe like you!"

"She's got *two* of them!"

"Cover your mouth when you talk!" says Lark. "It's disgusting."

"But the spell! You got—"

"Two! I heard you the first time! One for me, and another for *anyone but you*."

"Don't you get it?" Chad01 pleads. "You don't *really* feel this way about me, *remember?* It's the game that's making you hate me!"

"Whatever."

"It's just a spell! It's—"

"Oh my god, will you cover your mouth?"

34.

ONE HUNDRED YEARS OF SOLITUDE

"F■ckstain's turn is over," says the kid. "Who's next?"

You've gone this far. There's no turning back. It wouldn't be fair to Owlsy and Chad01. Actually, who cares about Chad01 — it wouldn't be fair to Owlsy. And you're thinking about maybe stepping forward when Lark does instead.

She takes a card and holds it so you all can see.

100 YEARS OF SOLITUDE

As you read the words, a memory comes flooding in. School. English. The class you weren't supposed to be in. All those reading journals. *One Hundred Years of Solitude*. You take a breath.

You think, *This card was meant for me.*

"What is it?" says Owlsy.

"It's a book," you say.

"No," says the kid. "It's one hundred years of solitude."

"What do you mean one hundred years?" says Owlsy. "She'd die in that time."

186

"Magic game, magic prizes," says the kid. "None of the cards are lethal—only painful."

"It's a *book*," you say again.

"Wrong," says the kid.

"How does it work?" says Lark.

"I open the magic red door. You step through the magic red door. I close the door. For the rest of us, only a moment will pass, but for you it will be one hundred years. I open the door. You come back out. Your turn is over."

And with that, the kid snaps his fingers, and the door swings open. Now instead of a backpack, it's just white, just blank empty space. A rectangle of nothingness against the desert.

"No," says Owlsy. "No way. That's—insane."

Lark tilts her head a little. "But it's like you were saying, right? We're so close to home. Just this one more thing." Lark stands before the door, chewing on her nail.

"It isn't worth it," you say. "Don't do it!"

"Listen," says Chad01. "*Lark*. Snorting ants is one thing—or like getting punched or whatever—but a *hundred* years all alone by yourself? That's a *really* bad idea."

"Shut it, Chad01," Lark snaps. "If I ever want your opinion, I'll ask for it! And you know what? The fact that your dumb ■ss thinks it's a 'really bad idea' probably means that it's *actually* a *brilliant* idea." She's walking to the door now.

"No!" Owlsy cries. "Lark!"

"See you soon, Owlsy. See you soon, Rainbow. F■ck off, Chad01." And before anyone can stop her, Lark slips through the open doorframe, grabs the handle, and slams the door shut behind her.

⁂

"Lark!" Owlsy cries. He runs to the door and tries the handle, but it won't open. "Let her out!"

The sky flickers. The sun sends off sparks.

The kid looks at his wrist as if checking a watch. "Yeah, should be done by now."

He snaps his fingers. The door opens.

Lark comes stumbling out of the white and onto the concrete. Her hair is sticking up in every direction and her mouth is hanging open, dried spit all over her chin, and a weird sound is coming out of her, this gurgling sound. She's holding something in her hand, a chunk of long dark hair, *her* hair, eyes glassy and wild, looking this way and that.

"Owlsy?" she says. She looks at the chunk of hair in her hands. "Owlsy?"

"Lark!" Owlsy goes to wrap his arms around his sister and— BRRZAP!—is thrown stumbling back.

"Owlsy?" She holds the hair up, gazing at it with glassy eyes.

"What have you done to her?"

"Wasn't me," says the kid. "A hundred years alone will do that to anyone."

"Owlsy?" says Lark blankly.

"I'm right here, Lark!"

"Owlsy? Owlsy?" She won't stop saying it. Just, "Owlsy? Owlsy? Owlsy?"

"Yeah," says the kid. "*Owlsy* for sure."

"You *psychopath!*" Owlsy lunges at the kid, only this time he's smart about it. With one hand he covers his eyes to avoid the screaming gaze, and with the other he punches the air wildly. One of the punches manages to make contact, *BRRZAP!,* sending the kid sprawling back on the concrete.

The three of you are on him now—you, Owlsy, and f█ckface —but then the kid opens his mouth and out comes the worst sound you have ever heard. This high-pitched screeching, like an audio version of his hateful gaze. It fills the air, everything vibrating with hate and sadness, and the nausea returns, and again for what feels like the millionth time, you're bent over puking up nothing.

.ิ.

"All right," says the kid at last. "Nice try. You almost had me. Who's next?"

Owlsy stands there with his red, swollen nose, Lark clutching the hair, stupid Chad01 with his stupid, bloody mouth. They've all gone. It's your turn now.

You step forward. You look at the cards fanned out in the kid's hand. You take one, slide it out, flip it over, and read the words:

CAN YOU KEEP A SECRET?

CAN YOU KEEP A SECRET?

"So actually there are *three* secrets," says the kid. "If you can keep the secrets, then nothing happens. But if you tell *anyone any* of the secrets —or even say them out loud—*all* the secrets come true."

"Wait," you say. "They aren't true unless I say them? How is that even possible?"

"Magic," says Chad01.

"Shut your stupid ▮ss face," says the kid. "But yeah."

⚡

You give it some thought. OK. Keep three secrets? It doesn't sound *so* bad. Whatever the secrets are, all you have to do is not tell anyone, and they won't come true, right? How hard can that be?

"Fine," you say. "Tell me the secrets."

The kid turns to you. "Well, I can't just say them out loud, or they wouldn't be secrets. Come here and I'll whisper them in your ear."

⚡

The kid is a little taller than you, and from a distance he smells, but up close there's another layer of stink altogether, something behind the bad breath and body odor, something wrong.

"Ready for the secrets?" He cups his hands and makes a little tunnel between the hole in his hoodie and your ear. His breath is hot vomit.

"*I am CJ,*" he whispers. "*You are crazy. All your friends are imaginary.*"

᠅

The words sort of hang there in the air as your world turns inside out.

For some reason you find yourself looking at the mountains. The cracks in the concrete. The flickering sky. Anywhere but the kid. No way. He is not your brother. You are not crazy. And your friends — you look at the others. The hair in Lark's hand. Chad01's stupid face. Owlsy's serious brow.

You look at the kid again. He's standing there silently, arms at his side, hoodie cinched up over his screaming eyes. He isn't your brother. He's a different CJ. Someone else. He could be anyone.

You take a breath and remind yourself that none of this even matters, because the secrets *aren't* true. And whether or not you believe the kid, you won't ever say them. It's that simple, right? As long as you don't say them, the secrets will never come true. Except — how could saying something make it true? That's just — it's *crazy*. This whole thing is. It's all just crazy crazy crazy crazy —

᠅

And now Owlsy is asking you a question. You are standing in the desert on the concrete pad and he is saying, "What did the two of you do?"

"*What?*" you ask.

"You and your brother! You were saying something about the beach. You were at the beach with your brother and there was something about a fire?"

"What are you talking about?"

"Your memory. You started to tell me and then you stopped."

191

"I did?" You can't remember it. You can't even remember telling him about it. The memory, whatever it was . . . it's just gone.

⁙

"Owlsy?" says Lark. "Owlsy?"

And stupid, toothless Chad01 sitting there like human garbage.

And the kid.

STUPID DANCE

"We played your game," says Owlsy. "Now give us the backpack and unlock the portal."

The kid doesn't answer. He's silent. This kid—this kid who is *not* and won't *ever* be your brother—he just stands there unmoving.

"Say something!" Chad01 yells.

"Shut up, Chad01!" says Owlsy.

"Owlsy?" says Lark.

"Open the portal!" you say.

The kid shakes his head. "The game isn't over until everyone has had a turn."

"We all went!"

"Not the fuzzy." The kid is pointing at the dumb■ss beside you. "I know it's there. I can see it glowing through that rip in your sling."

"What?!" Chad01 is standing now. "NO WAY!"

"Yes way," says the kid. "It's a member of your little crew, isn't it?"

"It's just a baby!" Chad01 says. "It can't even read!"

"Boohoo," says the kid.

193

"Listen," says Owlsy. "Chad01 is a complete idiot, but he's got a point. A magical baby creature can't reasonably be expected to read and perform written instructions, can it?"

The kid turns to Owlsy. "What are you, a lawyer?"

"I'm a scholar. So how about this: How about the fuzzy *picks* but someone else *does* the card?"

The hoodie tilts a little to the side. "Who would that be?"

You and Owlsy look at each other in silent understanding. "Chad-01!" you shout together.

"What?!" says Chad01. "I already went like *four* times! No way. One of *you* go!"

"It's your stupid pet. *You* do the card!"

"Stop being such a *baby!*"

Chad01 stands there, looking at you all with his stupid face.

"Owlsy?" says Lark.

❧

"Fine." Chad01 takes out the fuzzy, with its shining, incandescent eyes and halo of light, and it occurs to you how totally unfair and revolting it is that a loser like Chad01 should have such an adorable pet, and Echo Joy seems to agree.

You watch as it lets out a shriek and snaps at Chad01.

"Ow!" says Chad01. "You *bit* me! Why?"

"Duh," says the kid. "Now everyone loathes you."

"Nice," says Owlsy.

"This is f█cked," says Chad01.

"Owlsy?" says Lark.

"WHAT IS OWLSY?" says Echo Joy.

"Just do it, sh█thead!" you yell.

❧

So Chad01 uses Echo Joy to tap one of the cards in the kid's hand. He takes the card and tries to hand it to you, but you raise your arms and back away like he's got the plague because he probably does. In the process, Chad01 drops the card—he's such a klutz—and Owlsy picks it up and holds it out so you can read it.

DO A STUPID DANCE

"Wait, that's it?" says Owlsy. "All he has to do is dance?"

"Well, it has to be *stupid*," says the kid.

Echo joy chirps up. "WHAT IS STUPID?"

"Chad01 is," says the kid.

Owlsy snorts.

"Maybe you need some music?" The kid's holding a phone now. A familiar phone. You've seen this phone before. But no—there are lots of phones like this one, right? Millions, probably. It could be *anyone's* phone. He touches the screen. Music begins to play. Music you recognize. The Wandering Song.

"Where did you get that phone?" you say.

"I forget," says the kid. "Stupid song, though, right? Good for stupid dancing, right?"

You suddenly want to leave. You need to go. You need to get out of here. But there's nowhere to go. You can't leave until Chad01 is done.

But Chad01 just stands there, not dancing.

"Dance!" you shout.

"Now!" says Owlsy.

"Owlsy?" says Lark.

"Do it!" you scream. "Dance, you stupid sh■t!"

"WHAT IS A STUPID SH■T?" says Echo Joy.

"Him!" you say. "*He* is!"

The fuzzy giggles. Chad01 goes to stuff it down into his sling, and it bites him again.

"Ow!"

The music plays. *Happy . . . sad . . . dark . . .* You stare at stupid Chad01 standing there like a total lunk. How completely useless and pathetic he is. All he has to do is dance and he won't.

"Dance!"

"But—" he says. "But what does that even *mean*—a stupid dance?" His eyes are red. He's practically crying.

"Just get on with it!" Owlsy shouts. "Whatever you do, it's bound to be stupid!"

"Yes!" you say. "Exactly!"

"Owlsy?" says Lark.

"Someone needs to teach her a new word," says the kid.

"Dance, you dumb f█ck!"

"No!"

"Do it!"

"NO!"

Waaaay back in the corner of your mind, there's this little voice saying, *Hold on. Stop. This is mean.*

But you don't listen to the voice. Instead, you reach your hands toward Chad01's shoulders and cry, "Dance!" and *shove* him— *BRRZAP!*—and he stumbles back, and you stumble back, and it feels so good because he *is* crying now. He's trying to hide it but he can't. It's just so g█dd█mn beautiful.

"Dance!" Owlsy yells. "Dance, you pathetic, know-nothing loser!"

✼

The song plays . . . *sad* . . . *dark* . . .

Chad01 wipes his face with the sleeve of his hoodie, turns away from you, and begins to halfheartedly bob up and down.

"Make it more stupid!" Owlsy shouts.

Chad01 lifts one leg up, then the other. He swings his arms from side to side.

"Oh my god, you are just so . . . *blech!*"

"He sure is." The kid snaps a rubber band around the cards and slips them into his back pocket. "And that, my friends, is how you play One Precious Memory. Good job, everyone. Now comes the part when you die."

"What?"

He's holding something in his hand. A black remote control with a red button. You recognize it from your bedtime imaginings. You glance up at the massive cube hovering above you in the sky.

"Ready?" The kid who is not your brother turns to you with his sickening gaze. "Adios, Rainbow."

He clicks the button.

As you look up, you see the dark square beginning to grow. It's getting bigger and bigger, edges racing out in every direction, and someone is screaming, you aren't sure who, but there's just this scream ringing out as the cube grows bigger and bigger . . . blotting out the sky . . . plummeting down down down in a rush of wind and darkness and—

mem010760 (dance party)

Our parents are always stressed out and fighting about one thing or another. Mostly it's money. Bills to pay, groceries. Any little thing can erupt into a screaming match. Spoiled food. School clothes. Oh, and the thermostat. Mom says we can't afford heat. CJ and I take Dad's side. We complain endlessly about the terrible, bone-chilling cold that will surely freeze us to death, and Mom tells us to put on more clothes. We come to her in layers of sweaters, whining like orphans, and she puts one of her ancient Mom bands on the ancient stereo and tells us to dance or do jumping jacks or something.

◆◆

This is when we're little, six or seven, so we take her seriously, and we start doing jumping jacks, and pretty soon CJ and I are having a dance party. And over time it becomes sort of a thing.

◆◆

God, it's fun to dance. Especially when Mom and Dad aren't home. Those first few times they leave us alone. We find a song, almost any song will do, and off we go, the whole house is ours, the two of us flying from room to room, reckless and free.

CJ is a way better dancer than me, and I don't even really resent it. He'll squeeze his eyes shut and just let himself go, and his sense of rhythm and grace are indisputably a wonder to behold, and sometimes I find myself just bobbing around in the corner watching him do his thing.

Other times I lose myself in it. It's such an easy, abundant thing— I don't know about puberty yet, or awkwardness, or how the dancing will stop.

Right now, it's amazing. Right now, with our parents at the store or arguing in the car, now as I dance with my brother, it's like I have become some sort of beautiful, graceful space bird. Right now I unfold my wings and fly to the stars and back, bouncing off planets along the way, spinning fast enough to warp the fabric of space and time, until the end comes and I flop down on the floor, hair in my face, arms and legs outstretched, chest heaving, completely wiped out. All the fears and worries washed completely away. Absolutely, completely content.

ON THE BRIGHT SIDE

"Wake up! Hey, Rainbow, wake up!"

A voice you recognize, but you can't match a name to it at first. A dark shape hovers in the darkness beside you. You struggle into consciousness as the memories fade. A fire. Dark eyes. Owlsy.

"What happened?" you ask. "Where are we?"

"It was supposed to be the City of a Thousand Days and Nights," says Owlsy. "But I'm not sure that it is. There isn't a wiki entry. On a positive note, we've recouped Chad01's bottomless backpack."

As your eyes adjust to the darkness, you can make out the looming shapes of machinery, gears and cables and sharp, mathematical edges. Another machine forest.

Owlsy's nose is swollen and red. You remember the ants now. The hundred years of solitude. The loathing. The secrets. You turn to where Lark and Chad01 are curled on the ground, asleep.

"Are they OK?"

As you say the words, Chad01 coughs. He opens his eyes and sits up, blinking. Even in the dim light you can see the dried blood on his face, and when he speaks, you can see the gaps where his teeth used to be. You're speechless. All the loathing is gone, replaced by a burning shame.

"Oh dear," says Owlsy.

"Chad01," you manage to say. "About what happened—those things I said. I didn't mean them, and I'm just—I'm so sorry."

"Yes, and myself as well," says Owlsy. "Please accept my profoundest apologies for my shameful behavior and harsh words. We were under a spell. It was all that demented Keeper's game."

Chad01 runs his tongue over the place where his teeth used to be. "You f█cking █ssholes. I *told* you you were under a spell, and you wouldn't listen!"

"Because we were under a spell!" says Owlsy.

"I'm so, so sorry," you say.

"Yes," says Owlsy. "On the bright side, you've got your pack, right?"

"Kiss my █ss," says Chad01. He opens his backpack and lifts out a teddy bear . . . a shoebox . . . and finally a canteen. He tilts it back and drinks and drinks, the water running down his chin. He stops to gulp some air, then drinks some more, watching you and Owlsy. You suddenly realize how thirsty you are. Chad01 chugs some more.

A sigh in the dark. Lark begins to stir. She opens her eyes, sits up, and looks at the three of you in the darkness for a long time. She blinks, her lips part.

"Owlsy?"

Her brother touches her shoulder. "Lark, listen. You've got two heal spells. You've got to use them on Chad01 and yourself. Do you remember how that works?"

"Owlsy?"

"You need to say the words and then all this will be—"

"Owlsy?" she says.

"Here, you remember how to drink?" Chad01 hands Lark the canteen and instead of drinking it, she cradles it in her arms like a baby, and when Chad01 tries to show her how to drink from it, she turns from him and shakes her head, says, "Owlsy."

I SURVIVED 1OOO NIGHTS
OF DARKNESS

There's a path. You start out in single file through the machine forest—
Owlsy, Lark with the canteen, Chad01, and finally you. You are trying
not to think about the kid who is not your brother, or the secrets that
don't matter, or the night screamers, or how thirsty you are, or Lark's
condition, or Chad01's teeth, or any of it. You march along the dusky
path that winds beneath the dripping, mechanical canopy. It's cold out,
and dark, but not as dark as midnight. The air has that pre-morning
buzz to it. You can make out the contours of the ground now, the clinking screws and bolts underfoot.

Of course your friends are real. And that includes Chad01. He's
your friend too. And he's real. He's walking in front of you, and you
fight the urge to just sort of reach out and poke him in the back of the
neck to see if he actually is real. But of course he is.

Just forget it, you tell yourself. *Forget the secrets.*

At some point you stop, and Owlsy coaxes the canteen away from
his sister long enough for you and him to get a drink, and then Lark
begins to cry, so you hand it back, and her face goes blank again, and
you continue walking.

The path bends and you come to a high concrete wall. There's a big metal gate and a little guardhouse, with a window, and there's a kid sitting there. She's wearing a purple polo shirt and has long, braided hair.

"Hi!" she says brightly. "You're just in time!"

"Time for what?" says Owlsy.

"The celebration!"

"What celebration?"

"Really? You don't know about the celebration?!" She smiles and claps her hands. "Oh, wow! You are going to have *such* a good time!"

"We need some heal spells," says Chad01. "What level is this, anyway?"

"This is the City of a Thousand Days and Nights."

"Here?" says Owlsy. "*This?* That's incredible!"

"It *is* incredible!" says the girl. "And you know what's even *more* incredible? Today, right now, in like *ten* minutes, is the Dawn of a Thousand Days of Light!"

Lark looks up from her canteen and whispers, *"Owlsy?"*

"The sun!" says the girl. "Oh my gosh, we have missed it *so* much! I mean, a thousand nights of darkness is a looong time. You're super-duper lucky you showed up when you did—I was about to close the booth! Let me get you checked in . . . Let's see, I'll need to scan you, and do you have any quests to complete or items to turn in?"

"Yes, we do actually!" says Owlsy.

"Great!"

"Owlsy?"

The girl scans all your forearms and then she takes out a paper map of the city and draws a line with a pencil. "You can turn in your items at the main stage. It's right here, see? If you hurry, you'll still make it in time for the dawn! I'll be right behind you! Oh, and here are your gift bags!"

The big gate swings open and you follow the others through.

⩕

Inside, it's lit up like a party. You find yourself standing on a stone boulevard with wide lawns on either side and big glass buildings. Twinkle lights are strung across every bush and bench and lamppost. Bubbles float through the air, glittering in the light, and with every step, the crowd grows, and everyone is having so much fun, dancing and playing with glow-in-the-dark bracelets or light-up Frisbees, and some are juggling fire. And the kids, every single one as far as you can see, are dressed the same way, in jeans, flip-flops, and a bright polo shirt.

"OK," says Owlsy. "So now we just get some heal spells and turn in our quest for the home portal."

"If they really have one," says Chad01.

"They have one," says Owlsy. "They have to."

Chad01 shrugs and digs through his gift bag. "Do you guys just have a mug too?"

"Owlsy?" says Lark.

"All I got was a mug." Chad01 holds up a white mug with the words *I Survived 1000 Nights of Darkness*.

Everyone got mugs. You drop them into Chad01's backpack, along with the gift bags.

"I'm hungry," he says. "Was hoping there'd be some food or something."

"It looks like there are some booths over there," says Owlsy. "We could—"

EXCUSE ME, a voice booms down from the heavens.

EXCUSE ME EVERYONE SORRY TO INTERRUPT

EXCUSE ME SORRY

The crowd goes quiet. A few people whistle.

SO GUESS WHAT? the voice booms.

THE SUN IS ABOUT TO RISE!

The crowd erupts in cheers.

YES, I'M VERY EXCITED TOO! BUT LISTEN
IN ORDER TO BETTER ENJOY THIS MOMENT
HOW ABOUT WE TURN OFF ALL THE LIGHTS
AND GET ONE LAST TASTE OF DEEP DARKNESS
BEFORE THE DAWN.
HOW'S THAT SOUND?

The lights begin to wink out, strand by strand, and the cheering dies down like someone lowering the volume, and you find yourself standing in the predawn gray with thousands of other kids, everyone hushed and silent, the world holding its breath.

"Owlsy?" says a voice beside you.

THE WIZARD OF THIS LEVEL

Maybe all sunrises are wonderful. You haven't seen enough to compare, but this one is pretty spectacular. It happens really slowly at first, the black turning purple turning gray, and then all at once, the first rays *ping* over the buildings and the sky is suddenly streaked in orange and violet light, and the colors just keep getting more and more vibrant as the sun ascends the horizon, and then it's like you blink and suddenly the sun is overhead, just blazing down from a pure blue sky.

The crowd goes wild, a roaring ovation as the square erupts in streamers, balloons, and sparkling confetti.

YEAH! WOO!

THANKS FOR COMING OUT TODAY, EVERYONE!

YOU KNOW I LOVE YOU!

More cheering. They're very enthusiastic.

OK THANK YOU

WOW

WOO!

WOOOOO!

OK SO NOT REALLY VERY GOOD AT SPEECHES

BUT JUST TO SAY SOMETHING REAL QUICK BEFORE YOU ALL GO PARTY AND EAT FOOD AND DANCE IN THE SUN, LET ME JUST SAY THAT YOU ARE ALL JUST SUCH AMAZING AND INCREDIBLE PEOPLE! I'M JUST SO *FRICKIN'* LUCKY TO KNOW YOU ALL!

GIVE YOURSELVES A ROUND OF APPLAUSE!

The crowd claps and cheers.

AND ALSO BEFORE I FORGET WE NEED TO THANK OUR FRIENDS THE FUZZIES, RIGHT? BECAUSE WITHOUT THE FUZZIES ALL THIS WOULDN'T BE POSSIBLE. I MEAN COME ON, THEY'RE THE *REAL* HEROES HERE, RIGHT? LET'S SHOW THE FUZZIES SOME LOVE!

And everyone goes wild again, horns and confetti cannons and balloons and all of it, waves and waves of celebration, and just when you think it's starting to die down, the voice interrupts to say:

WELL, WE DID IT, EVERYONE!

WE SURVIVED THE NIGHT!

WOO! LOOK AT THAT SUN! FEEL THAT ON YOUR FACE BABY THAT IS SOME GOOD SUN. OH MY GOSH I'M SO FULL OF GOOD FEELINGS RIGHT NOW I SWEAR MY HEART'S JUST GONNA BUST RIGHT OPEN!

Everyone goes wild all over again, and when the cheering finally dies down, you turn to the person nearest to you, who happens to be a kid in an electric-blue polo.

"What's going on?" you ask.

"What?"

"That voice that was speaking—what was that?"

"That was the wizard," says the kid.

"This level has a wizard?" says Chad01.

"Yeah."

"Is he a good wizard or a bad wizard?" says Owlsy.

"Oh, he's good!" says the kid. "His name is Dave and he's definitely cool."

"That's right!" says another kid in a pink polo. "Dave's the best!"

OH, YOU GUYS, booms the voice. It's aimed in your direction now.

"Well, you *are,*" says the kid in the bright blue polo.

HA I JUST TRY TO BE THE BEST I CAN YOU KNOW?

"Dave is so awesome," says a kid in a canary-yellow polo. "You know what he did? He made a sanctuary here for the fuzzies, and—"

HA THAT'S RIGHT I GUESS I DID DO THAT

"But it's even better than that! It's this just *beautiful* glass tower. You can see the top poking up over there, and—"

AW YOU REALLY LIKE THE TOWER?

"Dave," says the kid. "You *know* we love it."

WELL THANK YOU

"Yeah so what he did was he built this tower and—"

WELL *I* DIDN'T BUILD IT

"Well, OK, not technically," says the kid to the sky, "but we couldn't have done it without you. Anyway, maybe I should just let you tell the story, or—"

NO YOU GO AHEAD YOU'RE DOING A GREAT JOB

"OK, let's see . . . So where was I?"

THE TOWER

"Right. Yes. The tower is the sanctuary for orphaned fuzzies. Dave built it. Not with his hands, but he *told* us how to build it. He's just so freakin' smart. And he came to us, and he was like—"

I DON'T HAVE ANY HANDS

"That's right. He, um, he isn't—"

I AM INCORPOREAL

I LITERALLY DON'T HAVE A BODY OR HANDS

"Yeah . . . it's so tragic."

IT COULD BE WORSE

"I guess that's true. You do always say that."

I'D RATHER HAVE GOOD FRIENDS THAN A BODY ANY DAY OF THE WEEK THAT'S WHAT I ALWAYS SAY

The kid nods solemnly. "That's a really good saying, Dave."

The crowd murmurs in agreement.

BUT SO YOU WERE TELLING THEM ABOUT THE TOWER

"Right!" says the kid in the yellow polo. "So Dave helped us build an amazing tower that is not only a sanctuary for orphaned fuzzies but which actually harvests their joy to power our city! We get lights in the darkness and air conditioning in the heat, and the fuzzies have a home and it's totally sustainable—and all thanks to Dave!"

AW STOP IT YOU'RE MAKING ME BLUSH

40.

JUST ABSOLUTELY REPUGNANT

"Um, *Dave*," says Owlsy, addressing the sky. "I was wondering if I could ask you a question."

YOU BET LITTLE BUDDY

"OK, well, so my name is Owlsy, and my sister, Lark, and I—and Chad01 and Rainbow—we came to this level because we were informed that there is a home portal here. Is that true?"

ABSOLUTELY JUST ASK ANYONE

"Yup," says a kid in a seafoam-green polo. "Can confirm. The tower was designed to open a home portal. We asked Dave to help us build it. Unfortunately, and beyond Dave's control, it turns out that home portals require like a *lot* of power. Like a lot. That's just basic physics."

LIKE *A LOT* A LOT OF POWER

"It wasn't sustainable," says the kid. "In the end, it made more sense just to use the power for the city. And anyway, we're all happier here with Dave than we would be at—"

AW YOU'RE ALWAYS SO SWEET!

"So now we just open the portal as a reward for those who have completed quests."

"Well, that's actually what I was getting to," says Owlsy. "You see, *we* were on a quest!"

"You were?"

YOU WERE?

"Yes! That's why we came here . . . to deliver a very rare and special item. Here." Owlsy holds out his hand. "Maybe this will make a good addition to your tower . . . I present to you this *power crystal!*"

AH, says Dave.

OH

UMMMMMMM

There's a sound, sort of a snicker, and at first it's coming from the sky and then the crowd around you picks it up and is snickering as well, and then suddenly everyone is laughing. You aren't laughing. Owlsy and Lark and Chad01 aren't laughing. But everyone else is.

AHAHAHAH OH WOW I'M SORRY, chuckles Dave.

IT'S JUST I DON'T KNOW HOW THIS FAKE "POWER CRYSTAL" STUFF GOT STARTED AND I'M JUST, AH GOSH I'M SO SORRY TO HAVE TO TELL YOU THIS BUT WELL THAT'S ACTUALLY NOT A POWER CRYSTAL IT'S A CANDY RING

"What?" says Owlsy. "No. We were promised one million gold for this!"

ONE MILLION? HA OH WOW I'M SO SORRY I MEAN WHOEVER TOLD YOU THAT . . . WOW . . . SO IT NEVER OCCURRED TO YOU TO *TEST* THE RING IN SOME WAY?

The crowd guffaws.

"But we were assured this was verified! My wiki said it was verified!"

"Is your wiki one hundred percent accurate?" says the kid in the seafoam polo.

"Well, no."

"So there you go then."

Owlsy's just standing there. His face is red.

"My sister," he says at last. "My sister endured a hundred years of solitude for this."

"Yeah!" says Chad01. "And I got punched and emotionally scarred and my teeth fell out. And she's got heal spells, but she can't use them because all she can say is 'Owlsy.' And you're up there making fun of us."

OH WOW, says Dave. **OH GOSH**

I AM SO, SO SORRY

"You don't sound like it," says Chad01.

NO REALLY I AM! I HAD NO IDEA!

SO LET ME JUST SAY I BET I SPEAK FOR EVERYONE HERE WHEN I SAY I AM SO SORRY I LAUGHED AND THEN EVERYONE ELSE LAUGHED TOO WE ALL REALLY NEED TO CHECK OURSELVES AND BE KIND TO OTHERS RIGHT? LOOK HERE'S WHAT I'LL DO:

I'LL GIVE YOU AN EASY QUEST, OK? AND LOOK I'LL ADD THIS TOO: IF YOU AGREE TO GO ON THE QUEST, THEN I WILL USE A STEAL SPELL TO TAKE YOUR SIS-TER'S HEAL SPELLS AND THEN I WILL USE THE SPELLS TO HEAL THE TWO OF YOU. I CAN DO THAT. I AM A WIZ-ARD, AFTER ALL HAHAHA, RIGHT?

SO WHAT DO YOU THINK? HOW'S THAT SOUND? AM I TALKING TOO MUCH? I JUST REALLY DON'T WANT YOU TO FEEL TOO BAD OK? YEAH? ARE WE GOOD? WILL SOMEONE PLEASE TELL THEM ABOUT THE QUEST?

A kid in a lavender polo steps up.

"Night Screamer Mini-Quest," he says. "Far outside the walls of this city, beyond the machine forest and the gap, there's a tree called the nightmare tree, and this is where the night screamers raise baby fuzzies as slaves, and then when they are done with them, they *eat* them, but—"

IT REALLY IS JUST ABSOLUTELY REPUGNANT

"But this time of year, if you are stealthy, you can sneak in and rescue the fuzzy eggs while the night screamers are sleeping and bring them back here to the city, where they will be free to live in peace in the tower. If you return with one dozen eggs, we will open the home portal for you."

SO WHAT DO YOU SAY?

Owlsy looks to you, then Chad01 and Lark, then back to the sky. It's clear you don't have much choice.

"Yeah. OK, we'll do it."

AWESOME! GIVE THEM THE ENVELOPE!

The kid in the lavender polo steps forward. "Here's an envelope with further instructions."

AND GIVE THEM A COUPON TOO

"Right. And here's a coupon for free curly fries."

"What about healing us?" says Chad01.

RIGHT, HAHAHA

DEAR ME I ALMOST FORGOT

OK

HERE WE GO

YOU READY?

LET IT BE DONE!

There's a brilliant flash and the sky erupts in thunder.

41

NIGHT SCREAMER MINI—QUEST

The curly fries are actually delicious. You can't remember the last time you've eaten something other than Chonk bars. They're so salty and crispy, and oh god, the cool, sweet ketchup. But that isn't what makes them good. What makes them so good is you are sharing them with your friends in the sunshine, on a blanket in a grassy field surrounded by shiny glass buildings. And they are well again.

Chad01's teeth are back, his face is better, and he's laughing with Lark, who, after the thunder crashed through the heavens, blinked as if she were coming out of a trance and couldn't remember anything after the door — not the hundred years, not the portal, not the sunrise. She keeps messing with her brother, pretending that she's slipped back into the trance again, and even though it gets him every time, Owlsy's spirits are high.

"All things considered, that could have been worse," he says. "I mean, actually it was good, I'd say. You're both healed and we've just got one more task, so . . . yeah. Love these fries too. Right?"

He's got a point. You look around. Music. Food. Dancing. Bubbles drift through the air, glittering with sunlight. It's a perfect summer day. In the distance a shining glass tower rises above it all, reflecting the pure blue sky.

"So I guess the question is *what next,*" says Owlsy.

Lark raises her hand. "Owlsy?"

"Knock it off," he says.

"No, I want to say something. My vote is we stay here and eat curly fries forever."

Owlsy shakes his head. "I meant in terms of the mini-quest. I meant do we leave now? Today? Or prepare first? What is a day in this place, anyway?"

"Um," says Chad01. "Who says we're doing the quest? You really trust that wizard after you got hosed on the power crystal deal?"

"Well, Dave wasn't the one who assigned us that quest, so—"

"Right," says Lark. "How *did* we get that quest again? Oh, I remember now. Your amazing wiki led us to it."

"Well," says Owlsy. "We agreed to it. That's how you got healed, remember?"

"We agreed to *try* it," says Chad01. "We didn't agree to finish it."

"But—"

"All I know is we can't stay here." Chad01 gestures at some kids playing Frisbee, and his voice lowers. "You seen their toes? *These kids ain't real!* None of them! And as for the mini-quest, whatever. What we *need* to do is find the goldfish moon."

"Have you even looked at it?" says Owlsy.

"The mini-quest? I don't need to. It's garbage."

"It's pretty straightforward, actually." Owlsy unfolds the paper for you all to see.

Night Screamer* Mini-Quest

1. Exit the city through the north gate.
2. Follow path to the gap.
3. Cross the gap.
4. Go to the cave.
5. Go inside the cave.
6. Climb the nightmare tree.
7. Collect twelve (12) fuzzy glower eggs.
8. Return to the city.
9. Congratulations!
10. The home portal is open!

*Caution: avoid eye contact with night screamers or you
will die screaming and bleeding out your eyeballs.

"Yep," says Chad01. "That is one hundred percent certified garbage."

"Really?" says Owlsy. "And how exactly do you decide just which wizard to trust?"

"What do you mean?" says Chad01.

"I *mean,* you trust the one who gave you the fuzzy, but you don't trust this one — even though he healed you?"

"Listen," says Chad01. "The wizard who gave me Echo, I could look him in the eye and *see* he was legit."

RIGHT BUT I HAVE NO EYES, booms a voice from above.

You look up at the sky with the others.

"Oh," says Owlsy. "You're still there."

**YEP ALWAYS AND FOREVER, CAN'T LEAVE THE CITY
WALLS, DOOMED TO DISEMBODIMENT**

"So you just basically overheard everything we said," says Lark.

HA HA YEAH BUT DON'T WORRY

YOU GUYS AREN'T THE FIRST TO NOT REALLY TRUST ME I MEAN I TOTALLY GET IT. IT'S A BAD WORLD OUT THERE FULL OF ALL KINDS OF CROOKERY AND DECEPTION LIKE FOR EXAMPLE WHOEVER SOLD YOU THE FAKE POWER CRYSTAL AND HONESTLY IT JUST BREAKS MY HEART THE STORIES I HEAR FROM OUTSIDE THESE WALLS AND ALL I CAN TELL YOU IS WHAT I TELL EVERYONE: I'M JUST A SEMI-OMNISCIENT DISEMBODIED PERMANENTLY-LOCALIZED WIZARD WHO WANTS TO GIVE THE WORLD A HUG

"You're the best, Dave!" one of the Frisbee players shouts.

42

MIND THE GAP

You exit through the north gate and start down the path into the machine forest.

"So what now?" says Owlsy.

"We need to find the Lake of the Goldfish Moon," says Chad01.

"Well, listen," says Owlsy. "There's no reason we can't multitask."

"What do you mean?"

"Well, there's also the mini-quest."

"Seriously? You're still on that? No one wants to do the mini-quest!"

"But it will open the home portal!"

"My ■ss it will," says Chad01. "You want us to go storming into something called 'the nightmare tree' so we can die screaming and bleeding out our eyeballs?"

"If it gets us home, it's worth it," says Owlsy.

"Uh, worth it to die screaming and bleeding out our eyeballs?" says Lark. "Not sure about that."

Owlsy shakes his head. "No one's going to die or bleed out of their eyeballs! My point is simply that we've already started the mini-quest, haven't we? We exited through the north gate. That was step one, remember? What's step two, follow the path? We're already on it. How hard can it be?"

"Ha," says Lark.

"Listen," says Owlsy. "We can do more than one thing at a time, yeah? We can look for the 'gap,' see what it's like, and meanwhile keep our eyes peeled for any sign of strange, fishlike celestial bodies, and if anywhere along the way a better opportunity presents itself, we'll take that. Yeah? I'm just saying we should keep our options open."

"Hey," says Chad01. "There's a sign up ahead."

It's a little placard beside the trail, among the scraps of broken machinery, like you'd see in a botanical garden or something. It says:

MIND THE GAP

"Interesting," says Owlsy. You head down the trail, and it makes a little turn, and then the trail ends, and the forest ends, and it all literally just drops off a cliff.

☾

You find yourself standing at the edge of an enormous chasm. You can't see the other side. The bottom is obscured by white mist. Across this space a bridge is strung, a long rope bridge with wooden slats that recedes into the horizon. Just looking at it makes your knees feel funny.

☾

Ding!

"An update!" Owlsy takes out his wiki. "OK, let's see . . . *bottomless chasm, avoid falling* . . . and that's it."

"And that's it?" says Lark.

"That's it." Owlsy snaps the wiki shut.

"Gosh. Whatever would we do without your little book?"

"Screw this," says Chad01. "You aren't getting me out there. That's insane."

"Really?" Lark sort of brightens. "Come on now, Chad01, there's nothing to worry about. It's just starting to get fun, right?"

She goes to the bridge and takes three big steps onto the wooden slats, stands there, shifts her weight. She bounces up and down a little, sending ripples out across the endless void. "See? Totally fine."

"Nuuuuuh, I'm gonna be sick." And with that, Chad01 turns and starts back the way you came. "Peace."

.ı.

You find Chad01 a short distance up the trail, sitting miserably on a rock. The truth is you don't want to go out on the bridge either, but it's like only one person can be scared at a time.

"You can do this, Chad01," says Lark.

"No."

"How about yes?"

"HOW ABOUT LEAVE ME THE HELL ALONE?" Chad01 hunches even further forward, glowering. "I've already had more than enough sh█t from you all."

"We were under a spell!" says Owlsy. "You're part of the team! The crew! You can't give up now! We need you! This might be the quest that brings us home."

"Uh-uh." Chad01 shakes his head. "*My* quest is to get Echo Joy to the Lake of the Goldfish Moon. *That's* what this is all about. *Then* I go home."

"Actually . . ."

"Chad01," says Lark. "So listen—"

"I'M AFRAID OF HEIGHTS OK? AND THAT IS MORE HEIGHT THAN I WILL EVER SET FOOT ON, AND IF YOU THINK—"

"Just listen!"

And she leans forward and whispers something into Chad01's ear, and he slumps forward, and she catches him in her arms, or tries to, but they're *BRRZAP!*ed apart and Chad01 tumbles to the ground where he lies, snoring softly.

Owlsy gives an approving nod. "Sleep spell. Good thinking."

"Let's get him across quickly," says Lark. "I never know how long these things are going to last. I'm getting low on sleep spells, and I'd rather not waste them all right here."

Lark takes his feet and Owlsy takes his arms, and you try to grab him in the middle but you are *BRRZAP!*ed away, so instead you help Owlsy with the arms, and the four of you start out onto the bridge with Lark in the lead, and although she's going backward, she's practically jogging.

"Can we slow down?" you say.

"The faster we go, the faster we get this over with."

"No, the faster we go, the faster we *fall*."

"The bridge is fine," she says. "Just don't look down."

You look down, past your feet into the yawning void. Bottomless? What would it be like to fall into a bottomless pit? What, you'd just keep falling forever? The mist swirls deep in the chasm. You've never walked so carefully in your life.

The mist keeps getting thicker. Also, Chad01 is heavy. Oh, wow, he's heavy. At some point, to your great relief, Owlsy and Lark decide they need a break, and you set Chad01 down and stand with the twins while he snores peacefully at your feet. You can't see either side of the gap now. Everywhere you look—up, down, it doesn't matter—it's just empty, swirling mist.

"Makes one feel somewhat insignificant, doesn't it?" says Owlsy.

"You think he's got any rope in that backpack?" says Lark.

She digs into Chad01's backpack and pulls out a potted plant . . . a coffee mug . . . an empty potato chip bag . . . and then an orange extension cord and a sleeping bag, which she uses to fashion a sledge to pull him on, and after this it's easier, the two people pulling and one walking behind to make sure he doesn't fall.

You walk across the bottomless void, four dots on a string, and after a long while, you see the other side rising out of the mist.

᠅

You're in a flat place now, like the top of a mesa. The machine forest is gone, replaced by wide slabs of slate rock cradling shallow pools of water, tufts of grass and short bushes growing here and there—moonscape tidal pools as far as you can see. You help Owlsy untie Chad01, and Lark wets her fingers in a pool of water and flicks it in his face. His eyes flutter open.

"Wha—?"

"Sleep spell. We're on the other side now."

Chad01 looks over his shoulder at the void. "You *carried* me across that? You coulda *dropped* me!"

"Well, but as you can see, we didn't."

"But you *coulda!*"

"But we *didn't!*"

᠅

You start up the trail, a dusty path that cuts along through the rock. Not far from the gap, it splits, and there's a signpost with two arrows pointing in opposite directions.

LAND OF THE NIGHT SCREAMERS →
← DARKNESS & DEAD BODIES

"Oh, this is nice," says Chad01. "We crossed the bottomless void for *this?*"

"Decisions, decisions," says Lark.

"How about *not* the dead bodies?" you say.

"It's agreed then," says Owlsy. "To the night screamers we go!"

⁂

You start along the path, weaving between the endless rocky pools on your way to the land of the night screamers. Infinite landscape, rocks and water. The sun is hidden behind a solid bank of gray. You walk. The light doesn't change. Just the pale gray. No one really speaks. You walk and walk, feeling ancient and rickety. Your feet are starting to hurt. Your back aches.

Finally it's time to stop and set up camp. Lark gathers some twigs and lights a small fire.

⁂

The others are soon asleep, but not you. It's still light out—light for another thousand days, whatever that means—but it's gray and cold, and you huddle by the fire. It's almost out now, and you stare into the flames and try not to think about home or your brother. There are memories there you don't want to remember.

You get up and add some more twigs to the fire, then you take one and hold it in your hands. One more time, you try the fire spell.

Wan shay wen ah—When she went out.

Sah shay tah dah—Saw she the dark.

Dah nah sah hay—Darkness saw her.

Ahn so tay dah — And so they . . .

Danced? Died? It doesn't matter. You can't get it to work.

You toss the stick in the fire. Then you take one of the white slips of paper from your back pocket and look at it in the flickering light. All the lines of code. The letters and numbers begin to buzz and vibrate, and you feel the weird nausea in your stomach, and then *snap!* Everything disappears, there is just emptiness, and then memory.

`mem01907i (the cliffs)`

I'm out on the beach looking for CJ. The sun is down and the wind is sweeping the fog in from the ocean and it's starting to rain. Drops zip randomly out of the twilight to sting my cheek. It's too cold to be out in just a hoodie. I pull my hands into my sleeves and hug myself against the wind.

⁂

I cross the ravine and head for the cliffs. I'm running, following the winding path, thinking about how I told him to throw Goldfish and himself into the ocean. It's foggy. Really foggy. I can barely see where I'm going. The ground is slippery and wet. When I get to the top, it's no better. I search around the rocks and puddles, but there's no one there. I follow the path to the wooden railing. The fog is so thick I can't see the ocean. I stand on the cliff and call to my brother over the edge.

"CJ! Hey! Are you down there? Hey, it's me!"

I'm shouting, but I can barely hear my own voice over the waves.

⁂

No answer. I have a sudden terrible thought, but I push it away. I shout his name again and start down the path, both hands out, basically hugging the cliffside. If the fog weren't so thick, I don't know if I could do this. But the waves are hidden. I can only hear them below, roaring and crashing, but I can't see the depths.

I come to the place where there's a gap. A couple feet of the trail have just eroded away. It's a short gap, but there are major consequences to falling.

I stop and think about this. The waves roar below. Fog swirls around me. I think about how stupid this all is. He's got to be OK. Of course he's OK. So why won't he answer my calls?

43.

I TOLD YOU NOT TO LOOK
AT THOSE THINGS

"Hey!" a voice is saying. "Hey, Rainbow!"

Chad01 slaps the paper out of your hands, and you watch it flutter to the ground. "I told you not to look at those things! You all right?"

Your mind is swimming with half-formed memories. For an instant, you see them all, then they fly apart again as you struggle to keep it all in order. School. Homework. *The cat.* Your brother. The cliffs. You were looking for CJ. You try to remember where he was; you try to remember finding him, but you can't.

"Are you all right?" Chad01 asks again.

"Memories suck," says Lark. "I used to look at mine too, but then I stopped."

"Why?" you ask.

"Because they suck."

"She saw things she didn't want to remember," says Owlsy. "We all have. It's like that for pretty much everyone. What were you seeing? Do you remember?"

You give it some thought. It's growing hazier by the second. "I was looking for my brother. I told him to jump off the cliffs. And I was looking for him, and I couldn't find him."

"Why'd you tell him to jump off the cliffs?" says Chad01.

"I—I was just so mad at him. He killed our cat. Or, wait—it was an accident, I think, and he was supposed to give me a ride to school, but she died, Goldfish died, and I told him to jump off the cliffs, and I was looking for him, and—oh God. I can't remember finding him . . . I don't know. I don't remember!"

"Well listen," says Owlsy. "People tell people all kinds of things all the time. *Jump in a lake. Climb a tree.* Basic figures of speech, yeah?"

"Seriously," says Chad01. "I wouldn't sweat it at all."

Lark says nothing but adds more wood to the fire, and everyone stays up for a while with you, and the talk is kind of light, and you start to suspect everyone's just waiting to see if you're OK. You eat a Chonk and tell everyone about pizza. They all agree it sounds pretty great. Chad01 makes you list out all the possible toppings. No one remembers what pineapple is. Eventually, one by one, the others drop off to sleep again in the gray light.

⁂

You stare at the fire. No way did CJ jump. He wouldn't. It's too horrible to be true. You reach into your pocket and you take out all the slips of paper you have collected. You hold them in your hands and look at them for a while, the way they seem to change shape in the flickering light.

You take the top one, crumple it in your fist, and toss it into the fire. It flares up, burns to ash. You take another sheet, crumple it, add it too. Then another.

You sit in the dirt feeding your memories into the fire until there is nothing left. Forget the past. Forget home. Forget cats. Forget pizza.

Forget your brother. From now on, in order to make it, you're only going to pay attention to what's right in front of you. This darkness. These flames. The cold ground below. You crawl into your sleeping bag and try to fall asleep. You dream about a god/dess who cannot die.

mem01614a ["The Eternal God/dess of Teen Depression"]

Alive as always but determined as ever, the Eternal God/dess of Teen Depression has built an enormous glass cylinder, twenty stories high, and filled it with 610 supersharp spinning blades — so basically a giant blender. The blades whir like angry fans as she ascends the spiral staircase. At the summit there's a diving board.

The Eternal God/dess of Teen Depression stands at the end of the diving board, toes curled over the edge, and looks at the furious blades below. She bounces a couple times, testing the board like an Olympic diver. This will be, she knows, one seriously beautiful and athletic dive. She is a god/dess, after all. This is the kind of thing she can make happen.

So she bounces one more time, and on the next touch, springs out in the air, folding herself like origami into the most graceful reverse jackknife triple-twist backflip the world has ever seen.

The sky spins. And the blades.

mem01615t ["The Eternal God/dess of Teen Depression"]

Today it's the slingshot.

The Eternal God/dess of Teen Depression manifests a bagpipe troupe and a flock of mournful purple doves to set the mood, and then she sits back in the hammock that is attached to the most powerful slingshot ever created, whose poles extend to the moon and whose stretchy band thing is so kinetically powerful that when it releases, it will propel her into the air at almost unimaginable speeds, the speed of gods, *godspeed,* shooting her straight into the sun, where she will burst into radiant fire, and for one luminous moment, that's all she will be, just a shining, heart-shaped explosion of pure light.

Which should be cool. For a moment, anyway. And then back to existence.

44

ALL BODIES OF SUNLIT WATER

You wake from your dreams to find the others eating Chonk bars, and you remember your decision: from now on you are going to just be here and do this thing and not think about anything else. No memories, none of that. You eat a Chonk and head out with the others across the rocky plateau and the pools of water, and then Owlsy stops and holds up his hand. "Hear that?"

You listen. Yes. Faint notes ringing out on the far edge of hearing. *Sad part . . . dark part . . .*

Over the next horizon you see it, out alone on the rocks with miles and miles of nothing in every direction—a call box.

You follow the others across the rocks, weaving among the pools. The box gets closer and closer.

"Why they always gotta put these things in the middle of nowhere?" says Chad01 as he swipes his wrist. Lark and Owlsy swipe theirs too, and when you swipe yours, the box goes *BLAP!* and you feel a sharp sting on your wrist and pull back your arm to see that your tattoo has changed:

LK
RAINBOW
STORYTELLER
61.39

"Hey," says Owlsy. "You got updated! Congratulations! You've got a class now: *Storyteller.* How's that feel?"

It's weird. You don't know what to say. Your arm has changed, but you don't feel any different.

"Storyteller?" Chad01 frowns. "What do they do?"

"Here's my totally uneducated guess," says Lark. "Maybe they tell stories?"

"Duh," says Chad01. "But telling *stories?* What kind of power is that?"

"Who says all classes have to have power?"

"Maybe it's a subtle power," says Owlsy, flipping through his wiki. "Well, I don't see it listed here. But this list isn't complete. I guess we'll just have to find out."

Lark turns to you. "So, *Storyteller,* do you have any stories for us?"

"Um . . ." You don't even know where to start. "What kind of story?"

"How about, 'Once upon a time, they all went home'?" says Lark.

"Yes, try that," says Owlsy.

It seems ridiculous, but you say it anyway. "*Once upon a time, they all went home.* The end."

The four of you stand there under the gray sky. Nothing happens.

Lark nods. "Not terrible for a first try. The plot was maybe a little thin, but I liked how it ended."

"Maybe you can only tell the story after it's happened?" says Owlsy.

"Well, what good is that? We need some directions." Chad01 slams the button again, and the call box spits out some more memories and a note that says:

ALL BODIES OF SUNLIT WATER LEAD TO THE CAVE

"OK, so we need to find some sunlight," says Owlsy.

"Which way looks the least cloudy?" says Chad01.

The four of you scan the overcast sky. In every direction it's the same, a solid bank of gray, like a sheet of hard iron overhead.

"Maybe that way?" says Owlsy.

You follow Owlsy and the others across endless pools in search of sunshine, but everywhere it's the same: gray sky reflecting in the pools of dark water.

You walk and walk.

"Is it just me," says Owlsy, "or are the clouds thinning a bit?"

"Just you," says Lark.

You walk some more.

· ·

And then all at once, it happens. The sky brightens, the clouds thin, you see a patch of flickering blue, and then the light pours down. Suddenly everything is bright again. And it's so beautiful — as far as you can see, the pools of water glitter with sunlight, like jewels set in stone.

"Sweet!" says Owlsy. "Now's our chance!"

You gather at the nearest puddle and look at the water glistening in the sun.

"What do we do?"

"We jump," says Owlsy. "Count of three. Everybody ready?"

"Let *me* count this time," says Chad01.

"Do we have to count?" says Lark.

"Well, no," says Owlsy. "But I—"

"Great, thanks!" And she plunges into the water, disappearing with a splash.

Owlsy looks at you and then Chad01.

"Would you still like to count?" Owlsy asks.

"Nah, it's cool." Chad01 jumps into the glittery pool.

And then Owlsy, and then you.

*

Sudden shock of cold. Every nerve screaming. And as you fall deeper into cold, black water, you can feel the panic beginning to rise. You're going to drown here; the water is getting darker and darker, you can hardly see now, you can feel the pressure on your face and ears, arms sweeping, legs kicking, lungs screaming . . . and then in a flash the whole world turns itself inside out; water becomes air, and you find yourself rising, gasping for breath as you pull yourself onto a dark and rocky shelf.

*

Someone is coughing, and then you hear rustling, and suddenly everything is lit in bright white as Chad01 lifts the sleeping Echo Joy out of its sling. You look around in the dazzling light. Earthen walls on either side. A deep, black pool of water behind you. Tree roots dangling from the ceiling.

The glowing fuzzy giggles. "WHAT IS WHERE *ARE* WE?" it says, echoing your whispered words.

45.

THE NIGHTMARE TREE

It's a cave — or more like a tunnel. You're following the others, Chad01 in the lead, awkwardly holding Echo Joy out like a torch. The brilliant light plays along the rock nooks and roots. No one speaks. Even Echo Joy is mostly silent, just sort of giggling to itself now and again.

Deeper you go, brushing past dirty cobwebs and roots. The cave narrows, and at one point you're forced to crawl on hands and knees, following the light of Echo Joy.

"I don't like this," Chad01 whispers. "Why are we doing this again? I'm telling you, the moment this starts to get sketchy—"

"Starts?" says Lark. "This is already sketchy as sh█t."

The tunnel gets narrower, then wider again, and wider still, until you find yourself standing in a dim but open place. You walk a little farther, and as your eyes adjust, you see that you are in an enormous underground chamber. You can just make out something big and dark in the distance. You follow the others to the big, dark thing.

"The trail ends here," Chad01 whispers. "There's just a wall."

"That isn't a wall," says Owlsy. "That's a tree."

"WHAT IS A TREE?"

Chad01 nestles the fuzzy back into its sling. There's enough light that you don't really need it now, milky beams dimly filtering through the high, misty ceiling from some hidden opening above.

The trunk is the width of a building, and it just goes up, up, up, into the mist.

"The nightmare tree," Owlsy whispers. "Up we go."

"Sorry," Chad01 hisses. "Not me. I'm not going up there. I'm done with high places. I'll stand guard or something. Here, take my backpack."

"What for?" says Owlsy.

"For the eggs, duh."

~

Up the tree you go, leaving Chad01 behind on the ground.

At first the tree is so big there's a winding path that spirals up the trunk, growing narrower until it gives out and you have to climb. The bark is rough and uneven, full of holes and pockets, and this makes climbing . . . not easy, but possible. An intricate ladder, enough hand-holds that your progress is fairly swift and sure. Still, as you follow Lark and Owlsy up into the darkness, you kind of wish you'd stayed back with Chad01 to stand guard. You climb what has to be three or four stories at least, and still you haven't encountered a single branch. The air around you is misty now, and the light is changing.

~

You come to a massive crook in the tree, as wide as a house. Three enormous limbs, wide enough for three people to walk along side by side, stretch in three directions out into the mist. One of the limbs is slightly bigger than the others, and this is where you go. You try not to think about how high you must be.

In a little while, the limb splits into three more branches, and these again split into smaller branches, and before long, you're in a matrix of branches, and it's like climbing a wooden web. There aren't any leaves, just dry branches, but as you climb, you begin to see faint lights here and there, like dim lanterns. Soon the tree is a constellation of lights, and then you see one up close, just above you, a bright yellow orb dangling from the tree like a glowing lemon.

While you and Owlsy watch, Lark climbs up to it, making her way silently among the branches. She stretches her arm to grasp the egg, but when she gives it a tug, it won't come free. She tugs it harder. She twists it. She yanks it. Nothing.

"Try twisting it!" Owlsy hisses.

"I *did* twist it!"

She twists it more, she tugs it again, and the branch bends and bends but will not give up the egg.

"What if you just keep twisting it in the same direction?" says Owlsy.

"Ohmygod will you shut up about the twisting? I am twisting, see? And the stupid thing isn't—"

Snap!

The egg breaks free from the branch, and Lark falls back and catches herself but fumbles the egg, and you and Owlsy reach out helplessly as it falls into the darkness below, and there's a moment of regret and reflection, and then you notice that the lights have grown dim. The eggs aren't glowing like they were before. And in the darkening silence that follows, you can feel a change in the air. Everything holding its breath.

And then whispering—the hushed murmur of a thousand voices all around you. And from the whispering erupts a laughing scream that echoes through the darkness, and then another scream, and then all hell breaks loose. A thousand laughing screams cry out all at once, and the tree is alive and crawling with dark and sinister shapes.

"Run!" Owlsy yells.

But you can't run down a tree.

The best you can do is scramble, branches whipping past as you scurry down in the darkness. You can hear them screaming and crashing through the branches around you.

You come to the path cut into the tree, sprint down the corkscrewing trail to the bottom, and you just keep running in the darkness, following Owlsy and Lark around the massive trunk, searching frantically for the opening to the passageway that brought you here. Where's the tunnel out? You're running and the screamers are right behind you now, you can hear them, they are going to catch you, there's no way out of it this time, and you hear a scream, and it takes you a moment to realize where it's coming from.

You. You're screaming.

As you sprint around the massive trunk, you suddenly see Chad01. He's running toward you, and he's screaming too.

"They're right behind me!" he shouts.

So you turn, but they are behind you too. There's nowhere to go. They are all around you, dark shapes screaming, laughing, moving in and out of view like fish in the water, horrible visions surfacing from the depths of a midnight lake. Screaming mouths. Dead eyes. Broken teeth. Blown-out faces. They chase you to a corner. And there's nowhere left to go.

You're huddled there with the others, hands up like a boxer ready to defend yourself against the horror that is coming. They are wailing, leering bug-eyed from out of the darkness, bloody and broken, and it's getting louder, all the screams joining into one horrible discord, rising in pitch like *eeeeEEEEEEEEEEE!*

And then suddenly it stops.

Silence.

What is going on?

The pause before your eyeballs start to bleed?

You stand with the others, mesmerized, waiting for the screaming death to come. You can see the glint of their eyes watching you from the dark.

They watch you.

And you watch them.

And then there's a sound.

Ding!

46.

THEIR GORY VISAGES

Owlsy pulls the wiki from his pocket, opens it, and flips through the pages.

He stands in the circle of screamers, reading from his book.

"OK," he says. "Uh . . . *Fuzzy Glowers, while magical and immortal, may have their form altered through the process of forced joy extraction, often to feed power grids. If this occurs, Fuzzy Glowers will gradually lose all joy and assume the look of nightmares, or 'Night Screamers' as they are commonly called, after which they tend to retreat to the darker corners of the Machine Forest. Due to their gory visages and famous laughing screams, Night Screamers are often portrayed as dangerous, even lethal creatures, but in fact Night Screamers are generally harmless, if also bereft of joy.*"

"Whoa," says Owlsy. "You know what this means, right? That wizard has been tricking Lost Kids to come here and steal eggs. He's not saving the fuzzies! He's extracting their joy and using them to power the city!"

"Dave's a bad wizard!" says Chad01. "An *evil* wizard."

You look around at the eyes watching you from the darkness.

"But wait, there's more!" says Owlsy.

"Ugh," says Lark. "Of course. There's always more! Do you not see how totally ridiculous this is?"

And you would tend to agree with Lark, except for the fact that you've been totally terrified for the last little bit and would much rather believe that these nightmare faces are not, in fact, going to make you die while bleeding out of your eyeballs. That would actually be very rad.

"Well, there *is* more," says Owlsy to his sister. "Do you want to hear it or not?"

"Just tell us!" says Chad01.

"It says, 'For those travelers who are brave enough to face the night screamers with pure intentions there is a reward: the night screamers will deliver them to the nearest home portal.'"

"No sh■t?" says Chad01. "How?"

"Uh, let's see . . . *be true of heart . . . brave intentioned . . . flawless in your vision . . .*"

"Yeah, yeah, we got all that."

"*Sincere in your hopes . . .* Oh, and *clap three times.*"

"What, like this?" Chad01 holds out his hands and claps three times.

In the instant of the final clap, you hear a sudden chorus of screams, and from out of the darkness pours another darkness, a whirlwind of shrieking, howling horror that wraps around you with hands and claws and broken, screaming faces, screeching and wailing, and you are screaming too as the ground begins to fall away. And you are being lifted into the air like a baby swaddled in the arms of a nightmare.

I look at my feet and the fog swirling in the gap on the cliffside. I think about my brother. I steady myself, take a breath. And then I jump.

It's such a small gap. I don't even know why it surprises me that I make it, but it sort of does. I totally make it.

I follow the trail along the cliffs. As I round a small bend, I can see it through the fog, this hole in the rock, and the trail disappears inside. But as I get closer, the hole becomes narrower and shallower, and I see that it isn't a cave at all, just this narrow depression in the cliffside. That's it. That's all there is. And there's no one here but me.

I stand in the depression, listening to the waves. What now?

I start back up the trail. I think about—I don't even know what to think about. I just need to be moving. The wet fog hangs all around like a curtain. The ocean roars. And all I can think is *Where is he?* I take out my phone. It's turned itself off again.

I turn it back on, and it vibrates cheerfully.

I've got six new messages, all from my brother. Of course.

> hey I took care of goldfish ok?

> please don't be mad at me anymore

> and feel free to apologize for being a b
> whenever you feel like it

> sorry I shouldn't have said that

> hello rainbow are you there?

hey please answer me ok?

I begin to text him back, but I don't even know what to say, and so I start to put my phone away, and then I second-guess myself and decide maybe I will respond, but instead what happens is my phone slips from my fingers and falls from my hand, and I watch as it disappears into the fog like a marble in a glass of milk.

I stand with my hand outstretched, looking at the place where my phone used to be, rushing through all the stages of grief: denial, anger, bargaining, and finally back to good old depression. F█ck.

I start up the trail again.

47.

SO DISRESPECTFUL

You're flying through the air being carried by the nightmarish screamers, and then you feel yourself falling and you think they've dropped
you, but no, they are setting you gently on the ground, and the next
thing you know you're watching from the edge of the machine
forest as the dark horde bleeds into the distance like black ink in
the sky.

⚡

You look around. It's familiar. You've been here before. The guard
house. The wall.

"What?" says Chad01. "Here again?"

"No, this is good," says Owlsy. "The fact that they brought us here
confirms it—there is an actual home portal in this city!"

"But we don't have any eggs, and the wizard is bad."

"Yeah, but we'll figure something out," says Owlsy. "I know we
will. We're *this* close!"

"Oh my god," says Lark. "We're *always* this close. *It never ends.* Don't
you get it?!"

"Are you still on this?"

"Yes! Don't you see? There's always going to be one more thing. They're always dangling a prize in front of your face. No one ever gets home. I used to think the only way out was to die, but I'm not even so sure about *that* anymore. Something always happens!"

Owlsy gives his sister a look. "What about the fuzzies, then? Are we just going to leave them in the tower?"

"No way!" says Chad01. "We can't do that. It's sucking up their joy!"

"You know what's sucking up *my* joy?" says Lark. *"This."* She gestures at the world. "All of it. I need a break. Like a complete break. The endless insanity is driving me crazy."

And you want to raise your hand, to be like, *Me too!*, and you almost do, but no, you can't because then you'd be admitting to the secret, which is that you *are* crazy, which is in itself crazy, this whole thing is just—

"Crazy?" says Owlsy. *"Crazy* would be to give up now. We're *so* close this time. We've never *been* this close before! *There is literally a home portal on the other side of that wall."*

Lark closes her eyes and shakes her head slowly.

"So what exactly is your plan?" Chad01 says to Owlsy.

"OK, well, let's see . . . We go inside, pretend we couldn't find the tree. We ask around, see if we can figure out some way to save the fuzzies *and* open up the portal . . . and in the meantime, we can *also* ask about the Lake of the Goldfish Moon too. How's that sound?"

Chad01 gives it some thought. "I guess," he says.

"What about Dave?" you ask.

"What about him?" says Chad01.

"You said he was *evil.*"

"Don't worry about Dave! Dude doesn't even have a body!"

᠅

Inside the walls, the kids in bright polos are dancing and playing volleyball on the grass. The smell of fried food wafts through the air. Bubbles drift past.

You turn and see Lark is no longer with you. She's walking across the grass toward the food carts.

"Hey," Owlsy calls. "Where are you going?"

"I told you," she says. "I'm out. No more. It's over. I'm getting curly fries to celebrate my freedom."

"No you aren't. Come on, don't pull this again!"

"I'm done."

"What do you mean, done?" you say.

"I quit. I'm dropping out. No more quests."

"Here?" says Chad01. "You're dropping out *here*?"

"No one's dropping out," says Owlsy.

"Not here, I wouldn't," says Chad01. "The wizard is whack and everyone else is imaginary."

"*I'm* imaginary," says Lark. "You said so yourself."

"No one's imaginary!" says Owlsy.

"It doesn't matter," says Lark. "I've made up my mind and it feels great. Adios. Goodbye. Farewell. I'm done. Love to you all."

"Come on," says Chad01. "You can't give up now."

"Watch me."

Lark does a neat little spin and starts walking away.

⚹

"She'll be back," says Owlsy as his sister disappears into the maze of buildings.

"You sure?" Chad01 asks. "She seemed pretty serious."

"Maybe we should go get her," you offer.

"Don't give her the satisfaction," says Owlsy. "I can't count the number of times she's pulled this stunt. Follow me."

You start down the boulevard with Owlsy and Chad01, but it seems so wrong to just leave Lark behind like this, and you're about to race after her when you hear a familiar voice booming from the heavens.

HEY THERE

WELCOME BACK Y'ALL!

HEARD YOU TALKING . . .

LITTLE BIT OF A DISAGREEMENT BACK THERE, HUH?

IT'S SUCH A BUMMER WHEN FRIENDS FIGHT

BUT THAT'S WHAT HAPPENS FROM TIME TO TIME . . .

SO ANYWAY I'M DYING TO KNOW: HOW'D IT GO?

YOU'RE BACK SO SOON!

DID YOU FIND THE TREE? DID YOU GET SOME EGGS?

ARE YOUR EYEBALLS OK?

"Well," Owlsy begins. "So, w—"

WAIT! DON'T TELL ME YET! LET ME MAKE AN ANNOUNCEMENT!

Dave booms louder:

HEY EVERYONE LOOK! THE BRAVE ADVENTURERS ARE BACK! HEY, COME ON OVER TO THE NORTH GATE AND GATHER 'ROUND THE BRAVE ADVENTURERS ARE GOING TO TELL US WHAT THEY FOUND ON THEIR BRAVE ADVENTURE TO THE NIGHTMARE TREE

It's like the crowd materializes out of thin air. You look around and there are suddenly dozens, if not hundreds, of kids in bright polos, surrounding you. Lark is gone. You don't see her anywhere. She's ditched you.

"Um," says Owlsy to the sky. "Well, the funny thing is, we actually never even, uh, found the tree, so . . ."

REALLY? ARE YOU *SURE?*

"Well . . . yeah."

"Listen," says Chad01. "Why are you even keeping—"

NO, YOU LISTEN! Dave booms.

YOU KNOW WHAT ONE OF THE LOOKOUTS TOLD ME?

SHE SAID SHE SAW YOU WERE DROPPED OFF BY A HORDE OF NIGHT SCREAMERS JUST OUTSIDE THE CITY WALL! THAT'S WHAT SHE SAID, AND ALL I CAN SAY IS WOW!

IT'S A MIRACLE THEY DIDN'T TEAR YOU LIMB FROM LIMB! IT'S ALMOST AS IF THEY WERE HELPING YOU OUT . . . LIKE GIVING YOU A RIDE OR SOMETHING . . .

PLEASE DON'T TELL ME YOU MADE *FRIENDS* WITH THE NIGHT SCREAMERS DID YOU?!

"All we d—"

BECAUSE THAT WOULD BE HORRIBLE

ABSOLUTELY *INEXCUSABLE*

THERE'S ONLY ONE WORD FOR PEOPLE WHO MAKE FRIENDS WITH NIGHT SCREAMERS . . . DOES EVERY- ONE REMEMBER WHAT THAT WORD IS?

"TRAITORS!" the crowd yells.

THAT'S RIGHT! THE WORD IS *TRAITORS!*

"Wait!" Chad01 steps forward. "Listen up, everyone! This wizard is bad! Dave's *evil!* He's tricking you! All your energy is based on a lie! This city is powered by sucking out the joy of the fuzzies! Owlsy's wiki said so! The tower turns fuzzies into night screamers and it's—"

WHAT?! HA!

HAHA!

NOT THIS CRAZY CONSPIRACY THEORY AGAIN!

WHAT A SNOOZE WHAT A LOAD OF BALONEY

The crowd boos. Someone throws a water bottle. It just misses Chad01's head.

YOU KNOW, says Dave.

YOU KNOW THIS HURTS

THIS REALLY ACTUALLY STINGS TO TELL YOU THE TRUTH

THAT YOU WOULD COME HERE AS GUESTS INTO *OUR* BEAUTIFUL CITY WHERE WE IN FACT HONOR AND PRESERVE AND *SAVE* THE FUZZIES . . . THAT YOU WOULD STRIDE RIGHT IN HERE AND ACCUSE *US* OF BEING BAD PEOPLE OR DISEMBODIED ENTITIES SUCH AS MYSELF THAT YOU WOULD ACCUSE *US* OF BEING BAD WHEN IN FACT *YOU* ARE THE BAD ONES OH WOW! I'M SO SORRY TO GET EMOTIONAL BUT I'M JUST ABSO-LUTELY SPEECHLESS

"We love you, Dave!" someone shouts. "We got you, buddy!"

YEAH THANKS I MEAN IT'S JUST—THESE TRAITORS ARE JUST REALLY BEING SO *DISRESPECTFUL!* FORGIVE ME EVERYONE IT'S JUST—I'M JUST SO VERY *FURI-OUS* RIGHT NOW! I WISH THESE BAD TRAITOR KIDS HAD NEVER SHOWN UP IN THE FIRST PLACE! DON'T YOU? I WISH THEY WOULD JUST GO AWAY FOREVER—RIGHT?!

"YEAH!" the crowd yells.

"Well, we can certainly leave," says Owlsy.

OH WOW OH HA HA, says Dave.

AND SO I GUESS IT'S JUST "SEE YA LATER" AND NOT EVEN AN *ATTEMPT* TO APOLOGIZE? WOW, OK. YOU KNOW WHAT? I'M NOT GOING TO LET IT BOTHER ME —I'M JUST NOT—BECAUSE YOU HAVE SHOWN YOUR-SELVES FOR WHO YOU ARE AND SO WHY SHOULD I EVEN BE SURPRISED, RIGHT?

UGH

OK

SO I GUESS WHAT HAS TO HAPPEN NEXT IS WE HAVE TO TAKE YOU AND LOCK YOU UP IN A BOX UNTIL YOU'VE LEARNED YOUR LESSON

"Well, actua—"

OK, EVERYONE! TAKE THESE HORRIBLE PEOPLE TO THE HALL OF TRAITORS!

LOCK THEM UP!

TAKE AWAY THEIR FUZZY!

The crowd begins to close in. Hundreds of kids in bright polo shirts of every hue.

"Awesome," says Chad01. "Mob time. I love a mob."

"What?" you manage.

"I'm a warrior, duh. I can take twenty of these little b■tches at once." And with that he rushes *into* the oncoming fray.

It's true—Chad01 probably *can* take twenty at a time. It's incred-ible. Better than kung fu. He jumps, and his legs swing through the air and two polos go down— *BRRZAP! BRRZAP!*—and as he lands, he grabs another by the head and bashes him into a fourth *(BRRZAP!)*, dodging a fifth, who he then trips and uses to leap onto a sixth before bashing a seventh, eighth, and ninth in rapid, vicious *BRRZAP!*s like some kind of violent and unhinged ballerina.

But there are too many of them; there are just too many. And you? You're not a fighter. You can't take even one or two. Owlsy the scholar is no better; you can hear him trying to *talk* his way out of it. He's trying to reason with them, but they aren't listening to reason. They're listening to *Dave,* who is shouting them onward, and they're on you now. They're all over you.

After the screamers, you're almost used to getting mobbed. You watch as Owlsy is thrown to the ground. Hands grab your arms, pinning them to your waist. Chad01 manages to shove two kids aside, but another three kids grab him from behind. They've got him in a chokehold, and you hear him gasp and sputter. *BRRZAP!*

Then the world goes dark as a cloth is shoved over your head.

You hear Chad01 shout "No!" and there's a thud, and he moans, and you hear Echo Joy giggle, "WHAT IS NO, UHHHG?"

48.

IT'S THE THOUGHT THAT COUNTS

They shove you into a room and rip the bag off your head, and you hear the door slam behind you, and the lock clicks. You look around. It's actually a pretty nice room. You're on, like, the third story of some building, and other than the bars on the windows, it's like a big, open hotel room. Your feet and hands are still tied. Owlsy is free, though, and he helps untie you, and then you help him untie Chad01.

As soon as he's free, Chad01 rushes the door, slamming it a half dozen times with his shoulder. It doesn't budge. After that he goes to the windows and sets to work on the bars, which are also immovable. He bangs on the door again, and then it's like something in him snaps.

He takes one of the wooden chairs and bashes it against the wall until it breaks. He isn't done. He punches a hole through a seascape painting, rips the minifridge out of the wall, dumps the pitcher of water on the floor, and then flings it against the wall in an explosion of pottery.

"Chad01!" you are saying. *"Chad01!"*

"WHAT?"

"Calm down, OK?"

"They took Echo Joy! And where's Lark? She's gone!"

"Yes," says Owlsy. "But you don't see anyone else breaking pottery."

"ARGH!" Chad01 upends a mattress, tossing it to the floor.

"We may have to sleep on those, you know," says Owlsy.

"THEY TOOK ECHO JOY!"

You rest your hand on his shoulder. *BRRZAP!* "Chad01 . . ."

He shrugs you off. "We need to get out of here!" he says.

"OK," says Owlsy. "Then how about we clean up this mess and think of a plan?"

"Bug off," says Chad01, slumping into a corner.

⠦

You help Owlsy tidy, and in the midst of it, you realize how worried he is. He's been running all over the place cleaning up stuff that doesn't even need to be cleaned, and now you're helping him put the sheets back on one of the mattresses, and you can see it on his face. Of course he's worried.

"She's going to be OK," you say.

Owlsy's face falls. He looks like he's going to cry. You drop your end of the sheet and walk over to the other side of the mattress and go to give him a hug, and *BRRZAP!*, you're thrown back against the wall. You hit it hard and slide down to the floor.

"Thanks," says Owlsy. "I would have enjoyed that hug."

"It's the thought that counts, right?" says Chad01.

⠦

The three of you lift the mattress off the floor and set it back on the frame.

"I'm f█cking tired, guys," says Chad01.

"Same," says Owlsy.

"Maybe it's naptime, then."

253

"Just a quick one. To recharge."

"Yeah."

"Just not too long."

"Right."

And you flop down with Chad01 and Owlsy on the big and surprisingly soft mattress. Lark is gone and you're all locked up, but you're so tired and it's a *really* soft mattress, and in about three minutes, you're totally asleep.

mem01908i (dark thought)

I start up the trail.

My mind is racing. My mind is always racing.

I think about how much it's going to cost to get another phone.

I think about Goldfish. I think about how cruel it was for me to make CJ deal with it all by himself. I think about how, even in an apology, he can't resist being a jerk.

I think about how I'm failing school. I think about how I always thought that I would be able to leave and go do fun things somewhere else and start a *real life,* and how am I going to do that if I don't even graduate?

I think about how I have no friends in this new place, not even my brother. I think about how I might never see my dad again. I think about how sad Mom is.

I think about how much harder literally millions of other people have it than me and what a self-pitying little sh█t I am.

I think about how I'm sick of it, all the thinking. I'm sick of my thoughts.

I'm sick of what a baby I am. I'm sick of how inadequate.

I think about how mean I can be, and I hate myself for it.

I don't want to be myself anymore. I don't want to be.

I think, *Oh, one more thing: now after you set out on this big dramatic trip all for nothing, now you get to walk up the sketchy AF trail again and all the way back to your mobile home eight miles outside town by a highway.*

And a dark thought wriggles up from some hole in my brain. *You could jump.*

I let the thought sit there. I don't do anything with it. I just let it sit there as I start up the trail in the fog again, not thinking about what it would be like to jump.

I come to the little gap. I leap across, and as I land, my foot slips on the rocks, just enough to make my heart beat faster, and I think, *Ha! That would be just like me, to accidentally die while I was looking for a place to kill myself.*

49.

THEY HAVE TO FEED US DON'T THEY?

"Rainbow! Hey, Rainbow!"

You open your eyes to see Chad01's face, eyes wide. Already the memory is fading.

"Hey!" he says. "Wake up!"

You look around the room. The smashed furniture. The bars on the windows. The light has changed. It's pale now, colder. Clouds have moved in again in this nightless level, blotting out the perpetual sun.

"It's OK," says Owlsy. "We're right here."

"And we're gonna get *outta* here, yeah?" says Chad01. He seems to have calmed down. "That's what Owlsy and I were talking about while you were asleep. We made a plan."

"We noticed there's no slot in the door," says Owlsy. "You know, to slide the meals in when they feed us. So when they come, they're going to have to open that door. We don't have any proper weapons, but Chad01 has inadvertently made us some. See?" He grabs a table leg, still partially attached to a tabletop, and pries it free.

"So here's the plan . . ." says Chad01.

◆

The plan is this: You and Owlsy will lie down on the beds like you're sleeping—but in your arms, buried under the blankets, you each hold a table leg.

Chad01 has taken up a position beside the door, armed with a leg of his own.

When the guards come to feed you, you'll overtake them and escape.

That's the plan.

⚡

You lie in bed. A breeze blows through the barred windows. It occurs to you that the plan has some potential flaws—what if a dozen kids show up to deliver your lunch? Or what if they don't feed you at all? *This plan is maybe not so great,* you think.

You wait, straining your ears to hear the approaching kids.

You wait and wait.

⚡

"Either of you wanna swap out?" says Chad01.

"Sure." Owlsy goes to the door and Chad01 gets under the covers, and you wait some more.

Nothing happens. No one shows up.

"Come *on*," says Chad01. *"They have to feed us, don't they?"*

⚡

Time slides endlessly by, but the light doesn't change; no one comes; the moment is frozen. You offer to switch with Owlsy, and he says OK.

So now you're standing at the door, holding a table leg while Chad01 gives you tips.

"Remember," says Chad01. "You gotta hit 'em hard, OK, Rainbow? Owlsy and I will be up in a split second, but you gotta make that first hit count, OK? I know you, Rainbow—you're basically like a

257

pacifist at heart—but these kids don't care about you or me or Owlsy or anyone. So you got one chance. Because after you hit them, they're gonna want to hit you back. So you gotta make that first hit count —you hear what I'm saying?"

You grip the table leg and think about what it would be like to actually hit a person with it. It's a horrible thought, wood on skull, so then you try to think of something else, but now it's *all* you can think about. Your hands are sweating. You wipe one palm and then the other on your pants.

You shift your weight from one foot to the other. You try to imagine yourself just confidently bashing in a skull.

No one comes.

"To hell with this," says Chad01. "They aren't even g—"

"Wait!" says Owlsy. "Shh! Do you hear that?"

⚡

A faint sound echoes from outside the door. Footsteps.

You grip the table leg, run your thumb along the splintered wood.

Chad01 is looking at you like, *You ready?*

You turn back to the door. You see the handle jiggle, just a little, so soft you probably wouldn't notice it if you weren't paying attention. And then, slowly, it begins to turn.

The handle turns some more.

The door begins to open.

You raise your club.

You gotta hit 'em hard, OK?

A kid in a neon-pink polo is standing in the doorway, unaware that they're about to be . . . Oh, wait. It's Lark.

"Hi!" she says brightly, and walks in grinning in her pink shirt, and you let the table leg drop to the floor.

50.

CONGRATULATIONS
YOU GOT ME TO BE SINCERE

"Lark!" you say.

"Lark!" says Owlsy.

"Surprise! It never ends! Also, I brought presents." Lark gestures to the gift bag in her hand.

"Wait, so how'd you escape?" says Chad01.

"I ran," says Lark. "But the wizard could see me and he kept telling everyone where I was, so I put a sleep spell on him and then I ran some more and—"

"You put a sleep spell on *Dave?*" says Chad01.

"Haven't you heard him snoring? He was *really* going at it for a while. Just a terrible racket. Yeah, I put a sleep spell on him, and then I stole some shirts and went to the tower and here I am! Bearing gifts, even." She holds the bag up. "Check it out. Have a look."

As Owlsy lifts off the tissue paper, beams of white light shoot out.

"Echo!" Chad01 lifts the sleeping fuzzy into his arms. It's so impossibly cute. "Where? How?" he asks.

"In the tallest building—the tower. There was a room with fuzzies in it. It took me *forever* to find the right one. And then it wouldn't shut up, so I had to use a sleep spell on it. And then I had to use another sleep spell on a couple of kids. We should go. I've only got *two* sleep spells left. But first, you need your disguises." She reaches into the bag and pulls out three pink polo shirts.

"Wait," says Owlsy. "I don't get it. Suddenly you're all gung ho about this? Why the change of heart?"

Lark gives her brother a look. "Well, I love you, duh. Congratulations, you got me to be sincere. Also, it was boring without you all. Here, have a shirt. You too, Chad01. Here, Rainbow."

She hands you your polo and turns to give Chad01 his, but Chad01 is standing back by the window, looking at the creature in his arms.

"This isn't Echo Joy," he says.

"What?"

"This isn't Echo Joy."

"What do you mean it isn't Echo Joy?"

"Look. Look at this. You see this?" Chad01 runs his fingers through the glowing halo of hair. "This one's got *golden* fur with *orange* tips; Echo had *orange* fur and *golden* tips." Chad01 snaps his fingers, and the fuzzy opens its eyes and giggles. "The eyes are different too! You see that?! Echo's eyes are *blue*. These eyes are *green*."

"THE FUZZIES HAVE DIFFERENT EYES!" it says.

"It's the wrong fuzzy!"

The creature giggles. "THE KID IS HOLDING THE WRONG FUZZY!"

"This can't be!" says Chad01. "This is NOT Echo Joy! Echo Joy asks *questions!* This one—"

"THE KID IS ANGRY AND FLUSTERED!"

"This one gives *answers!*" He opens his sling and plops the glowing creature inside, covering it with fabric.

"THE KID IS DISHEARTENED!"

"THE DARKNESS IS ALL AROUND!"

Yawn. "The fuzzy is sleepy . . ."

"We gotta go back to the tower," says Chad01.

"Right," says Owlsy. "I agree. Let's get our disguises on and get out of here!"

᠅

Everyone has their shirts on but Chad01.

Chad01 holds up his pink polo and examines the tag. "I think you gave me the wrong one. This says *girls small.*"

"When I stole them, I didn't exactly have time to check for sizes," says Lark.

"So gimme a different one then."

"Sorry. They're all the same size."

"Seriously?"

The shirt is tight on Owlsy, but it's *really* tight on Chad01. He's a big kid, and he can scarcely get it on. He has to squeeze himself into it, and the sleeves barely cover his shoulders, and the tiny collar presses into the flesh of his neck. Lark tugs at the hem, but the material won't stretch any further.

"Maybe," you suggest, "maybe with your gear on it won't be so noticeable."

So Chad01 puts on his backpack and sling.

"Hmm," says Owlsy.

"It's . . . sleek," says Lark.

"It's f█cking cutting off my circulation," says Chad01.

᠅

In your bright pink polos, the four of you hurry down the hall past two sleeping kids in green polos and onto the crowded streets, and you

261

don't know why, but you feel suddenly optimistic. You've been through some stuff, but at least you're all alive and together, a team. Outside, the sky has cleared. Sunshine pours down. Bubbles float through the air, bright lights dance up and down the buildings, music plays from hidden speakers.

⚬

The tower is a tall building of glass and steel, and out front in the plaza, there are screens playing informational videos about fuzzies, how they are sustainably and organically raised, how their joy is harvested and turned into energy, and how that energy is even enough to generate a home portal, which attracts Lost Kids from all over the Wilds, vying on quests to earn the one million gold fee to open it.

As you walk past, the screens zoom out on a bright tower of singing fuzzies, each one dancing in a little white box. The energy grid. Words flash across the screen:

SAFE. HAPPY. SUSTAINABLE.
ENERGY FOR LIFE.

Inside, through the big glass doors, there's a wide lobby with tall ferns and abstract metal statues and a waterfall cascading down brick platforms inlaid into the granite wall, and in the middle at a booth, a kid in a turquoise polo looks like he's just waking up from a nap. When he blinks and asks to see your IDs, Lark leans across the desk and whispers something in his ear, and he slumps forward, resting his head on his arms. She slips the lanyard from his neck and holds up his ID card with a smile. "Didn't know I'd need this again."

⚬

She leads you down an empty corridor. There are more video screens and then a glass wall separating you from a small room with some baby fuzzies in it, each one swaddled in a blanket and encased under more glass.

"This part's for show," says Lark. "The real stuff is in back."

At the end of the corridor is a door marked AUTHORIZED PERSONNEL ONLY. Lark swipes the kid's card over a black pad. The light turns green; the lock clicks.

"This way."

⁘

You find yourself in a large, well-lit room full of shiny glass boxes, like incubators. But they're all empty. Electrical wires and panels and blinking lights line the high walls.

"Where are they?" says Chad01. "What happened?"

Lark searches the empty aisles. "I don't know! I swear they were all here when I left! This whole place was full of them!"

"Hey," says Owlsy. "Where does this door go?"

It's more of a hatch than a door, and so big it looks like part of the wall, but you can see the latch on it now—and the security pad.

Lark takes her stolen ID and swipes it across the black square, and the door begins to open.

51.

THE TOWER IN THE TOWER

You find yourself standing in an enormous glass room. Not even a room. A tower. A vertiginous glass tower with the blue sky outside, and inside this tower, in the middle of the tower, is *another* tower, also glass but made up of a grid of thousands and thousands of glass boxes —like what you saw on the video screens.

"The power grid," says Owlsy.

You gaze up at the lofty, shining boxes.

It isn't *quite* like the videos though. There's a different feeling to this place—a darkness despite the light. Sparks crackle. A massive lattice of metal stairs rises alongside the tower of illuminated glass boxes, and over it all, a song blares cheerfully from hidden speakers, and thousands of voices answer back in anguished screams and cries of unbounded pain.

**IF YOU'RE HAPPY AND YOU KNOW IT, CLAP
YOUR HANDS!
*[ANGUISHED SCREAMS!]***

264

**IF YOU'RE HAPPY AND YOU KNOW IT, CLAP
YOUR HANDS!**
[ANGUISHED SCREAMS!]
**IF YOU'RE HAPPY AND YOU KNOW IT
AND YOU REALLY WANT TO SHOW IT,
IF YOU'RE HAPPY AND YOU KNOW IT, CLAP
YOUR HANDS!**
[ANGUISHED SCREAMS!]

The tower glows brighter, and the song repeats.

．．

"Look!" says Owlsy.

You see it maybe ten stories up: a kid in a Day-Glo-orange polo and buglike sunglasses is standing on the catwalk.

"And there!"

Several levels up from the first kid, another kid in a matching polo and sunglasses rounds the corner with a garbage bin. You watch as he stops at a glass box, opens it, and removes a glowing body. It struggles a little, and he whangs it against the metal guardrail a couple times, tosses it in the bin, and replaces it with another fuzzy.

You watch him, and the kid below him, and then the kid below sees you.

"Hey!" he says.

"Crap," mutters Chad01.

The kid is marching down the stairs now, *clang, clang, clang.*

"Hey, what are you doing here?" His sunglasses give him a sinister, insect look.

"Hi," Owlsy calls. "You see, we got a bit lost and—"

"Lost?" The kid walks up to you. "How did you get in here? You're not authorized to be here! You need to leave immediately."

"Right," says Owlsy. "Absolutely. The doors were open and, um, who's your friend back there? Is he the only other attendant?"

The kid's holding a walkie-talkie to his lips now. "Yeah, hey. It's me. There are four unauth—"

Lark slaps the walkie-talkie out of his hands and whispers in his ear. He slumps forward, and she catches his limp body under her arms—BRRZAP!—and he tumbles to the ground, asleep.

"Hey!" yells the other kid from high on the catwalk. "What's going on down there?"

"Um . . ." says Owlsy. "Well, your coworker has had an accident!"

"What? Who are you?"

"No worries! We called the, uh, medics!"

"Medics? What medics? What are you doing?"

Now he's marching down the stairs too. The song keeps playing.

IF YOU'RE HAPPY AND YOU KNOW IT, STOMP YOUR FEET!

[ANGUISHED SCREAMS!]

"So by the way, that was my last sleep spell," says Lark.

"No worries," says Chad01. "I got this."

"How about you let me talk to him?" says Owlsy.

"When I'm done with him, sure."

"Well, don't just hurt him needlessly," says Lark.

"Oh, I won't."

"What are you going to do?" you ask.

"Just some warrior sh■t," says Chad01.

He shrugs off his backpack, opens the flap, and pulls out his djembe drum, a couple folding chairs, a slinky.

A bucket.

A pillow.

A potted plant.

A baseball.

A pair of socks.

A sweater.

A chocolate peanut butter Chonk bar.

Finally, the end of a yellow rope.

Chad01 pulls the rope out of his backpack, and it keeps coming and coming, yards and yards of it, coiling on the ground beside him like a magic trick.

⁘

The kid in sunglasses comes up to you. "What are you doing? You aren't authorized to be in here! What on earth is all that stuff? What are you doing with all that rope?"

"Tying you up," says Chad01, and he lunges forward, and before you know it, the kid is on his butt and Chad01 is wrapping him up.

"Dave!" the kid calls out. "Dave, they're tying me up!"

"Be quiet. Dave can't hear you."

Around and around Chad01 goes, bundling the struggling kid in layer after layer of endless rope. And when he's done, the kid looks like a fat bug in a yellow cocoon, only his head and feet poking out. And still there's rope left over.

"Dave! Help me!"

Chad01 pats him on the head. "I told you, Dave's out of commission, man."

The kid's eyes are wide. "What did you do with Dave? Is he OK?"

"Here," says Chad01, cutting the rope. "Let's tie up the other one too."

"Dave!" the kid yells again.

But Dave does not rouse from his sleep.

The kid eyes you from his cocoon. "It doesn't matter. It really doesn't. Someone is going to come looking for us, you know. We work in shifts, duh. It isn't like—"

"Don't talk anymore," says Chad01. "Just sit."

"You w—"

"What did I say?" Chad01 looms over him. "NO TALKING."

⁓

The rope just goes on and on. You wrap the sleeping kid in a matching cocoon of it, then Chad01 turns to the other kid again. "I'm looking for a fuzzy. Orange with golden tips, on the fuzzier side, blue eyes. You seen it? Its name is Echo Joy."

The kid doesn't answer.

"WELL?" says Chad01.

"Oh, can I talk now? Nice shirt, by the way."

"Where's my fuzzy?"

The kid squirms. "I can't move."

"That's the point, duh. Where's Echo Joy?"

"Look, buddy, they're all the same to me. I have no idea. I just work here. If you want your fuzzy, it's probably up there, wouldn't you think?"

You turn to gaze up at the enormous tower of shining boxes.

52.

ANSWER BRIGHT

You find yourself heading up the metal catwalk with the others in search of Echo Joy.

The boxes appear to be color coded. The first levels are all blue—thousands of glowing blue and bluish fuzzies trapped in glass cases that wrap around the tower. As you are heading up to the next level, you notice one that isn't lit up, and you pause a moment.

You see a dark form thrashing around inside. A fuzzy with the light off. It's moving in a blur, hurtling itself against the wall, screaming and laughing in an insane frenzy.

More blue fuzzies, and then higher up they become green. Level after level, box after box, thousands and thousands of fuzzies dancing wearily to the song, screaming out at the end of each chorus. It's freaky and unreal and right in front of you and all around.

IF YOU'RE HAPPY AND YOU KNOW IT, SHOUT HOORAY!
[*ANGUISHED SCREAMS!*]

269

Higher still, and finally the glowing bodies become golden yellow. Chad01 moves from box to box, peering inside, moving on, opening a door, and lifting a fuzzy out, then practically flinging it back in. "Where the hell is it?"

You search the boxes, hundreds of golden-orange fuzzies.

"What about this one here?" says Owlsy.

"No. Too big."

"And this one?" says Lark.

"No! Look at the eyes!"

More boxes. Hundreds and hundreds and none of them are quite right.

·•·

And then you see them—a pair of iridescent blue eyes gazing at you curiously. You open the glass and take it in your hands. The brilliant, glowing body.

"Echo Joy?" you say.

The little creature giggles. "WHAT IS ECHO JOY?"

"Oh hell yeah!" Chad01 comes running and takes the fuzzy in his hands and gives it a long look. "It's you!"

"WHAT IS YOU?"

"Yes!" Chad01 opens his sling and the other fuzzy pops its head up, and the two fuzzies gaze at each other for a moment.

"WHO ARE YOU?" says Echo Joy.

"*I* AM ANSWER BRIGHT!" says the other one. "*YOU* ARE ECHO JOY!"

"WHAT IS ECHO JOY?"

"*ECHO JOY* IS YOUR NAME!"

"WHAT IS YOUR NAME?"

"MY NAME IS ANSWER BRIGHT!"

Chad01 swaps them out, placing Answer Bright in the enclosure and returning Echo Joy to his sling.

"WHAT IS ANSWER BRIGHT?"

"ANSWER BRIGHT IS MY NAME!" says the other fuzzy from its glass box.

"WHAT IS MY NAME?"

"*YOUR* NAME IS ECHO JOY!"

Chad01 pushes the glowing creature down into the sling and zips it in.

Yawn. "What is Echo Joy?" it whispers one more time, and the other answers brightly from its glass enclosure,

"YOU ARE!"

"Wait, we're just going to leave it there?" you say. "This place, it's—"

"THE TOWER IS A NIGHTMARE OF PAIN AND SUFFERING!" chirps Answer Bright.

"Right," says Chad01. "OK." He opens the glass door, grabs the fuzzy, and shoves it into Lark's arms. "Here."

"Me?" she says.

"You're the one who found it in the first place!"

"What about the others?" you ask.

"Let's go talk to the kids," says Owlsy. "They might—"

"Hey!" says Lark.

You turn to see the fuzzy floating in the air above her.

"WHEE!" it chirps. "I'M FREE AS A BEE!"

"What happened?" says Chad01.

"It just slipped from my hands!"

"FREE AS A BEE!" it calls again as it floats upward like a lazy balloon.

You run down the catwalk and gather the two kids you've tied up on the concrete floor. The first one is still snoozing, a trickle of drool running down his cheek. The other is looking up at you with mild amusement.

"The doors," says Chad01. "How do we open them all? There's got to be a switch or something."

"Open the doors?" says the kid. "Why would you want to do that?"

"To free the fuzzies."

"That's dumb. If you free the fuzzies, you can't open the home portal."

Owlsy turns to the kid. "And how does the portal work? Is it possible to open it and not harm the fuzzies?"

The kid looks up from his rope cocoon. "Ha. Like I'm gonna tell you."

"Tell us and we'll take you with us," says Chad01.

"No way. You know how much trouble we'd be in?"

"We'd be home, you dumb sh█t!"

The kid gives it some thought. "Look," he says. "You can't just *turn on* the home portal. It takes up all the energy. You've got to charge the reserve batteries first; otherwise, you'll have no power for the city. And you can't just charge up the reserve batteries, because the grid's already running at full capacity. But there is a way . . ."

"What is it?" says Chad01.

The kid turns his head, defiant. "Nah. I don't trust you."

"We're pretty much begging you," says Owlsy.

"It isn't really in the spirit of begging if you've got me tied up."

"We'll take you with us!"

The kid pauses. He stares intently at each of you. "You wanna know how to open the portal? Fine. You flip the switch." He nods toward the wall, the maze of wire and blinking lights.

"What switch?" says Chad01. "Where is it? Point to it!"

The kid looks out from his rope cocoon. "Well, I can't *point* to it, now can I? It's over there. See?"

⁂

There's a little gray panel on the wall. It's locked.

"Where's the key?" says Chad01.

"Bet you wish you knew," says the kid.

Chad01 takes a footstool, a dog leash, a scented candle, and finally a crowbar from his bag. Using the bar, he breaks the hinges on the box and pries it open.

"OK, OK, fine!" says the kid. "But you gotta take me too, OK? You said you would, remember? You can't just leave me here!"

"Shut up," says Chad01. "No one's leaving anyone, just be quiet for a second!"

Inside the panel there's a single ON/OFF switch in the OFF position under a little placard that says: HOME PORTAL.

"Wow," says Owlsy. "OK . . . here it is."

"Be careful," says the kid in the cocoon.

"Let's do it," says Chad01. "Let's see if your crystal quest was legit or not. Turn that sh█t on!"

"You know, I'm actually kind of excited to see how this fails," says Lark.

Click. Owlsy flips the switch to ON.

CLAP YOUR HANDS

There's a sound, a low humming that gets louder and higher in pitch, and the song is getting louder too, and the anguished screams, and the boxes in the tower are starting to glow brighter, and everything just keeps getting louder and louder and brighter and brighter, a nightmare of light, and the screams turn to wailing shrieks, and the air fills with the sharp odor of metal and electricity and singed hair.

"No!" Lark shouts. "It's going to kill them!"

"But this is our way out!" Owlsy answers.

"It's not worth it!"

You agree with Lark, you're reaching for the switch now, and the roaring grows louder.

...HAPPYANDYOUKNOWITCLAPYOUR *HANDS!!!*

And you're all going for the switch now, all four of you. The suffering is just unbearable, laughing and shrieking and screaming in anguish as the white light pouring from the grid grows brighter and brighter and still brighter and—

Chad01 gets to it first and flips the switch to OFF. There's an enormous POP! and all at once the lights go out and the music stops and a single scream rings out into the darkness and then there is nothing but silence. Smoke curls in the air above you.

"Wow," says the kid from his rope cocoon. "Way to go. You killed the whole grid."

Silence.

Darkness.

Smoke.

⁘

"Look," says Owlsy.

You see it, a box high in the tower. A little glow.

And then another glow. And another. Twinkling lights. Like stars coming out in the evening sky.

"They're waking up! They're alive!"

There's something else too. High in the tower, a bright shape is swooping around, and as it passes by the boxes, the doors open, and more fuzzies come out to join it.

"FREE AS A BEE!"

"Uh-oh," says the kid. "Dave is *not* going to like this."

As you watch, the air fills with thousands and thousands of magical, glowing creatures. They pour out of their boxes and swirl in the air, a whirlwind of light that sweeps around the inner tower, gathering in size until the air is a glowing tornado that rises higher and higher and then comes the sound of something breaking, and the tornado sweeps upward, funneling through the jagged hole in the roof and into the sky. Glass rains down from above.

An alarm is sounding.

BOOOOP! BOOOOP! BOOOOP!

"Oh *snap*," says the kid. "I'm not even kidding. You guys are in *so* much trouble."

54.

RUN

You're heading out the front doors of the tower when Dave wakes up and starts shouting from the heavens above.

WHAT? HEY! HEYYYYYYY!

WHAT'S GOING ON?

DID SOMEONE—OH NO! OH MY GOD LOOK AT THE TOWER!!!! WHAT HAPPENED TO THE TOWER?! WHO FLIPPED THE SWITCH?!

You're running down the street with the others. It's different out now. The lights on the buildings are gone; the flashing screens are blank. No videos. No music, no bubbles. The power is off. It's just sunshine and Dave.

HEY, EVERYONE! HEY! EMERGENCY! BIGTIME EMERGENCY! THE BAD KIDS PUT A SLEEP SPELL ON ME AND DESTROYED THE POWER TOWER!

THERE'S FOUR OF THEM!

THEY'RE HEADING NORTH FROM THE TOWER!

THEY'VE GOT PINK POLOS ON THAT ARE WAY TOO SMALL! HURRY! HURRY! GET THE EVIL TRAITORS!!

You turn down an alleyway, sprinting along the narrow corridor. It opens to a wide boulevard, and you race after the others toward the distant wall.

THEY'RE GOING FOR THE NORTH GATE! DON'T LET THEM GET AWAY! OOH THESE FILTHY TRAITORS DESTROYED THE ENTIRE TOWER!! OOH I AM SERIOUSLY SO MAD I JUST WANT TO BASH THEM REPEATEDLY IN THE FACE WITH A CROWBAR, FRYING PAN, OR SOME OTHER EASILY-ACCESSIBLE HEAVY METAL BLUDGEON

You feel a tug on your sleeve.

"This way," Chad01 whispers.

HEY! OOH! OOH! I HEARD THAT! *I HEARD THAT*, YOU ROTTEN TURD! OK, EVERYONE, HEY! THEY'RE CHANGING DIRECTION! THEY'RE HEADING TOWARD THE WALL JUST TO THE *LEFT* OF THE NORTH GATE! HURRY! GET SOME FRYING PANS!

You get to the wall, and Chad01 shrugs off his backpack, reaches inside, and for once grabs the exact thing he's looking for. You watch as he lifts his wooden ladder rung-by-rung up and out of his bottomless bag. He sets it on the grass and leans it against the wall. Dave is still shouting.

You look back. *Where are the kids?* As far as you can see, it's just the empty boulevard, a wide grass field bordered by glass buildings. Then from behind one of the buildings, you see a couple bright polos appear, and then more, and then a tide of them, pouring out onto the boulevard like neon water rushing your way, *hundreds* of kids, and Dave is shouting,

HURRRRRY, THEY'RE CLIMBING THE WALL! HURRY!

RUN! RUN! RUN! RUN! RUN!

GET THE BAD KIDS!

"Up up up!" says Chad01, shoving you toward the ladder. You're climbing the rungs behind Owlsy. With every step, the ladder shakes. You can hear the crowd shouting behind you. You're scrambling as fast as you can.

"Here!" Owlsy is helping you onto the wall. Next comes Lark, then Chad01.

And the four of you start to pull up the ladder at the same instant the candy-colored mob of kids collides with the wall, yelling and cursing below you, and one of them, a girl in a canary-yellow polo, manages to jump and grab on to the last rung, and the others grab her by the legs and now it's a tug-of-war.

KNOCK THEM OFF! yells Dave. **PULL THEM DOWN!**

Chad01 takes a basketball from his bag and tosses it down, and the girl drops from the ladder to dodge it. The four of you lift up the ladder and use it to scramble down the other side while Dave shouts,

NOOOOOOOOOOOOOOO!

TO THE GATE! GO! FRYING PANS!

55

RETURN TO THE GAP

You are running down the trail through the machine forest, cords and pipes whipping past, and the sign comes into view again.

MIND THE GAP

You find yourself standing at the edge of the void once more, with the rope suspension bridge and its wooden slats stretching out into the emptiness.

"All right!" says Owlsy. "We just have to get to the other side and then we can cut it!"

"Wait!" says Chad01. "I can't do that! Put me to sleep!"

"I used my last sleep spell!" says Lark.

He turns from the gap and stands there with his face scrunched up. "F█ck."

"Chad01." You wrap your arm around him—or try to. *BRRZAP!*

"We could still carry you," says Owlsy. "You could close your eyes and we could just—"

A shout in the distance. You see bright polos beginning to emerge from the mechanical foliage. Frying pans. Crowbars.

"Come on!" says Lark. *"You can do this!"*

"Yeah, yeah." Chad01 takes a breath, turns toward the bridge, and starts walking. But then he stops again.

"Well, I'm not gonna be first. I wanna be in the middle or something."

"Fine, yes, let's just go!" says Owlsy.

᠅

Somehow you're in the lead. You didn't want to be first, it just ended up that way. It's you, then Chad01, Lark, and Owlsy—in that order. You hurry along the bridge, wooden slats passing in a blur underfoot, the bottomless void swirling below, moving swiftly but safely, not quite running.

You're almost out of sight of the edge when you realize you can't hear Chad01 and the others anymore, and when you stop and look back, you see them far behind you. Chad01 is just standing there, holding the railing with both hands. Owlsy and Lark are behind him, gesturing furiously.

Beyond them, you can just barely see the other side, and the horde of kids in bright polos. They aren't following you. At least, it doesn't look that way. It's like they're doing something else, too far away to see. And you are standing here wondering if you should go back for Chad01 and the others, when you see the first curl of smoke. It grows thicker, rising into the shimmery air, and as you peer into the distance, you can see yellow flames curling up along the handrail.

"Fire!" you call out to your friends. "Hurry! They're lighting the bridge on fire!"

Lark shoves Chad01, and they're moving toward you now.

Owlsy is shouting something.

"Run!"

Yes. Run.

You start off again and immediately trip, and the bridge jerks under your feet, and you're thrown to your knees, grabbing the railing as the emptiness sways back and forth below. You pick yourself up. You run. The boards are a blur at your feet.

You run and run with the fire behind you, and then you can see it —land. The bridge sways sickeningly as you dash for solid ground. You leap from the last slat and onto hard rock. The other side. Safety.

You look back to see how your friends are doing and find to your horror that they've stopped again. No—they're moving, but just barely. Lark and Owlsy are log-jammed behind Chad01 as he picks his way carefully from board to board. The flames are rising higher behind them, leaping up at billowing, black smoke.

There's a sound, a *snap!* And then again. And then it happens. The bridge breaks—it rips apart at the center of the flames—and you find yourself watching helplessly as the entire span seems to fall from beneath your friends—but no, they are falling too. And there's nothing, *nothing,* you can do but watch as their bodies drop like stones and disappear into the chasm below.

56.

WHEN SHE WENT OUT

You find yourself standing at the edge of the cliff, looking into the void where your friends used to be. The wind blows your hair around your face. The mist curls in the emptiness. Everyone is gone. You are alone again. You stand on the cliff in the wind. You watch as a gray bird darts out over the chasm.

It's too much. It's just way too much. You're either crying or it's raining, you don't know which. You wipe your face and take a breath. You have this thought: *Maybe the kid was right. Maybe they were just imaginary.* But what about the secrets, then? If your friends are imaginary, then the kid is your brother. And you are crazy.

No. You don't want to think about it. Any of it.

You are moving. You just need to be walking. You are heading up the path.

You come to the fork again, and the same sign from before:

LAND OF THE NIGHT SCREAMERS →
← DARKNESS & DEAD BODIES

You stop a moment to consider it, and then you head down the trail to the left.

⠒

It isn't dark. Not at first.

The path meanders out across the rocky mesa, weaving among the pools of water, but gradually turns back the other way, back toward the gap, and before long you can feel it nearby, the yawning chasm, and then in the distance you see a railing, and the path takes you there and you are walking alongside the endless, empty void, the chasm you crossed. You can't see the other side.

As you walk, the light begins to seep out of the world, the sky darkens, the ground goes from brown to dark gray, and then there's a gap in the railing, and the trail swings toward it and disappears over the edge.

⠒

You're standing on the edge again. The trail doesn't end here. In the fading light, you can see it disappearing at an angle down into the chasm, a path carved into the side of the cliff.

You hesitate a moment, and then you start down the path.

It's steep at first, but then it becomes less steep, and after a while, it switches back in the other direction. And then again.

Down you go, following the trail as it snakes back and forth down the cliffside, and the darkness rises out of the void. How deep does this go?

It doesn't matter. More than anything you just want to keep moving, keep your mind on that, but it's getting too dark; you're going slower now, keeping both hands on the sheer wall as you descend, straining to see the trail.

At some point you realize you can't see it anymore.

You find yourself clinging to the side of a cliff in the dark above a bottomless chasm of nothingness. Darkness, you, and that's it. You are alone—no friends, no portal, no way out.

And you think, *This is crazy.*

And you think, *Don't think like that.*

Not the crazy thing.

Really, really don't need that right now.

So what do I need?

You look around in the swirling darkness.

You take out your phone, run your thumb along the rounded edges, push the button. Nothing happens. You push it again. It's dead. You need light. You feel around in your pockets, wishing for a lighter, and instead you find something else. Something sort of gritty and sticky, covered in lint. You hold it up, squish it a little with your thumb. You can't see it, but at the same time you *can* see it, even if the image is only in your mind. You can see it in your hand: a translucent white Ghost Punch Sour Patch Kid.

According to Chad01 and the twins, if you smoke the sour, you will unlock a portal. Which is crazy. But then all of this is.

Fire. You need fire.

You raise the Sour Patch Kid to your lips, remembering the story. You just have to get it right.

OK.

When she went out.

Saw she the dark.

Darkness saw her.

And so they—

Died? Danced? Both? Neither?

It doesn't matter.

Just say it.

"Wan shay wen ah," you begin. "Sah shay the—"

No.

Not "the."

Try again.

You start over, and this time you make it to the part about *darkness saw* before messing up.

Third time's a charm, you think.

And maybe it is, because this time the words just flow out on their own, the whole story, syllable after syllable in a steady stream . . . *dah nah sah hay ahn so tay* . . . it feels strange, like instead of you speaking the words, the words are speaking you. And on the last word, *dah,* it happens. A spark flares up in the darkness, just like magic, and your Sour Patch Kid is on fire.

You've only got a moment to inhale before it burns down to your fingers, but that's all it takes. The smoke is hot and noxious, stinging your nose like burned rubber, and the instant it hits your lungs, you drop the Sour Patch Kid and begin to hack and cough, tears in your eyes, and you take a step forward to steady yourself, but where the path should be, there is nothing, only an emptiness that rises up to embrace you as you fall off the edge.

.ɰ.

In the darkness, you can't see it, but you can feel it—the void rushing up, the sudden weightlessness, your breath leaving your lungs as you gasp. You are falling. You feel your whole body squinch up as you brace for impact. Every muscle tightening like a coil. The wind rushing past.

The darkness absolute. You brace for impact, and you keep bracing, but nothing happens. You just keep falling. *Right. The hole is bottomless.*

.•.

You are falling and falling, and in the darkness, it feels like the rushing turbulence is almost pushing you up somehow, but that's just a trick of your acceleration. You try not to think about how fast you must be going.

You find yourself falling through blank, empty space. And as you grow used to the wind, it's almost like it disappears. You are just there. Here. Floating. Everything timeless and empty. You are a formless being in a formless void, and mixed with the terror, a strange, inevitable peace begins to overtake you. *OK, so this is me now.*

And then you remember something else: *Hey, I smoked the sour. Wasn't I supposed to see a portal or something?*

And that's when you see it—a flicker in the distance. Just a spark at first, but as soon as you see it, it begins to grow larger. It grows and grows, rushing toward you like a subway train, wider and wider, illuminating the walls of the chasm in rippling light. The wind roaring. The train speeding closer. The blinding light. There's a flash, and you are somewhere else.

mem01908m (stop being)

My foot slips on the rocks, just enough to make my heart beat faster, and I think, *Ha, that would be just like me, to accidentally die while I was looking for a place to kill myself.*

.•.

I'm standing at the edge of the cliff, overlooking the fog and the hidden waves. My mind fills with all the things: dead cat, dead phone, failed class, no friends, Dad gone . . . and part of me is just weighed down by the hopelessness of it, and another part of me is like, *Stop being so dramatic. Lots of people have it way worse than you.*

And the first part of me is like, *Oh, that's supposed to make me feel better? I can't remember the last time I've been happy.*

I think about how mean I've been. I hate myself for being mean.

The waves roar below like an angry god.

So <u>do</u> something about it, I say to myself.

Show some motivation.

And then it happens.

I do something really stupid.

I don't even know why.

I step off the cliff and out into space.

57.

IS THIS DEATH

You wake up screaming under a blue sky.

A sunny hilltop.

Tall grass. Wildflowers.

A voice calling out to you.

Someone is calling your name.

"Hey!"

Chad01's face appears above you. Bright-eyed, smiling.

"Hey! Thought you'd *never* wake up! How's it going? You were really screaming there. Dang!"

~

You sit up, blinking in the light.

Already the memory is fading. The cave. The cliffs. The waves.

Did I die? you wonder. *Am I dead? Is this death?*

And now here you are. Again. Still.

You take a breath.

You *are* breathing, aren't you? It *does* feel like air.

~

"What's up?" says Chad01. "You OK? You got a funny look on your face."

"I think . . . maybe . . . uh . . ." You're having a little trouble getting it out. You stand up to give yourself a moment. "I think maybe I died," you say at last. "I think maybe I killed myself by jumping off a cliff, and now I'm dead. But I didn't mean to! I wasn't thinking right. It was just this one dark moment and—"

"Wait," Chad01 says. "You think you *died?*"

"Yeah."

"Seriously?!"

"Yeah."

"Ha," Chad01 laughs. "Wow, that's crazy. You aren't *dead*. How could you be standing here talking to me if you were dead? Come on, you're smarter than that! You're right here, Rainbow! Alive and well! We *all* are—see?"

You look to where he's pointing, and you see them now, Owlsy and Lark, strolling down the hillside with sunlight in their hair and flowers all around.

"Hey," Chad01 calls to them. "Got a question. Does Rainbow seem *dead* to you?"

Owlsy considers you a moment. "Dead people aren't generally upright."

Chad01 nods. "That's what *I* said!"

"Hi, Rainbow." Lark gives you a little wave. "Welcome back to the endless journey."

.ʌ.

You look around again—the flowers, the sunshine, the sky. OK, so you're here. That doesn't mean you're *not* dead. This could be the land of the dead. Is that what you're doing here?

"Wait," you say. "Are we *all* dead? Maybe we're all dead."

"What?" says Owlsy. "No, of course we're not all dead!"

"But the bridge," you say. "You *fell*. I saw — it was —"

"Yeah," says Chad01. "*Totally* bottomless. We just kept falling and falling for *hours* and *hours*!"

"It was quite a terrifying trip," says Owlsy.

"Followed by *boring* and *tedious,*" says Lark.

"Followed by terrifying again," says Owlsy. "Because as we were just idly falling through seemingly infinite space, the nature of our predicament began to dawn on us. Given our velocity, if we hit the bottom — if there *was* a bottom — we would die upon impact. But if my wiki was correct and the chasm we were falling in was, in fact, bottomless, that would mean that, if nothing changed, we were fated to just keep falling and falling until we eventually perished of thirst and malnourishment. Neither possibility was at all desirable."

"Death by splat or death by dehydration," says Chad01. "We were double-f■cked."

"Yes," says Owlsy. "And we debated for some time about what we should do, and that debate quickly turned into a fight . . . how'd it go? First, we argued about whether we might sort of paddle or kick through the air over to the edge, but our efforts proved futile. We debated different swimming strokes. At some point Lark suggested Chad01 kiss her ■ss. Then Chad01 suggested that Lark might instead kiss her own ■ss. Then Lark suggested Chad01 could crawl into his bottomless bag and disappear, and I thought, *Not a bad idea* — not the disappearing part, but the crawling into the bag part. So we did, all of us. Falling through the bottomless void, we wiggled into Chad01's bottomless bag, and I'm not quite sure how it worked, only that the two bottomlessnesses must have canceled each other out, and this contradiction of powerful magical forces somehow ripped open a portal because —"

"Because the next thing we knew — *blam!*" says Chad01. "We're tumbling outta the bag and we're here! Blue sky, field of flowers, and who do we see curled on the ground? Our good friend Rainbow . . . Incredible, right?" He grins in the sunshine. "But so how'd *you* get here?"

᷈

You tell them about the darkness and the fall and how you smoked the sour.

"Ah!" says Owlsy. "OK, *now* it makes sense! It wasn't the backpack. You opened a portal in the bottomless hole, and we all fell into *that*. And *that's* why we all wound up here!"

"It doesn't matter," says Lark.

"Right," says Owlsy. "We're together — that's the point."

"No," she says. "The point is it never ends. There's no escape. It just keeps going."

"Where are we?" you ask. "What is this place?"

"Oh, man!" says Chad01. "Don't listen to Lark. Wait until you see the surprise! Come check it out for yourself!"

He takes your hand and practically drags you through the flowers to the top of a little grassy rise. Somehow, it's evening now. Birds chirp and insects hum and every flower is a delicate lantern holding the light of the sun, and the whole thing is just impossibly beautiful, bright, and incandescent. With the sun at your back, you stand and look out at endless hills and flowers, and the darkening horizon, and the deep blue sky, and the thing floating in the sky.

"*So?*" says Chad01. "You recognize that?"

There's this bright round object floating in the sky. Like a moon. Only it isn't a moon. It's a cat. It's a cat and a moon. It's a giant, orange, glowing cat curled up in a perfect little ball, eyes closed, asleep, serene.

"Goldfish," you say.

Chad01 pumps his fist. "Yes! I knew it! The wizard said to me, he said, *Bring Echo Joy to the Lake of the Goldfish Moon, and it will open the portal home.* And then I saw that moon and I remembered what you told me about your dead cat and how its name was Goldfish, and I was like, *This has to be it!*"

You can't believe it. But it's true. Your dead cat has been resurrected as a celestial body. You want to call out to her, to hold her in your arms. How far away is she? How big? There's almost no way to tell, the perspective is all off, but anyway, she must be gigantic. She's a moon.

"Told ya! I told you guys we'd find it!" Chad01 is absolutely radiant. You've never seen him so happy. "Now we just gotta find the lake!"

THE LAKE OF THE GOLDFISH MOON

You're walking through the wildflowers and tall grass with the sun behind you and the goldfish moon rising in the sky ahead, and it feels really good: the sweet smell of the air, the warm breeze, the humming insects and fluttering birds. It's just so beautiful.

The others are in a pretty good mood, even Lark, and you are too. It's hard not to be. Even if you are dead, this place is pretty nice right now. The sun is warm on your back, but not too warm, and the breeze and the sweet smell of the grass and the flowers . . . You stroll along, listening to your friends' back-and-forth, watching the serene sleeping cat floating in the sky, and pretty soon you are humming to yourself, and your humming becomes a song, and the song becomes the Wandering Song, and you see a call box appear on a hill in the distance.

"And just think," says Chad01, "all this time I was searching for the wrong kind of goldfish. I was looking for a *fish*. If I hadn't run into you, Rainbow, I never would have made it here or even recognized it if I did. That's pretty awesome."

"A truly remarkable journey," says Owlsy. "A lesson in teamwork and courage."

You swipe your IDs, and something whirs inside the box, and it goes *BLAP!* and spits out a piece of paper:

YOU ARE CLOSE

"Nice," says Owlsy. "We're close."

"Yeah, but how about some actual *directions?*" Chad01 pounds the button. Another paper.

YOU ARE VERY CLOSE

"Fine. So we keep going."

"What's it going to take?" says Lark. "When will you two realize that it never. *Ever.* Ends?"

~

You start off again through the wildflowers.

You walk and walk.

"Got any stories for us, Rainbow?" asks Chad01.

Maybe? You don't know. You need to think.

"I've got one," says Lark. "How about this? Once upon a time, there were four crazy kids who got lost in the Wilds, and a wizard told one of them that to get home, they just needed to bring a magical, glowing fuzzy to the Lake of the Goldfish Moon! And guess what? They were just on their way to the lake — they'd found the moon, in fact! — they were *just* on their way when, what do you know, they suddenly discovered that it was *actually* hidden in the giant subterranean kingdom of the Mole Wizard! Guarded behind a superspecial, *secret* entrance that could only be opened after all four magic runes had been returned to the lost pillar of, of, um . . . oh."

You've come to an overlook. The wildflowers bleed out onto a rocky outcrop, and you find yourself standing with the others, looking out over an enormous, wide-open valley, and in the middle of the valley, there it is: draped out like a shining blue cloth, and in its still and tranquil waters floats the reflection of the goldfish moon.

"Told ya!" says Chad01. "It's the g█dd█mn lake!"

⚡

You run with the others down the slope, through flowers and grass. Insects leap from out of the foliage. Tiny birds dart past.

At the shore, there's a dock.

The boards creak as you walk out over the water. At the end of the dock, where the waves lap against the wooden pilings, Chad01 opens his sling and lifts out the little, glowing creature.

"Holy sh█t here we are. We made it. This is it."

Echo Joy looks out over the waves and giggles. "WHAT IS IT?"

"The Lake of the Goldfish Moon!" says Chad01. "Way to hang in there till the end!"

"WHAT IS THE END?"

"*This* is, buddy!"

"WHAT IS THIS IS BUDDY?"

Chad01 kneels at the edge of the dock and holds Echo Joy out over the darkened water. "You're home now, little friend. Take us home with you, OK?"

"WHAT IS OK?"

Chad01 lets go, and the fuzzy slips from his hands and plunges seamlessly into the water, and as you watch, the glow fades away under the waves, smaller and smaller until it disappears.

⚡

At first, nothing happens.

You stand at the lakeshore, peering into the darkness. No one says anything. The world holds its breath. You begin to wonder if you have just drowned the adorable little creature.

"Look," says Owlsy.

"Right on time," says Lark, following her brother's gaze to the sky.

And then you see it: something white drifting down from above, tumbling this way and that like a leaf falling from a tree, down, down, down. At last it lands, coming to rest right at Chad01's feet. It's an envelope. A little, white envelope. Like a birthday card or something.

⁂

Chad01 tears open the flap and takes out the card. On the front, there is a picture of a lake, like a postcard. Inside, there's a message:

THANK YOU FOR RETURNING ME TO MY HOME!
I AM SO HAPPY NOW! HERE IS A BONUS POEM OF ANCIENT
WISDOM I WROTE JUST FOR YOU!

DAY IS SHORT
NIGHT IS LONG
PAIN IS PAINFUL
LIFE'S A SONG

BUT LOVE IS REAL
LOVE IS RIGHT
AND EVERY DARKNESS
SHINES WITH LIGHT

THE HOME PORTAL IS NOW OPEN!
HUGS & LOVE FOREVER!
ECHO JOY

".. . knew it!" Chad01 is saying. "*I just knew it!* I just *knew* that little fuzzball would—*Ohmygod will you look at that?!*"

The moon. It's growing.

The sleeping cat is swelling overhead, bigger and bigger until it is the size of the sky, and everything above you is just an enormous, glowing cat. You stand stunned in the orange light.

"Wow," says Owlsy. "So this is it then."

"Wanna bet?" says Lark.

The silvery whiskers tremble, an ear twitches. Goldfish yawns and opens her eyes. There's a bright flash.

`mem01909m (i am falling)`

My chest swells with horror and sickness as the fog rushes up. Behind the screaming terror, my brain is just firing off one thought after another, about how oh my god I am falling and how I can't believe what just happened, how it can't be happening, and how it *is* though, and how much I regret it, with every ounce of my being. I've never regretted a thing so much in all my life.

My mind is on fire, one thought after another.

Mostly I just see it all rushing away: CJ and Mom and my life and the sun and the wind and bean burritos and warm socks out of the dryer, and all the million other memories I'm leaving behind, and all the future memories that won't happen, and all the unfinished things.

Things I should have done that I didn't even know I had to do until this exact moment. Like talk to CJ and tell him I'm sorry and I love him, and he is a good brother and the thing with Goldfish wasn't his fault, I didn't mean to yell at him, I just wasn't thinking straight, I've been so down it wasn't anything to do with him and oh god — *what if he thinks this was somehow his fault?* And I'm falling, I'm thinking *oh sh█t oh no,* and I just want to talk to my brother one more time and tell him I love him, it's cool, everything is OK, but everything *isn't* OK because I am falling and the dark waves are racing up to greet me and then I hit.

WAKE UP

You find yourself standing just where you were, on the shore of the Lake of the Goldfish Moon. It's darker now. The moon is gone. Goldfish is gone. But you are here. Again. Still. You listen to the waves gently lapping at the darkness. The sky is filled with dark clouds; it feels like rain. For a long moment no one speaks.

". . . the f■ck?" says Chad01 at last.

"It never ends," Lark says quietly. "It just goes on and on and —"

"No," says Owlsy. "No! There's got to be *something!*" He flips through his wiki, snaps the book shut. "Let me see the card again, Chad01."

"What card?"

"The one we just got from your fuzzy!"

Chad01 hands the card over. Owlsy opens it and reads it intently.

"*There,*" he says. "See that? See what it says? It says, *the home portal is now open.* It doesn't say *which* portal is the home portal. It just says it's open! So maybe that means that we opened the portal *adjacent to* the home portal or —"

"Oh my god, will you wake up!" Lark glares at her brother. *"There is no home portal!"*

"Listen," says Owlsy, "this attitude of yours, this insistence on cynicism—just because *you* haven't seen it with your *own* eyes doesn't mean it's not true or possible! We're in the Wilds! *Anything* is possible, and that includes—"

"No!" she says. "No more inspirational speeches! I refuse to listen to another—"

A distant screech cuts Lark off, a squealing sound, metal on metal, followed by a booming crash that echoes through the night.

"What was that?" you ask.

"Ugh, no," says Chad01. "Not here."

"Yep, here," says Lark.

"A machine quake," says Owlsy.

"What's that mean?" you ask.

"It means this level is being eaten by the machine forest, and if we don't—"

But that's as far as he gets because there's another crash, closer, and you hear in the aftermath the sound of crunching metal and broken glass, and then you see it, a cascading tower of machinery rising out of the darkness to topple into the lake. And it just keeps coming, pouring up out of nothing, spilling into the lake and onto the shore in a maelstrom of tumbling debris, drawing closer and closer.

"Run!" says Lark.

⁂

You run. You sprint with the others away from the lake and the crashing metal death. You run through the darkness—you are always running —but finally the terrible crashing ceases, the machine quake is over, and everyone stops. You see now that the machinery is everywhere.

You are standing in a forest, creaking stacks of bloody mechanical parts looming in every direction. "OK, everyone, be quiet," Owlsy whispers. "We don't want to start an avalanche."

"Portal," says Chad01. "We've got to find a portal."

"*Shh.*"

The forest rumbles and creaks.

"Hey, do you hear that?" Chad01 asks.

"Yes, it's going to collapse!" Owlsy hisses.

"No. *Listen,*" says Chad 01.

You hear it now. Music is playing, a melody floating over the debris . . . *triumphant, happy.*

⚡

You are running again. You are running with the others through the dark, overgrown maze of broken machinery, following the song. Owlsy trips on a cord and goes tumbling onto the trail. He picks himself up and brushes the greasy, black bits of metal off his pants.

The music is louder now, right on top of you almost, and then you spot it — a call box, half-buried in the machinery.

Everyone swipes their wrists.

The music stops. The machine whirs. *BLAP!* A paper appears.

```
HOME PORTAL WILL REMAIN OPEN
AS LONG AS SACRED FIRE BURNS
```

"Nice!" Owlsy turns to his sister. "You see that? The home portal!"

"What about the sacred fire?" she says.

"What about it?"

"It's another quest, right? We'll have to search everywhere for the sacred fire, and after that, another quest. It never ends."

In the distance, the forest rumbles. You hear a crash, broken glass. Chad01 slams the call-box button. "OK, so tell us where the fire is!" *BLAP!*

SACRED FIRE IS A MANIFESTABLE OBJECT

"What the f█ck does that mean?" says Chad01.

"Manifestable object!" says Owlsy. "It means we need Lark to manifest!"

"Ugh, no," she says. "You know it's just another stupid—"

"Listen to me," says Owlsy. "This level is unstable. The machine forest is taking over as we speak. If we don't do *something,* it's going to crush us. So please just—"

A squealing explosion of metal erupts from out of the darkness. Owlsy stops talking and everyone freezes, listening for the sound to subside, but it doesn't. In fact, it's getting louder. Closer.

And again you're running.

You race through the maze of machinery, below broken stacks and dripping meat, and at some point it begins to change, the machinery gives way to sand, and the air becomes salty and you hear a familiar sound, a dull roar, and you can see it now through the fog, the dark expanse in the distance: the ocean. You are running down a beach toward the ocean. Waves wash in, spilling onto the sand, then retreat. The fog is up, ghostly clouds wandering along the beach.

You stop with the others near the waves. You know this place.

The ground rumbles behind you, followed by a crashing cascade.

"You need to manifest!" says Owlsy.

"Fine!" says Lark. "But I need a—"

"Here." Chad01 is handing Lark a stick, and now she's sitting on the sand drawing circles as you look out into the fog.

Lark goes into her trance as another quake spills machinery onto the beach. She sits a long time, shuddering, and finally she falls over, and her brother catches her. *BRRZAP!*

And in the same instant, you see something.

᠃

A light. Far in the distance. Something flickering.

"Look!" says Chad01.

"The sacred fire!" says Owlsy.

Lark blinks, rises to her feet, wipes the sand off her jeans.

Owlsy goes to hug his sister and gets *BRRZAP!*ed away. "Good job, Lark! I knew you could do it!"

"There's someone there," she says.

"What?"

She doesn't answer but starts walking, so you follow her. As you draw closer, the flickering becomes a small bonfire on the beach, and the cliffs take shape behind it, and you see another light rising from the waves beside the rocky walls.

It isn't like the others. It's bigger, brighter, and it's pulsating, ascending like fire out of the ocean waves, disappearing into the darkness above. The fog glows in a halo around it, bathing the sheer wall of the cliff in shimmery light.

"The home portal!" says Owlsy.

"Look," says Chad01. "Down by the fire."

You see him now. Through the fog, you can just make out a shadowy figure in a hoodie standing by the dancing flames. You instantly know who it is.

"I have to talk to him," you say.

"Who is it?" Chad01 asks.

"Him."

"Who?"

"The kid. From the desert."

"Him?" Chad01 peers through the fog. "What's *he* doing here? It *better* not be him. Because if it is—"

"I have to talk to him," you say.

"No you don't!" says Chad01. "You see that big g■dd■mn shining light up there? That's the *home portal!* You don't gotta *talk* to the kid. You gotta get into the light!"

"Yes, I would really advise against talking now," says Owlsy. "We're *so* close and Nobodies are no match for Keepers."

"I'm not a *Nobody*. I'm a *Storyteller,* remember?"

"So what are you going to do," says Chad01. "*Tell him a story?* You w—"

There's a loud boom that rings out over the roar of the ocean, followed by a crunching, clanking, tinkling, breaking sound, and you turn to see piles of broken machinery tumbling onto the sand just down the beach.

"This forest," says Owlsy, "is going to crush us!"

"I have to talk to him."

"Why?"

"Because he's my brother!"

"What?" The others are all looking at you.

"I'm pretty sure of it," you say. "I'm pretty sure he's my brother, CJ."

It feels good to say it. It feels good to just get the secret out there.

※

"No," says Chad01 at last. "No way. You think that piece of sh■t is your *brother?* That's crazy."

"Yes!" you say. "That's just it! *I'm* crazy. That's the secret he told me. In the desert. He's my brother, and I'm crazy."

"You're *crazy?*" says Lark. "I thought you were dead."

"Maybe I'm both, who knows?"

"That doesn't make sense," says Chad01.

"Exactly! *Nothing* makes sense. None of this does. Because I'm crazy, and the kid is my brother, and you're all—" You catch yourself.

"What?" says Chad01.

"Nothing."

"We're all *what?*" he says.

You don't want to say it, but they're all looking at you now.

"Imaginary."

Chad01 flinches like he's been slapped. "Imaginary? You think *I'm* imaginary? Me? Are you out of your mind? I'm not imaginary! What about my *toes?*"

"Well . . ." you begin. He's so hurt. You try to walk it all back. "Well, OK . . . the truth is, I don't know anything, no one does, so I'm probably just—"

"And that kid?" says Chad01. "That kid isn't your brother! He can't be! A psychotic douchebag like that? Are you crazy?"

"Yes!"

"Enough!" says Owlsy. "No one's crazy, and no one's dead—and no one's imaginary either! OK? Everyone just needs to keep it together right now because the home portal is *right there,* and we are *this* close. *Please,* everyone!"

You feel a gentle hand on your arm. Lark.

"I believe you, Rainbow," she says. "At least, I don't *not* believe you. Why wouldn't we all be imaginary? It makes as much sense as any of this. And if you want to talk to the kid, you should. Owlsy and Chad01 can calm down and help me look for more firewood for this supposed sacred fire . . ." She turns to Owlsy and Chad01. *"Right?"*

"This is a terrible idea," says Owlsy. "Five minutes. Be careful."

"Listen, Rainbow," says Chad01. "The second that kid tries to pull anything, you just scream, OK?"

SORRY

You find him warming his hands by the fire. His dirty hoodie is cinched around his face; there's just that little hole. Behind him, the column of light rises out of the waves, reflecting off the sheer walls of the cliff.

"Hey," you say.

The forest rumbles.

"Hey, we need to talk. There's something I have to tell you."

He turns your way a little.

His awful gaze. You can feel the nausea rising.

"Got any sour?"

You shake your head.

"Then please kindly f■ck off," he says.

"I want to tell you a story," you say.

"No thanks."

"It's about my brother."

"Double no thanks."

You clear your throat. Metal crashes in the distance.

"Once upon a time," you say, "there was this kid. He was my brother, and—"

"No f█cking thanks! OK?"

He's staring at you. You feel like you're going to puke. You make yourself step closer. You gaze into the empty, black holes of his eyes. The endless scream.

"He was my brother," you say. "And he wrote this song. He composed the whole thing on his phone by himself, if you can believe that, and it was super impressive and catchy and beautiful, but I never told him because—"

Something in the forest falls behind you with a whining screech, some stack of machinery interrupting your words, but you keep talking.

"Because, I don't know, I just let the opportunity pass I guess, and then the song got kind of annoying because he kept playing it all the time ... but there was this one day—I'm just remembering it now. It was a really sunny day and I was coming back from the beach. It's like the only sunny day I remember, actually, and I was coming back from the beach walking up the drive and I—"

"Wow," says the kid. "Not only is this story endless, but it also doesn't have a point."

"And I heard the song blasting from the trailer, and at first I was like, *Ugh, the stupid song again,* so I went up to his bedroom window to yell at him to turn it down, but then I saw him. He was wearing this ridiculous lime green polo shirt with the collar popped, dancing with his eyes closed. I hadn't seen him dance in probably *years,* and it's hard to describe—he was just so graceful and goofy at the same time, moving his arms, making pictures with his hands in the air. I should have said something, but again I didn't. I guess I was just caught up in the moment ... anyway, I loved him, and if I had it to do over again, I would have told him so ... The end."

Another crash in the distance.

"Listen," says the kid. "I don't know who you are or what you're talking about, but if you could *please* f█ck off, that would be awesome. The forest is coming. Let me get crushed in peace."

"I'm Rainbow," you say.

"I don't care."

"And you're him. You're my brother. You're CJ."

The kid tilts his head, his screaming eyes. You feel the nausea rising, but you fight through it.

"The secrets," you say. "Remember? You told me if I said them, they'd come true. And I did, and you're CJ."

⁂

You take him by the shoulders, you look into his hoodie at the darkness in there, the howling gaze, and you make yourself keep looking, and the darkness looks back. For a moment, it's just that — just you and the darkness. CJ squirms out of your grip and gives you a shove, *BRRZAP!*

"You know what *I* think?" he says. "I think you dreamed me up. I think this is all some kind of f█cked-up nightmare you dreamed up as a twisted excuse to prove what a piece of sh█t I am so you could —"

"No," you say. "That isn't it!"

"Yeah it is!" he says. "You dreamed me up to prove what a piece of sh█t I am so you could make it OK in your mind that you f█cking chewed me out for an *accident* and made me clean up Goldfish's dead body, and then you told me to go jump off the cliffs and kill myself, and I probably did, and you're just feeling guilty so —"

"It was *me*," you say.

"What?"

"*I* was the one who jumped."

"You?" the kid, your brother, steps back.

It's raining now, lightly. You can feel it on your face and see droplets falling into the firelight.

"I'm sorry," you say. "I just—it was this one dark moment, and I'm so sorry. I wasn't thinking. I'm so sorry for all of it. If I could do it again, I would do it differently. I'm just so sorry I hurt you. And you have to know, I forgive you for everything. And *none* of it was your fault. And I'm so sorry. And I love you. OK?"

As you look into the darkness, you see something in there: you see eyes peeking out. Your brother's eyes.

"No," he says. "No. Where are you?" He looks around as if seeing everything for the first time. The bonfire. The glowing portal. The looming machinery on the beach. "What is this place? What's going on? Are you OK? Where *are* you, Rainbow? I'm worried. Mom's worried. She's been—"

"Listen," you interrupt, because you can't bear to hear about your mom right now. "Listen, I don't know where I am, but I'm trying to get back home. OK? And I'm not giving up."

And all you want to do is untie his stupid hoodie and see his face again and hug him and feel him hug you back and squeeze each other like you used to when you were little kids and everything wasn't so f█cked.

But when you go to wrap your arms around CJ, there's a sound, *BRRZAP!,* and you're thrown back, and you stumble and nearly trip into the fire, and when you look up again, he isn't there. Your brother, the kid, whoever he is—he's just disappeared.

THE HOME PORTAL

You stand by the fire watching the rain fall through the space where your brother used to be, and for a while, your mind is just that — the rain and the fire — and then it occurs to you to add some wood to the flames, and as you are doing this, you come to a decision. You don't even know what it is yet, but you can feel it. Something has shifted inside you.

The others return, their arms loaded with driftwood.

"Where's the kid?" says Chad01.

"I don't know," you say. "He disappeared."

"Probably teleported," says Owlsy, stacking wood onto the fire. "Of course, upper level Keepers have powers of teleportation and —"

"And how are you, Rainbow?" Lark searches your face with her dark eyes. "You seem . . . Are you OK?"

"I think so?" you say. "I don't know. I got to talk to him. I guess that's what I wanted."

"What did you say?"

"Well . . . I told him I was sorry and that I was trying my hardest to get back home. And . . . yeah."

"Speaking of home, we should go now," says Owlsy. "There isn't much time." He's looking at the column of light rising out of the ocean beside the cliff. "The question is, how do we get there?"

"My inflatable swan!" says Chad01. "I never shoulda left—"

There's another booming crash, so loud it feels like the ground shakes—the ground *does* shake, and you turn to watch an avalanche of bloody machinery spill onto the sand.

"This way," you say. "Follow me."

⁂

You lead your friends down the beach, past the machinery, and then up the winding path in the dark. Cold spray blows in off the ocean. You flip up your hood and tie the strings. There are carvings here and there in the sandstone, kids' initials. The ground is hard and slippery.

The trail makes one more turn and goes almost vertical for a moment, and then you are at the top, and the wind is blowing harder, and raindrops zip through the dazzling column of light rising up out of the ocean and into the sky. And standing between you and the portal is the little guardrail—DANGER KEEP OFF—and eight to ten feet of empty air.

⁂

You lead them around the guardrail and stand at the edge in the wind and the rain, four lost kids side by side in a line. The forest groans behind you in the darkness. The light rises out of the water, into the sky, illuminating the rain. You look down at the boiling waves. It's farther down than you remember. But the light—the light is so beautiful.

The ground rumbles, or maybe it's the ocean, or the sky, or all three, the whole world vibrating in a low bass rumble.

"So you think this is it?" Chad01 shouts.

Owlsy's got his wiki out. But something happens. When he goes to open it, it slips from his fingers, and the wind catches it and blows it away down the darkened trail.

"Hey!"

He starts back for it, but Lark grabs his arm. "Forget the book!"

"What?"

"You won't need it if we're going home, right?"

"But I was going to check and see if this is in fact the home portal, or at least—"

"You see that fire down there?" she says. "It won't last another minute in the rain. There isn't time to go stumbling through the dark!"

"I need that wiki!"

"It's OK," you say. "It's going to be OK."

"But what if it isn't?" says Owlsy.

"Hold on," says Lark. "Wait. After all your speeches? No, you don't get to just give up all faith at the end!"

"It isn't faith! It's a book of annotated, probabilistic odds!"

"Owlsy," says Chad01. "Owlsy, *buddy*."

⸱⸱

And as you stand on the cliff, you realize you don't know *what* happens next, but you are the storyteller and you've made your decision: you want to tell a good story; you want to tell how everything works out, how everyone returns home to their families, and real food, and fields of grass, and trees, and sunshine, and happiness. Chad01 on a bike, laughing as he jumps a log on the trail. Lark and Owlsy on a train, high in the mountains.

And yourself too—you want to tell that story.

⸱⸱

How after you jumped . . . how you clawed your way through the roaring waves and climbed onto the beach and he was there—CJ was there, he was out searching for you—and how you hugged him freezing wet in the rain and breathed in the ocean air.

"I'm so sorry," you said.

And how you stood there, shivering with your brother, and you didn't want to go home just yet, you just needed a little time, so you gathered driftwood and dug a pit in the sand. The wood was damp, but you found some dry grass in a grove of pine trees by the dunes, and using CJ's lighter, you managed to get the fire lit.

How you stood shivering by the flames with your brother.

God, it was cold.

"We could dance," you said.

And your brother gave you a look like, *?*

"To warm up," you said. "Like we used to, remember? Like when Mom and Dad were arguing about the thermostat. Remember? We just need some music. Play a song on your phone. Play that one song."

You got him to play it. He was reluctant at first, but you told him how good it was. *Happy part, sad part, dark part, triumphant part.*

And you started to dance. CJ wouldn't, of course, he was way too cool for it, but you were persistent. That was always one of your better qualities. You never gave up easily.

You took your brother's hand, and you bopped around, singing his song for him, swinging his arms for him, and just when you were getting too embarrassed to keep it up, he started to shuffle his feet a little. Just a little. But enough.

How he closed his eyes and began to move.

Under the stars and moon.

By the waves and the darkness.
In the light of the fire.
You danced.
. . . Remember?
You and your brother danced.

THE FOREST RUMBLES

The forest rumbles behind you, pulling you from your story. The waves roar, the column of light shimmers in the rain.

"If we're going to do this," says Owlsy, "we'd better do it now. Count of three, yeah?"

"Do we *always* have to count?" says Lark.

"Wait!" says Chad01. "I got a question."

"Now?" says Owlsy.

"Yeah. I always wondered: Do you think we're going to the same place?"

"What do you mean?"

"We're going to our *homes,* right? But I don't remember you or Lark or Rainbow from my home . . . Do you remember me?"

"Huh," says Owlsy. "No . . . I never thought about it that way."

"Who knows?" says Lark. "Only one way to find out, right?"

⋰

As you take one last look at your friends, you realize that you love them. Whether or not they are real, whether you are real, whether any of this was real, you love them. And you wish you could tell them all their stories, all the good things to come, but there isn't time because the rain is falling, and the fire is going out, and the column of light is beginning to flicker. All you know is whatever happens, with whatever power you have, you're going to take this nightmare and turn it into something good.

"Count of three!" Owlsy says again.

But there isn't time to count.

The beach rumbles, the cliff shakes, part of it drops off, Owlsy falls to the ground and grabs the guardrail. You can hear it, another cascading wave of destruction coming your way. And you have no choice —the cliff is disappearing from under your feet, you are already in the air, you have already jumped, you are already falling.

`mem01910a [in the waves]`

And then I hit.

Icy shock. Water rushing up. Darkness all around me, my clothing a dead weight dragging me down. It's like swimming in sand. Bubbles, cold darkness, hands waving in front of me. And as I fall deeper into cold, black water, I can feel the screaming panic clawing inside me, and the water is getting darker and darker. I can hardly see now, I can feel the pressure on my face and ears, and I'm kicking, arms sweeping, as the current bats me back and forth.

⁘

And I'm losing it. The water is pulling me down, I'm swimming through an infinity of water, there's no way I'm this deep, I'm not going anywhere.

I'm—

⁘

And there's this voice talking to me, it's me, I'm talking to myself. I'm saying, Hey, *now* is the time, you've got to try to make this work *now* because you have a life. You have a *life*. OK? You have a life, and it isn't gone yet or you wouldn't be thinking this, right? And yeah life is a nightmare sometimes, a total f█cking nightmare, but it's happiness too, and even joy, and family, and all the things, all the ten thousand million good things there are, like wind and rain and flowers, and it's there and you just have to not give up right now, just don't give up just —

The water pours away as my head breaches the surface, my eyes stinging, my mouth open and gasping for breath, gulping in the sweet night air, bobbing up and down in the waves.

And for a moment it's just that.

And all around me there's this glow, the light of the moon and stars is cutting through the fog, and I'm bobbing up and down in the black water, dreamy and beautiful.

And then another wave washes over me. I am kicking. I am sweeping my arms.

64.

WAVE AFTER WAVE

Wave after wave of terror and darkness and water, and then the sudden boundless joy of feeling sand under your feet, and you drag yourself soaking wet onto the glistening beach like a creature of the darkness, sputtering, gasping, alive. You puke ocean water all over your shoes, and then you straighten up and hug yourself, soaked and shivering in the icy wind. You're *so* cold. You've never been this cold in your life. It's so good. Every nerve screaming. You are here. Stunned, freezing, alive.

And then you see something, a light flickering in the distance.

You hear a voice drift across the darkness.

Someone is calling your name.

mem01899i (EPILOGUE I)

I'm sitting in her yellow office again. Another meeting. It feels like I've been talking for hours. I keep watching the sky through the window. It's a blue sky, a sunny day in early spring, and I'm stuck inside. But that's OK. Because I've got this question I want to ask. I've wanted to ask it for a long time. We talk about some random stuff, and I tell her some memories about me and CJ, and finally after all the talking, I make myself ask her the question.

"Am I crazy?"

She pauses, pen hovering above her notepad. "Are you crazy?"

"Yeah."

"What makes you ask that?"

"Sometimes I think of the most f█cked-up things."

"Such as?"

"I don't know. All kinds of things. Dark stuff. My imagination's always going."

"Can you give me an example?"

"Um . . . like what I wrote about in my paper, a god/dess who keeps killing themself over and over. Or just random mind trips. Sometimes I'll imagine like a tower of suffering. Or a room of blood. Or that I'll never be able to afford my own apartment or have a job."

The counselor sets her pen aside. She pushes her glasses up into her hair and rubs her face. "Well, first of all, *crazy* isn't a clinical diagnosis. Crazy is a very subjective and nonspecific word, OK? Your mind, my mind, the human mind—it's like a river: very powerful, always moving, always thinking, always doing *something,* and you can't always control it, but you can learn to exist with it, be friends with it, and maybe even help it to transform."

꙳

Transform into what? It doesn't really answer my question, but I find myself outside later, thinking about what the counselor said, and also my story, and how even if I never turn it in, I should probably still change the ending (but I'm keeping the epilogues).

꙳

It's spring, and the trees along the side of the school are blazing green in the sun, and the sky above it is blue, and the air is still kind of crisp, and it's just really, really nice out.

I take a breath. I let it out. I take another.

mem01616t (EPILOGUE II)

The Eternal God/dess of Teen Depression wakes up one day, makes breakfast, and decides that instead of killing herself by becoming triple-berry vanilla juice and vaping herself, today she will do something entirely different.

Today, on a whim, she decides she will make everything all better. In the entire universe. To the best of her ability. After all, she is a god/dess.

So that involves taking care of all the suffering that has ever or will ever happen—and that begins with greeting all the souls of the recently departed as they return to the infinite unity from whence they came. But first she has to create an infinite unity. So she does that.

※

She creates an infinite unity. She makes it blazing, luminous, and brilliant beyond mortal comprehension, a shining supernova of pure love and effervescence forever and ever and ever, like a fuzzy, warm, eternal squeeze, only better, and this is where she decides all the souls will go— ALL of them, past, present, and future—and everyone and everything will be made light again in this place.

※

Next, the Eternal God/dess of Teen Depression sits herself in an absolutely flawless lotus position at the gateway of this boundless land of sunshine. From there she welcomes everyone who arrives like a supermarket greeter, all the dead cats and old people and children and all the suffering souls who will soon be free again, and her tears become water for the thirsty, and her laughter is music for lost souls, and from the crack in her broken heart, there radiates an endless, infinite love that fills every corner of creation.

Yeah, it's seriously kind of a big day for her.

And as it comes to an end, the Eternal God/dess of Teen Depression begins to realize just how truly exhausted she is. Ten thousand doves sigh from the rooftops and trees. The sky brightens from blue to magnificent pink. She goes inside and changes into something comfortable, makes herself an absolutely unparalleled grilled cheese sandwich, eats, brushes her teeth, flosses. And then it's bedtime.

She doesn't know what comes next, but as she tucks herself in under her twin blankets of darkness and light, the Eternal God/dess of Teen Depression is surprised to discover she's actually sort of looking forward to tomorrow. She closes her eyes, snuggles into her pillow, and slowly drifts away. All night long, she dreams and dreams. It's the same thing over and over: a flickering sky, an endless field of waving grass, and a kid so lost they can't even remember their own name, but who manages to find themselves anyway.

THE END.

THANK YOU

Thank you to Tara and Cedar for being first readers, and thanks to Elliot just because. Thanks to Lynne, Eleanor, Andrea, and everyone else at Clarion. Thanks to Jen and everyone at DC&L. Thanks to Laura. Thanks to Jesse. Thanks to Michele. Thanks to Zach. Thanks to Alison. Thanks to Mom and Dad. Thanks to my students, who help me to see the light. Thanks to the light! And finally, thanks to you, person reading this.